Left Turn at Cloud 9

Left Turn at Cloud 9

Sarah J. Faulkner

Left Turn at Cloud 9

Copyright © 2012 by Sarah J. Faulkner

ISBN-13: 978-1-47810-717-0
ISBN-10: 1-47810-717-0

Cover design by Vic Jong

Cover photograph © 2012 by Sarah J. Faulkner

I dedicate this book to all those who dream of flying.

And to all those who've helped me fly.

June 21, 1961

Happy birthday to me! I am celebrating this extraordinary life I have; I definitely have the best of both worlds! I spent the morning with Rhein, splashing in the stream and climbing trees and watching butterflies. I know he is much older than I, but it is hard to remember that, because he seems so young in his appreciation of every little detail of his world and, I must admit, of me. Delicious! I am 61 years old today, and I feel younger than I have in years.

He does not share my interest in birthdays; he thinks every day is worth celebrating. And when I am with him, I have to agree. I have learned so much from him and from his family. His sisters teach me about their plants, and then I take those plants home and cultivate them and use them in my teas, getting wonderful results for my friends, and now their friends are coming to me also. There is a beautiful farm for sale north of town, with plenty of land. I am thinking of digging out the old valise that I brought with me from New York so long ago, opening up that false bottom, and finding out what all that fancy jewelry might be worth. Of course I would never sell Henry's alexandrites, but as for the rest? It has been useless to me for almost 30 years now. If I could use it to buy this farm, maybe I could turn my tea making into an actual business. I would miss seeing everyone at the restaurant every day, but I do believe the trade-off just might be worth it. I cannot keep waiting tables forever.

And speaking of forever . . .

Walter and Mary had me over for dinner tonight, to celebrate my birthday. Of course, Walter had out his camera, as always. We got to looking at old photographs. Funny thing, I look younger now than I did last year, two years ago, three. I had not even thought about it, but as we were looking at the photographs, I realized that I have not dyed my hair in, well, I cannot remember the last time. I used to have to do it every month or so, did I not? I snuck a few of the photographs to bring home with me. It is quite odd. But is it really so strange? When I am with Rhein and his people, I eat as they eat and drink as they drink, including drinking the water from that amazing stream. They seem ageless . . . is it really so strange that I should be affected in this way? If this is true, though, I need to be more careful than ever. No one must ever suspect that there really is a place where aging can truly be slowed, or even (as seems to be the case if the photographs are to be believed), reversed. . . . It does not bear thinking about! Up until now, all of this has been a delightful, thrilling secret, my own little mystery. Now I realize I cannot treat this as a lovely game, for if I am careless with this knowledge, I can open Rhein and all that he loves up to terrible exploitation. That I will never do. As for the other? I believe I will take a trip to San Francisco next week, and see what old Russian jewelry is worth these days. Perhaps I shall purchase some property. Perhaps it is time for me, finally, to have a home of my own.

Chapter 1

On the morning of my fiftieth birthday, I dreamed of flying. I lay stretched out under the soft sheet and tried to keep the dream going, tried to resist the tide of consciousness as my dream self soared over an ocean, a bluff, a stretch of land with a lone house watching over the surging tide. I'd flown here before; this was familiar landscape to my dream self. The music of the wind sang in my blood, "Fly, Emma, fly!"

But the day I woke up to, well, it wasn't a flying sort of day. June 21, summer solstice: you'd think it would be bright and sunny, but noooo. It was gloomy, chilly, the clouds too tired to even rise up above the houses. Typical, and a perfect match to my mood. This whole turning fifty thing? Just not my idea of a good time. I'd been divorced for ten years, had no children, and was working as an assistant manager at a giant (read "heartless") chain bookstore. This was not the life I'd pictured years ago when I'd looked forward to my fiftieth birthday. As far as I was concerned, it was going to be pretty much like any other day, to be gotten through as painlessly as possible.

Of course it wouldn't be that easy. My best friend, Petie, was insisting on taking me out to dinner, and she'd probably drag some other people along to make it seem more celebrational. Why, oh why, couldn't Petie ever just let something slide when I asked her to?

On my lunch break, I had one voice mail on my cell phone. Probably Petie. I'd listen to it later.

I skipped out of work an hour early. At least Petie was taking me to a really great restaurant, one I certainly couldn't afford to take myself to. I'd been wanting to try it out for ages. I allowed myself to cheer up a little. If I couldn't avoid it altogether, I might as well touch up my makeup, put on better clothes, and do my best to enjoy the unusual treat.

Only three pieces of mail were in the box. I could save HUNDREDS on car insurance if I switched carriers, and I could transfer my ENTIRE credit card balance and pay ZERO INTEREST FOR ONE WHOLE YEAR! If only they knew I never used credit. And a thick manila envelope, hand addressed, from . . . California? I didn't know anyone in California. I'd never even been to California. I tossed my purse on the couch and cautiously opened the envelope. Inside was a letter, a photograph, and a packet of something. I flipped over the picture and a chill washed over me from the heels up. It was a picture of an ocean, a bluff, a stretch of land with a lone house overlooking the surging tide. The picture was straight out of my dreams.

I closed my eyes and shook my head. No. Coincidence. It just looks sort of something like it, I told myself, trying to take myself back to my dream, to the lift of the wind, to the view down below. I looked at the picture again, and the chill was chased by a hot flush. It was the same view, exactly. I stared at it for a long minute, thoroughly shaken, and then I remembered the letter. It was handwritten in a strong, slanted script.

"Happy Birthday, dear Emma!" it began.

I'm sorry we will never have a chance to meet, but I have been keeping an eye on you since you were born. You are perfect, absolutely perfect. I know you haven't been very happy, but please believe me when I tell you that either you make your own happiness, or you never really have any. Although, now that I think of it, why should you believe me? I imagine you never even knew I existed.

No matter! All that is changing. I hope you will be brave, dear one. I hope you will look deep into your soul and pull up the courage you will need. I hope you will follow my dream and find your own. I hope you enjoy my birthday present to you for the rest of your life, which, if you do all of the above, may be very long indeed.

Blessings to you, child! Think of me with fondness, if you think of me at all,

Your Great-Grandmother,

Emma Rae Wright

P. S. Please enjoy the enclosed tea. It will do you 2 worlds of good."

I stood, motionless, staring at the letter, the picture, the packet of . . . tea, apparently. How bizarre was this? It has to be some kind of joke, I told myself. It's weird, just too darn weird to be anything but a joke.

But how could some anonymous jokester have taken a picture right out of my subconscious and printed it out on a brilliant 8 x 10 glossy?

And did I even have a great-grandmother? I didn't remember such a person. I remembered my Father's mother, a washed out, timid little old lady with a sweet smile who lived with us when I was little but died when I was still quite young. And my other grandmother, my mom's mom, who was tall and flamboyant, though not always very nice. She'd died when I was in my early twenties. But I remembered nothing about a great-grandmother.

I went to the couch to grab my purse, and dug out my cell phone to call my mom. Oh, yeah, I had a message. Automatically I pressed the key for voice mail. An unfamiliar man's voice spoke into my ear. "Hello, my name is Daniel Connor of Connor, Black and Connor in Boast Point, California.

I'm looking for Emma Wright, daughter of Henry Wright Jr., the son of Henry Wright. It is in the matter of an inheritance Please return my call at your earliest convenience. I'll be available until 7 tonight, that's California time, uh, yes, that would be 10 p.m. your time. I look forward to speaking with you."

I pulled the phone away from my ear and stared at it. What was going on? I checked the time: 4:30. I should be getting ready. But first I had to find out what the heck was going on. I dropped down on the couch to return the call.

"Connor, Black and Connor. Daniel Connor's office" said a bright female voice.

"Hello," I started, but my voice came out more like a croak. I cleared my throat and tried again. "Hello, this is Emma Wright. I'm returning Mr. Connor's call?"

"Yes, hello, Ms. Wright, I'll put you through directly."

There wasn't even time for canned music, he came on the line so quickly.

"Emma Wright?" he asked, foregoing a more conventional greeting.

"Yes, this is."

"Thank you so much for returning my call so promptly," he said. "I hope you won't mind answering a few questions, just so that I can establish your identity?"

"Mr. Connor, you called me," I said. "Before I answer any of your questions, perhaps you'd tell me what this is about."

There was a brief silence. "Forgive me. I assumed you'd know, or at least have some idea."

I've never been much of a one for surprises or secrets or games. I preferred to at least keep an illusion of control at all times. I was very much off guard, and that made me crabby. "I have absolutely no idea whatsoever what this is about. However I am in a hurry, so if you wouldn't mind getting straight to the point?"

"Forgive me," he said again. "This is concerning the estate of Emma Rae Wright, who passed last Thursday. I offer my condolences."

"Mr. Connor, the only Emma Rae Wright I know of is myself, and I have most definitely not *passed*," I said sharply. But even as I said it, I thought of the name on the letter that lay beside me on the couch: "Your great-grandmother, Emma Rae Wright," it was signed.

Another brief silence. "Well, if you are indeed the rightful heir, she was your great-grandmother on your father's side."

I thought about that. "If that is the case, how is that she just passed last Thursday? My father is . . ." I thought a minute, "seventy-three years old. Somehow I doubt that his grandmother was still alive just last week."

"Well, yes," he conceded, "I admit that it is somewhat . . . unusual. Nonetheless, it does appear to be the case. She was 111 years old. That is, she would have been. Her birthday was today."

Once again I had that creepy feeling all over my body. "You're telling me that I have a 111 year old great-grandmother whose name is the same as mine, and whose birthday is the same as mine, that I know nothing about?!"

"Had," he said gently. "Yes, I believe that is what I am telling you."

My brain struggled. "But she knew about me?"

"Yes, she apparently did, Ms. Wright. She's left her entire estate to you."

Forget my mom. It was Petie I needed to talk to.

Petie had been my best friend my whole life. The only two "only children" in a neighborhood full of big families, we'd stood in as sisters for one another. My mom worked as a secretary back then, and Petie's mom was practically an Earth mother, so I spent as much time as I could at their house. Mrs.

5

Singer was always baking something, or sewing something, or canning something, and the whole house was always warm and welcoming. Petie always complained about having to weed the garden or help in the kitchen, but I loved to join right in and get my hands dirty.

We both got married straight out of high school. Petie's marriage was a disaster from the start, and lasted eight awful years. She swore off marriage, but had sustained a quite alarming dating life ever since. She was optimistic, upbeat and goofy, whatever life threw at her. In fact, when my own divorce came around thirteen years after hers, she's the one who kept me on the vertical. If not for her nagging, I would have lain right down and died.

"So then what happened?" Petie asked, leaning forward across the table, forgotten appetizer cold, martini warm. She had, in fact, invited no one else, telling me that as part of her birthday present she was honoring my request for a quiet, understated evening. Of course she also let me know that it was a real hardship for her, and that I had better make it up to her on *her* 50th by inviting every person we'd ever met in our entire lives, and telling them that presents were absolutely required.

"That's pretty much it," I said. "I was so overwhelmed by it all that I told him I had to go. He didn't like it, I can tell you that, but I really couldn't take in any more."

"Are you kidding me? Did you even ask about the estate? Was she rich?"

"Petie, I don't know. She was 111 years old. She probably lived in a nursing home and has nothing left but bills, taxes and old cookbooks. I'm probably inheriting 111 years worth of debts."

"Wow," Petie said, "You're a real buzzkill, you know that? This is the most amazing thing ever, and you're turning it into something awful."

I didn't know how to tell her how freaked out I was. I hadn't told her yet about the package. I wasn't sure I could handle how over the top she was going to be about it. But Petie was my absolute best friend, and she knew me better than, well, probably better than I knew myself. She was not only smart, but she was also wise, and I loved that about her. She could act like a royal flake, but in fact she was one of the most grounded people I'd ever met.

"Okay," I said cautiously, "there is just one other thing."

She'd started to pick up her martini, but at the tone in my voice, she put it back down. She looked into my eyes, saying nothing, just waiting. It made me so nervous I almost told her to forget about it, but clearly that was never going to happen now. I sighed and reached into the oversized bag I'd switched to. "I got this in the mail today," I told her. The look on her face was so intent that a little imp in me made me pull it out in the slowest of slow motion, dragging it out to see if I could make her snap (have I mentioned that we've been friends a l o n g time?).

I timed it to perfection. Just one fraction of a second before she launched herself across the table and ripped the envelope out of my hand, I pulled it the rest of the way out and handed it to her. "Careful, *careful!*" I cautioned as she started to tear it open.

I sat back and let Petie investigate at her own rate. I really didn't know what to say about any of this, so I just said nothing. Eyes open to maximum, she scanned the letter, examined the picture, sniffed at the tea. Finally, she too sat back. "Wow."

I nodded. "I know."

"This is some kinda crazy," she said softly.

I nodded again. "Yeah. I know."

"Do you think that's her house?"

"I don't know. Maybe."

She looked up from the picture. "It's probably in California."

Oh, yeah. She'd hit it dead on. What was I going to do with property in California? If it was anything at all, it was more than I had here in Michigan. Here I had a crummy apartment I could barely afford, supported by a job that only just paid the bills. And with the economy the way it was, the way it had been in Michigan for years now, there was very little hope for something better anytime soon. My parents lived here, and Petie. Petie was the only one I was really close to. In the years since the divorce, most of my old friendships had become remote, at best. What was there for me here anymore?

I sighed. "Probably. But you know what? I really don't know anything about it. Let's not think about it anymore tonight."

She shook her head. "Oh, hell no, Emma, no way are we dropping this! Are you crazy?"

"What do you mean?"

"Well, just look around. Do you see camera crews? Are we on Candid Camera or a reality show or something? It's your fiftieth birthday. . . ."

"Thanks for reminding me," I muttered, but she ignored me and kept talking.

". . . and out of the blue you get a letter and photograph from a long lost relative you've never even heard of, who is way too old to even still be alive for pity's sake, talking about a birthday present. And on the exact same day you get a phone call from a lawyer telling you you've inherited the estate of this stranger who, let me remind you again, is way too old to have even been alive in the first place! And you expect me to *not talk about it*??"

"Well, I was kind of hoping . . ."

"Well you can just forget about it!" Petie declared passionately. "And all of that doesn't even touch on the really bizarre part!"

8

It didn't? "Which would be . . ." I prompted cautiously.

"The TEA!" Petie almost shouted, grabbing up the little bundle. "For real? Are you kidding me? *TEA*???"

She had a small point there. The tea was, no contest, a bizarre twist to an already inexplicable tale. I picked up the packet. I hadn't even unwrapped it yet; there'd been no time. She leaned in once again as I untied the string that held the brown paper wrapping closed. A scent arose as the paper came away, seeming to fill up the space between and around us. I suddenly thought of the circus, sunny fields on a breezy day, flying. It was delicious, strange, evocative. "Wo-o-ow," I breathed.

Petie's eyes were glazed. She blinked at my voice, then seemed to struggle to focus. We both looked at the innocuous looking packet in my hands, open now to reveal what looked like, oddly enough, loose tea. The scent lingered. I remember noticing that I felt, I don't know, happy. Which I have to admit was a rare feeling in those days. I grinned at Petie, and without even thinking about it, I signaled a server, who hurried over.

I smiled up at him. "George, is it?" He nodded. "George, would you be so kind as to bring us two cups and some hot water for tea?"

He nodded again, and I noticed him sniffing, his nostrils flaring. His eyes seemed to shift to some far away vision, then he started and came back to us.

"Uh, yes, ma'am, certainly," he said, hustling away.

I swayed toward Petie. "What are you thinking about?" I asked, almost in a whisper.

She grinned like a little girl. "Remember the pond out behind the old Wilson house? Remember how it used to be full of tadpoles every spring, and we'd go scoop them up, and how cool and tickly they felt, squirming in our hands?"

I nodded, and she went on.

"And how summer nights used to be so magical with fire flies. And you know how thick and charged the air is right before a thunderstorm, and so sweet after?"

When I think back on that night, I picture us sitting across from each other, quiet, smiling like we were high or something, our eyes gazing off at lovely, distant memories. We drank some of the tea, leaves loose in the bottoms of our cups. I don't remember us talking much more at all. And as I drove myself home, let myself into my crappy little apartment, and got ready for bed, I remember thinking that maybe things were about to turn around for me. Maybe, just maybe, the sad times were over and now everything was going to be just wonderful.

Sheesh. I hadn't a frikken clue.

Chapter 2

"Hello?"

"Hi Mom! What's going on?" I was trying to ease into this conversation. When I woke up the next morning, the rosy glow still had a grip on me, but I was once again thinking clearly, and I didn't want to come off as unhinged when I talked to my mom.

"So," I started after the pleasantries were covered, "Do you know anything about Dad's grandma?"

"Emma Rae? Sure, you were named after her." She laughed, "Against your father's strong objections, I might add!"

"Really? Why's that?"

Mom was quiet a minute, thinking, I guessed. "Well, she was a wild gypsy type, so the story goes. When your Grandpa Henry was still just a baby, Emma Rae left him. She was still a young woman, quite young, widowed from World War I, and she wasn't willing to settle down. She left the baby with her parents and took off, to New York or some such. When I was carrying you, I thought about her a lot. Your Grandpa Henry was such a quiet, colorless little man, and I thought that if I had a girl, I'd rather she be like Emma Rae, who I imagined was beautiful and bohemian, a very romantic figure to my way of thinking! Your dad was against it, he'd never heard a good word about her. And I thought Grandpa Henry would have a coronary! But I was a real hellion when I was pregnant, and you can bet your pink booties I got my way." She laughed again, a warm, rich sound.

This story was so typical of my parents. I never understood their relationship, why it apparently worked so well. My mom was much more like the Emma Rae she'd imagined, independent and artistic, and my father was somber, stern, unimaginative. When it came to disagreements, my mom always got her way, because my dad really did worship her, and he hated confrontation of any kind. I often felt that he was only vaguely aware of my existence, not quite sure who I was. My mom was his first, last and only love. Lucky for us, my mom's love was absolutely gigantic, plenty big enough for both Dad and me.

"Whatever happened to Emma Rae?" I asked.

"Hmmmm. You know, honey, I don't really know. I think she just disappeared and was never heard from again. You'll have to ask your father. But why the sudden interest?"

"Well, um, it, uh, seems she's been heard from again."

"What? What do you mean?"

I sighed. This was not going to be easy to explain. "You know, Mom, I think maybe I should talk to you and Dad together. Are you gonna be home tonight?"

Her voice sharpened. "Emma, what is going on?"

"It's just, well, it's kind of hard to explain. I think this is more of a show and tell than just a tell."

"What on earth are you talking about? Is anything wrong?"

"Mom, I'm sorry, I don't mean to be mysterious. No, nothing is wrong. I just, oh, sheesh, it's really hard to explain. Please, can you just wait and let me tell you about it tonight?"

My mom hates it when I do stuff like that. Come to think of it, I hate it when people do it to me, too. But this was one time I thought I really should wait and do it in person.

"Well," she said with a huff, "that doesn't seem very nice of you."

"I know, and I'm really sorry. But I'll make it up to you. I'll bring dinner, from that Chinese place Dad likes so much."

That was really sneaky; it was Mom who loved that place, and we both knew it.

"Oh, fine," she grouched. "Bring extra eggrolls."

"Connor, Black and Connor. Daniel Connor's office."

"Hello, this is Emma Wright. . . ."

"Hello again, Ms. Wright. I hope you're well today. I'll put you right through."

"Hello Ms. Wright, thank you for calling. Are you ready to hear more?"

I sighed. "Mr. Connor, please call me Emma. I'm sorry I sort of hung up on you yesterday. . . ."

"The fault was entirely mine, Ms. Wright, I had no idea you would be caught off guard as you were. I should have approached it . . . differently."

"Yes, well, thanks. I talked to my mom this morning, and yes, apparently I do have a Great-Grandmother Emma Rae. Um, had. Whatever."

"Excellent. Naturally, you understand, we will need proof of identity, but that can wait until you get here."

I cut him off. "Get where?"

It was his turn to sigh. "I'm sorry, Ms. Wright. . . ."

"Please, Emma."

". . . yes, all right, Emma. And you may call me Daniel. But as I was saying, I'm sorry I seem to keep making assumptions here. Not like me at all, I assure you. So, would you mind if I start over, begin at the beginning, so to speak?"

"I would really appreciate that, Mr. Connor."

"Daniel."

Okay I admit it, at this point I almost dissolved into nervous giggles. We seemed to be stuck in some idiotic script, unable to communicate like normal people. But I managed to maintain control, and he went on.

"My family has represented Emma Rae for, well, for about 50 years, since she became a woman of means," (Do people really still talk like that?) "I personally have known her since I was a boy. I was surprised that you didn't know her, or in fact, know *about* her, because she has always spoken of you."

"What?!"

"Yes, I can imagine that is surprising to you. Nonetheless, it is the case. Emma Rae was well known, and well respected, in this area, even though she was a bit, well, unusual."

"Unusual?"

He cleared his throat gently. "Um, well, yes. As you observed yesterday, she was nearly 111 years old. That in itself is unusual. I never actually knew how old she was until after her death. I'd never before had reason to look back that far into her file."

He paused again, and I said, "I assume she was living in a nursing home?"

"Well, actually, no. She still lived in her own home, and she lived alone."

"Are you kidding me? You're telling me that she still lived alone at 111 years old?"

"Yes, well, the thing is, well . . ."

Once again he came to a stop.

"Mr. Connor, uh, Daniel, I'm sorry, but none of this is making any sense to me, and the way you're presenting it is making me very uncomfortable. Is this really so difficult? Is there some weird mystery here? I mean, besides how she got to be so old in the first place?"

"Well, yes, actually, that's the thing. As I told you, I've known Emma Rae since I was a boy. And I have to tell you, in all that time, she never aged. I mean that quite literally. She never aged in any discernible way. If I'd had to guess, I would have said she was in her fifties, sixty at the most."

"Wha . . ."

"Please, Ms. Wright, let me go on, as this is very difficult. I am not a man who is comfortable with mysteries, though I have lived closely with this one for many, many years. Emma Rae was a lovely, active, vibrant woman. Exactly the same as she was when I was a boy. I don't expect you to understand this, or even to believe it, especially given that her very existence was unknown to you. I considered Emma Rae my friend. Her death was very sudden, very unexpected, and the loss is quite, well, quite difficult for me."

I was speechless. I realized that my mouth was hanging open. This whole thing just got increasingly bizarre, more and more Twilight Zone. But either this man was genuinely grieving, or he was one hell of an actor. I couldn't imagine how to respond appropriately, so I remained silent. At last he cleared his throat again, and continued.

"Be that as it may, it is my job to administer her estate. She was careful in handling her affairs, and there is nothing messy here. In fact, she was determined that you wouldn't be bothered with estate taxes, probate, or any other annoyances that are often passed along with an inheritance."

I finally found my voice. "What do you mean?"

"Emma Rae created an irrevocable trust in your name. Based on the precise terms of that trust, as of her death you own her entire estate outright. She spent many years structuring the details so that there would be no taxes on your inheritance. Of course, you will be responsible for property taxes, but that is a different matter.

"How is that possible without my knowledge?" I asked, stunned.

He chuckled. "It is the easiest thing in the world, Ms. Wright. I'm sorry, I mean Emma. People out there are stealing identities all the time. Using many of the same techniques apparently, Emma Rae has been building one for you."

"That's crazy," I breathed.

This time he laughed outright "I guess it is. But if you had known her, none of this would surprise you in the least." Then he added in a softer tone, "Believe me when I tell you, your Great-Grandmother Emma Rae will be truly missed, and by many, many people."

"I don't believe any of this," my dad said.

Mom and I just looked at him. The remains of a Chinese feast (that I could ill afford) cluttered the table. The extra eggrolls were long gone, the fortune cookies remained untouched. And my father was clearly furious. It wasn't a sight I was familiar with, and I didn't want to do or say anything incendiary, so I remained silent.

"What game are these people playing?" he said through his teeth. "Emma Rae was dead and gone a long time ago."

Mom leaned across the table to put her hand on his. "Do you know that for a fact, Henry?"

He snatched his hand away as though he'd been burned. "What do you know about it?" he growled.

Her mouth dropped open, then her own temper flared. "Henry Wright, what on earth! How dare you talk to me like that!"

He scowled at her. "You and your fantasies, how wonderful she was, what a gypsy, what an adventurer. Let's name our daughter after her! But you never knew her, Meg, you didn't know what she was like!"

"For heaven's sake, Henry, *neither did you!*"

I jumped up. "Stop it!" I shouted.

They both looked up at me, startled. I've never been a shouter. But they were really scaring me. I'd never seen my dad look like that before. I turned and went into the kitchen, standing at the sink, staring out into the yard without seeing anything. What was going on? I heard them talking in low voices, but I left them to it. I'd told them about the inheritance, about the things that Daniel Connor had said. But I hadn't told them about the package I'd gotten from Emma Rae. I went to my bag, and pulled out the packet of tea. I put the water on to boil. It was a hot and muggy evening, but I didn't care. I needed to do something, and I was too upset and confused to want to continue the conversation with my parents right then.

I poured some tea into a tea strainer. The aroma floated up. I thought about swimming with Petie in our friends' pond out in the country. We used to float on our backs late at night, watching the stars, cooling off after the heat and humidity of a broiling summer day. I remembered the almost transcendent feeling of peace as we rocked gently on the water.

I fixed a tray with teacups, the teapot, sugar, spoons. I carried it out to the dining room, where both my parents were red-faced and angry looking, and set it on the table. I watched the steam rise between them. I watched them stop and breathe in the scent, and I watched as their eyes lost that angry intensity, and their faces relaxed into smiles. I felt so much better. And so, clearly, did they.

Into this interesting calm I drew out the manila envelope. "Hey guys," I said gently, not wanting to rock the boat any more than necessary, "there's more to this story."

I pulled out the letter and the picture. Mom leaned toward Dad, resting her shoulder against his and reading the letter with him. They read it, then they looked at the picture. Into their silence I said, "I don't know, but I'm guessing that was Emma Rae's house. I'm guessing that's the property I'm inheriting."

I said it, but I really didn't believe it. This whole thing still seemed like a crazy joke, and I figured sooner or later someone was going to walk in laughing. A lot of my life had seemed like that. Somehow, I usually wasn't the one who was amused.

Dad let out a big sigh and slumped back in his chair. "I don't understand this at all," he said. Mom sat back and held his hand. "They're saying that a woman who left my father with his grandparents back in 1918 and was never heard from again was alive and well last week, and has left a considerable estate to you? How does any of this make sense?"

"I don't know, Dad. Mr. Connor, the attorney, wants me to fly out to California. They need to make a positive identification, prove that I'm the right person, although he said that it's kind of just a formality, since Emma Rae provided all the particulars. They didn't have to track me down at all. She provided my name, address, phone number. . . ."

At that my mom's head snapped up, little lines forming between her brows. "That's kind of creepy. Isn't it?"

I nodded. "Yeah, Mom, it is. So much about this is creepy."

"Why do you need to go to California?" Dad asked. "It's not like you can really afford the plane ticket, let alone the time off."

I looked down at my hands. "Well, um, they're paying for that out of the estate. It's important because, well, I guess it's actually a pretty big estate."

He looked at me. "How big?"

I shook my head. "You know, this is all so weird, I haven't asked. I'm not sure I want to know. It just doesn't seem real, so I'm kind of just pretending it isn't real. I'm not asking those kinds of questions."

"Emma?" Mom said. "What kinds of questions *are* you asking?"

I couldn't answer Mom's question that night. I felt numb, wrung out; I think we all did. I tried to help with the clean up, but Mom waved me off, and Dad walked me to the door. Clearly, they were as ready for me to leave as I was to go.

But the next day at work I found a good question. It was, "May I take a few days off to deal with an unexpected family crisis?" It was June, you know, not a particularly booming time for book sales. Still, my boss just didn't see how she could part with me, even for a few days, without several weeks notice and a written request. I didn't think to play the "someone died" card; that part felt no more real than the rest of it. So instead I unpinned my name badge, said, "Well, in that case I quit," and walked off a job for the first time in my life.

"You did what!?" Petie gasped when I told her.

"I quit."

"Well it's about time! You've been putting up with their shit for ten years. Good for you!"

I had another surprise for her. "And I've got a first class ticket to California. I'm leaving Monday, and I'm staying for two weeks."

"Monday?! In four days?! And you're staying two *weeks*!?!"

"Well, he wanted me to leave tomorrow, but . . ."

"Emma, who's going with you?"

"No one. Just me."

She looked at me in astonished concern. "Honey, you haven't gone five miles down the road without someone to hold your hand since your divorce."

"That is so not true!"

She thought a minute. "You're right. You never did before your divorce, either."

I tried not to think about it. The truth is, she wasn't far off. I'd never been what you could call adventurous, at least not that I could recall. And the thought of flying across country alone, with no one to meet me but a stranger, to deal with a situation that I still couldn't wrap my mind around, was more frightening to me than I cared to admit. I'd never even flown before. But it had to be done, and no one could do it for me. At least I was going first class.

Meanwhile, I dreamed of flying every night. It seemed that as soon as I'd close my eyes, I'd hear the wind whispering down through the stars, calling me. I'd rise up off my feet and soar, over the waves, over the sand, over the tawny hills. On the morning I was to leave for California, I actually woke up laughing. I stopped soon enough, but the memory stayed with me all the way across the country, as I peered out the window to watch the changing landscape.

I had plenty to think about on that flight. I'd had dinner with my parents again the night before, and we'd talked late into the night. I understood my dad better now, why he was so upset about all of this. His father, my Grandpa Henry, had been raised by his grandparents. They were stern, bitter people, and had raised Grandpa Henry with virtually no kindness or love. Also, they'd missed no opportunity to tell him how horrible Emma Rae was, leaving her baby for them to raise. They brought him up to believe that his mother was a wild, uncaring, selfish beast of a woman, and Grandpa Henry had passed those beliefs along to my dad. It was impossible for him to believe that the woman who had disappeared ninety some years ago was making an appearance in my life now.

Admittedly, it was impossible for me to believe, too.

Furthermore, even if it was true, my dad was convinced that there must be some sort of malicious intent involved, so strong was his belief in Emma Rae as a truly horrible person. My mom argued long and hard against that viewpoint, and I agreed with her. If Emma Rae had lived to 111 years old, that meant she'd been very young when she disappeared. Married, widowed, and had a baby by eighteen years old: I could believe in her as a desperate, tragic, romantic figure, maybe even selfish, thoughtless. But I was hard pressed to think of her as evil.

Dad supported his viewpoint by arguing that if she wasn't horrible, surely she would have returned for her child as soon as she'd gotten settled someplace, that sooner or later she would have at least tried to make contact.

I couldn't believe we could drum up so much emotion over this ancient history.

Not all ancient, Dad accurately pointed out. Last week was barely ancient history.

I bit my tongue just in time to keep from saying, "Yeah, and see? She did come back after all."

Things were a little strained when I finally headed home, but Dad did bring himself to wish me good luck. Mom, on the other hand, wrapped me in a gigantic hug and offered to come with me, if only it wasn't too late to buy a ticket. Why did everyone think I couldn't handle this on my own?

Oh, yeah. Maybe because I'd never been one to handle much of anything on my own.

Well, and maybe it was time for some things to change.

I survived the flight. In fact, I almost enjoyed it. I'd never flown before, and here I was in first class. The food was pretty good and I took advantage of the bar service. As long as I didn't think about where I was going or what I was doing or that I'd be all alone in a strange place or that this still seemed like a cosmic set-up that couldn't possibly end well, I managed not to panic completely. However, as we neared San Francisco, I rather desperately ordered one last vodka and cranberry and slugged it down. What the hell was I doing?! I'd be getting off the plane alone, navigating through a big city airport, alone. At least someone was supposed to be meeting me by the baggage claim, but this whole thing was crazy, wasn't it? I was probably being set up for, I don't know, alien abduction or something, and like the first Emma Rae, I would disappear without a trace forever. Or, okay, ninety plus years. Of course, if someone simply wanted to abduct me, why fly me first class? Why fly me at all? Why not just slink around outside my crappy Michigan apartment, whack me over the head with a baseball bat, and throw me into an old, beat up Caddy, saving all the drama and expense that Connor, Black and Connor were putting out on my behalf?

I discovered in the San Francisco airport that reading is an invaluable skill. Much to my relief, if I simply kept my eyes up and read the signs, I could get just about anywhere, including Baggage Claim. I could even stop part way there and use the ladies room and still not get lost. Even as my chest swelled with a sense of accomplishment when I positioned myself beside the correct baggage carousel, I realized how ridiculous it was that this simple process, one that small children no doubt could accomplish single-handed, seemed like such a challenge to me. Was I really so pathetic? Sadly, I had to admit that, yeah, I really was.

I looked around for someone with a big sign reading "Ms. Wright," but didn't see anyone. No sweat, I told myself. My luggage hasn't even come up yet. They'll be here.

And there it was. Petie had loaned me two pieces of her gorgeous, bright red luggage, and as I struggled to pull the big one off the carousel, strong hands suddenly slipped in front of mine, grabbed the bag and easily hoisted it free of the conveyor. I turned, startled, to look up at the tall, slim man beside me. He set the suitcase down and turned to me.

He had short, well cut brown hair that was turning to grey, brown eyes, and a nice smile. "You are obviously Emma Rae Wright," he said confidently.

Somehow that did not reassure me. He was supposed to wait on the sidelines with a big sign. I was supposed to find him. I didn't smile back.

His smile wavered. "You look so much like Emma Rae."

"I *am* Emma Rae," I said stupidly.

"Yes, of course, I mean you look so much like your . . . You know, it's impossible to think of her as your great-grandmother."

"No," I said, "I don't know. You just told me I look just like a 111 year old woman. Forgive me if I find that a little . . . offensive."

He shoved his hand through his short hair, barely mussing it. "I'm so sorry. I certainly meant no offense. Quite the opposite, in fact." He sighed. "Please, Emma, let me start over." He stuck out his hand. "I'm Daniel Connor. I am so pleased to meet you. Thank you for coming all this way."

After a pause that was long enough to be almost rude, I gave in and shook his hand. "Hello, Daniel. Thanks for meeting me. I expected you to send a lackey or something."

He laughed. "Well, yes, I normally would. But this is not a normal situation."

I looked up at him. "Isn't it? I mean, it's sure unusual for me, but for you?"

He shook his head ruefully. "Look," he said, grabbing the suitcase and picking my carry-on bag up off the floor, "let's get moving. We've got some driving to do, and I thought we'd stop for something to eat, if you're not too tired?"

I thought about that, then sighed. "No, I'm not too tired, and I am hungry. That would be nice, thank you." I didn't know why I was being so crabby with this poor man, he was only doing his job, right? Why did I have to make it so hard on him?

I got goose bumps at my first glimpse of the Golden Gate Bridge. I'd seen so many pictures, seen it in so many movies, but here I was, seeing it up close and personal, about to actually go over it. At my excitement, I inwardly laughed at myself again. I really did need to get out more!

But before we crossed, Daniel exited and drove us up into a little park area. "There's a great view here," he told me, "and I thought you might enjoy a picnic."

Wow, really? Though it was a hot day, there was a nice breeze, and he quickly found us a spot at a picnic table. "It's nothing fancy, but I thought this would be a nice introduction to California. You did say you've never been here before, right?"

I nodded as he pulled a baggie with turkey and cheese sandwiches out of a cooler. He went on, "And I also didn't want to wait too long to get started. We've got about four hours driving ahead of us."

Carrot and celery sticks and a personal sized bottle of white wine came out of the cooler. "Welcome to California!" he smiled, toasting my wine bottle with his own bottled water.

I squinted out over the water. It was a whole lot bigger than Lake Huron, that was for sure. I loved the sweet smell of the air, and what I assumed was the "salt tang" that I'd read about in so many books. The sunshine was plenty hot, but I could get used to this, this heat without the humidity. Gorgeous flowers were blooming everywhere, and, much to my surprise, a lot of trees were flowering, too. Back home, trees only bloom in the spring. Beyond all that, there was the ocean. The real, actual Pacific Ocean! My heart seemed to be tripping, and I couldn't wipe the silly grin off my face: the Pacific Ocean!

We made small talk, but I was clearly distracted, so we ate fairly quickly, packed up and got back on the road. Daniel seemed content with silence, and I was happy to just enjoy the scenery. It was so beautiful, far prettier than I had imagined. It was incredible to me, the road twisting and turning inland and then, just like that, bringing us back for another gorgeous view of the Ocean. I'd never even seen an ocean before, and I felt something rising up in me, an almost irresistible desire to just dive into that cool blue vastness. I noticed my hands were gripping the edge of my seat, and I deliberately relaxed them. In all the craziness of the past five days, it had never once occurred to me that I was headed off on a Grand and Glorious Adventure. Now, skimming along beside that great, wide ocean, smelling the sea and the eucalyptus trees that shaded the road, sitting beside an attractive stranger and headed up to *my own property*, I was gripped with an excitement unlike anything I'd ever felt before. I imagined I must have felt something like this 30 years ago as my wedding day approached, back when I'd still believed in happy endings and dreams coming true. But that was a long, long time ago.

And maybe this was all the more exciting because I was so much older now, and had lived for so long with disillusionment and disappointment. To feel such a Christmassy sense of possibility at this point in my life was incredible. I wanted to savor it, mostly because I believed it couldn't possibly last, that at any moment it would be ripped away from me, like all of my other dreams.

So I rested back against the comfortable leather seat and enjoyed the scenery and the silence, and once again did my best not to think about these crazy life changes that seemed to be spinning outside of my control. Time enough for that, I told myself. Time enough for that when I sat in the offices of Connor, Black and Connor and heard more of the story of Emma's New Life: Whether You Want it or Not.

"Emma. Emma?" I must have fallen asleep. The car was stopped; Daniel's hand was gentle on my arm. I struggled to open my eyes and clear the fog out of my brain.

"We're here. Are you okay?"

My mouth tasted horrible, probably from the wine. "Yeah, I'm fine" I would've killed for a drink of water. I looked out the window at an old fashioned two story house. Some brilliant fuchsia flowers climbed up the side of it, and roses lined a flagstone walk to the front entrance. "Is this Emma Rae's house?"

"No," he said, letting himself out of the car and coming around to open my door. "I thought you could stay this first night in town, since we have the memorial service in the morning, and we can head up to Emma Rae's property in the afternoon. It's about another twenty minutes up the coast. I thought maybe a good night's sleep first . . . ?"

I glanced at my watch as I climbed out of the car. Almost 9:00, midnight Michigan time. "Sure. Yeah. Good idea."

I woke up to a soft breeze blowing through the room, and a low noise humming through the room that I eventually identified as the ocean, curling up onto the shore several blocks away. I've never been one to jump out of bed in the mornings, but this morning I crawled out pretty darn briskly, and in a moment was staring out the window, suddenly wide awake. The Bed and Breakfast was on a hill, and I could see over the houses below, straight out to the water. Absolutely mesmerizing. Now at last I knew what all the fuss was about. It was so vast, so brilliant. It seemed like a living thing, a beast of extraordinary beauty, exotic beyond imagining, playing there at the very edge of my normal everyday existence.

I breathed in that salty tang, and breathed out tension. If I could just stand here for about a year and a half, I thought, breathing in the sea and breathing out, well, everything else, maybe I could begin to smile again. Maybe I could begin to laugh again. I had done so little of either in such a very long time. Maybe this really was a chance for me, an opportunity to live in a different way.

Finally I pulled myself away from that glorious view. So much was happening today: Emma Rae's funeral, then the funeral lunch that Daniel insisted I should attend. After that we had to go and attend to "official business" at the offices of Connor, Black and Connor. And then, at last, we would head up the coast to Emma Rae's property. My property. What was it like? How big was it? Was it run down? Were there neighbors nearby? Shoot, I didn't even know if she had a phone, running water, indoor toilets! Daniel and I had barely talked at all yesterday; he'd been very respectful of my need to keep myself insulated from all these changes. When had I become so terrified of change? Had I always been this way? I remembered comments that my folks and Petie had made in the past few days. It made me so uncomfortable, re-hearing them, thinking about what sort of a person I must be, that they were so worried about me now. I wondered again, had I always been this way? Or were these recent changes, maybe since the divorce that had left me stunned and reeling.

I firmly shut that door in my mind. Again. Not going there. No way, no how. I went to my suitcase, lying open on the floor, and pulled out my uncrushable black dress. Mom had insisted on taking me shopping, saying that I really had to have something decent to wear, somber but not unfashionable, something that would travel well but still be attractive. Sounded like a tall order to me, and I really didn't care much, but Mom said it was necessary, that to not pay attention to this kind of detail was to be disrespectful. Dad had snorted at that, but said nothing. I, on the other hand, figured she might have a point there, and so I submitted to being dragged around the mall until she found something she thought was acceptable. One thing is unquestionable: my mom does have great taste in clothing. And better yet, she managed to meet all of her criteria, and my one request. It was comfortable.

I slipped the cotton/lycra sheath over my head, and it slid down over my body neatly. It was loose enough to hide any minor flaws, snug enough to emphasize my curves, yet was somehow still modest: a true miracle dress. I slid my feet into dressy flats, ran my fingers through my curls, and put on a touch of eye shadow and mascara. I looked at myself in the mirror and shrugged. That was as good as it was going to get.

I headed down the stairs to the dining room, steeling myself for my hostess's reaction. My arrival last night had been terribly uncomfortable, since apparently I looked so much like my dead 111 year old great-grandmother that the owner of the bed-and-breakfast thought that a miracle had occurred and that I actually *was* my dead 111 year old great-grandmother, returned from the grave all hale and hearty. It had taken Daniel a few minutes to convince her otherwise, after which the poor woman had been upset and apologetic and had finally practically forced a cup of tea on me. "Emma Rae's tea," she explained, "My own special blend." I didn't really want any, but the poor woman was practically overcome with several kinds of remorse, so I accepted more out of compassion than desire.

As it turned out, I was glad I'd accepted the tea. It was a very different blend from the one Emma Rae had sent me. Still, as I breathed in the spicy aroma and let the warmth of the brew relax me, the bone-crushing exhaustion I'd been struggling against gradually eased into a lovely, ready-for-bed sleepiness. When I'd made my escape and crawled into bed a half hour later, I slid directly into a deep, restorative sleep.

This morning my hostess, Jeanne, simply apologized once again for her gaffe of the previous night, and then bustled about in a competent and friendly manner, directing me to the sidebar laid out with eggs scrambled with ham and Swiss cheese, bacon done to crispy perfection, fried potatoes and a fragrant loaf of braided sweet bread. She brought me a sized-for-one teapot, confiding with a laugh, "I don't usually serve my special blend to guests, but you're really family, now, aren't you?" Thankfully she didn't seem to expect a response to that ridiculous statement. And again, I was grateful for the tea as it seemed to smooth away my reawakened anxieties and allow me to enjoy the excellent breakfast.

Daniel arrived at 9:30, accepting a plate of eggs and his own cup of the special brew. He grinned ruefully at me over his dainty teacup, whispering so Jeanne wouldn't hear, "I already had a cup of my own, but Jeanne's mix is much better for anxiety. Just what I need today."

I looked at him with new interest. "Why are you anxious?"

He set the cup down. "I haven't known how to prepare you for this. The service this morning . . . well, to say it will be well attended is an understatement of significant proportions. Emma Rae was an extremely well loved woman."

He seemed to be struggling for what to say next. I waited. At last he continued.

"Also, I don't think you understand at all how like her you look. That's startling enough under normal circumstances, but under these . . ." he trailed off again.

"You're right," I said, "I don't understand, not at all. But even so, why is it such a big deal that I look so much like her? I mean, other than the initial shock."

He shifted in his seat, took another sip of his cooling tea. "Well, her body wasn't recovered."

A long silence passed. His words didn't seem to register at all for long moments. And when they did, they still didn't make sense. "What do you mean, her body wasn't recovered?" I had assumed she'd died of a heart attack, or in her sleep, or some other quiet way like any self-respecting 111 year old woman would die. "How did she die?"

He shifted again, cleared his throat. "Okay," he said finally, "You're not going to believe me, but I am telling you the truth. She died in an ultralight crash."

"What? In a what kind of crash?"

He sighed. "Emma Rae flew an ultralight. It's a very light, very small one-person airplane. She was flying over the ocean near her home, and she went down."

I stared at him. Did he think I was stupid? I shook my head and looked around. Maybe I *was* stupid. I was here, in Cali-frikken-fornia, in a tiny little town where I didn't know anybody, on the say-so of this man I'd never met before. What was I thinking? Why hadn't I looked into this more closely? I hadn't even thought to google Connor, Black and Connor, or Daniel Connor, or even Emma Rae Wright. In spite of how strange this whole set-up was, it had never even occurred to me to do any kind of cross checking, and here I was, listening to the biggest crock I'd heard yet. What was I *thinking*?!?

Daniel nodded sharply. "Right. Didn't think you'd believe that." He sighed again. "But it is the truth, Emma. You're going to have to trust me just a little longer, and then you'll see. Strange as it is, you'll see." He ran his hand over his short hair in that gesture I'd noticed before. "And you might as well get used to it. Probably any story you ever hear about Emma Rae is going to be a strange one. She was no ordinary person. Never was."

I stood up without speaking, and went back up to my room. I opened my packed suitcase and rummaged around till I found the now familiar paper-wrapped packet. If I had to listen to shit like this, I needed my own tea.

Daniel had not been exaggerating. The service was held in a small country church, and we got there well before it was scheduled to begin. Already the place was jammed with people. Places had been set aside for us at the front of the sanctuary, so we made a slow, laborious journey through the crowds to our seats. Over and over I heard gasps of surprise, I felt Daniel's hand on my arm, saw out of the corner of my eye as he shook his head repeatedly, and steadily guided me forward. We didn't speak to anyone. I was grateful to my mom for making sure I was dressed appropriately. I was grateful to Daniel for the steady hand and his tall presence shielding me. At the same time I felt a rising tide of . . . was it anger? Anger toward this person, this Emma Rae Wright, my namesake, for plunging me into the middle of this circus. Okay, maybe circus was too strong, but I certainly felt as though I was flying through a space I hadn't chosen, toward a landing I didn't understand, being guided by those I didn't know.

Yet even as I had these bitter reflections, other thoughts sprang to mind, thoughts of the life I'd been leading, closed off and miserable, of the worried looks Petie and my mom so often slanted my way, of the hopelessness that so often seemed as though it might drown me. I'd longed for a change. Cautiously, surreptitiously I looked around. This was certainly a change! Be careful what you wish for, I muttered under my breath.

At last we made it to our seats. I slid into the waiting pew, looking up at the sole occupant. It was a man about my age. He had dark brown hair that had started its run to silver, longish and curling across the back of his neck. He looked up as I sat beside him, and hazel eyes widened in surprise, then narrowed thoughtfully. Daniel, settling in beside me, reached across me to greet him, which surprised me as he'd so carefully avoided speaking to anyone else. "Emma," he said, "this is Ben Rainey. He was Emma Rae's good friend, nearest neighbor, and business associate. He, um . . ." He trailed off in an odd discomfort, as Ben shook my hand.

Ben's lips tightened a little as he said, "It's a pleasure to finally meet you, Emma, though I'm sorry it's for this reason.

What Daniel doesn't want to mention is that I was with Emma Rae when she, uh, when her plane went down. Well, sort of."

My eyes must have asked the question, because although I didn't speak, Ben went on softly. "We used to love to fly together, Emma Rae and I. We'd been doing it for years. I was in my plane, she was in hers. . . ."

His face expressed deep grief and, if I read it right, some sort of odd reticence as well, though maybe, under these circumstances, it wasn't so odd after all. My hand, somehow still in his, tightened briefly before I let go. "I am so sorry, Mr. Rainey. I can't imagine how terrible. . . ." I, too, seemed unable to finish my sentence.

He hunched a shoulder. "I imagine you'll want to know more about it. Anytime, later, I mean after." The shoulder twitched again. "Emma Rae was very dear to me. It would be my privilege to try to answer any questions you have."

The grief in his face was so raw, I simply turned away with a murmured "thank you." And then I sat in that pew, between two men who carried such deep sorrow over the loss of my mysterious benefactor. I tried to hold myself apart from the feelings that ran so thick in this building, but they swept over me in waves, threatening to wash me away. My breathing thickened, and I remembered times past when I'd been caught off guard like this by others' emotions, and how I'd learned to build up a thick defense against them. Here, now, I needed those defenses, but they seemed to have abandoned me. In their wake I was left gasping, face to face with years of my own anguish that, like the pains of others, I had insulated myself against. As I struggled to breathe, both Daniel and Ben reached for my hands, and as music began to play, I was comforted by the touch of these strangers in a way I had seldom been comforted before.

Chapter 3

I had not been to many funeral services in my life, so I didn't have much to compare this one with. But it was simple, straightforward, and moved me more than I can say. Opportunity was given for mourners to share a few words about Emma Rae, and so many people crowded forward that finally the pastor had to step in, bring the sharing time to a premature close, and suggest that they be continued more casually at the luncheon which was scheduled after the service.

The sharings had been beautiful. All those who spoke had a story about how Emma Rae had made a difference in their lives with a well-timed word, and generous act, or through her teas. It seemed impossible that the woman so lauded could have heartlessly walked away from her own child, even when she was young and grieving. Surely at some point she would have gone back.

At the close of the service, Daniel and Ben both stayed near me, guiding me to an exit at the front of the sanctuary. We slipped into a shadowy, cool space, and there in the gloom was an old man, all alone, sitting extremely upright and gripping the top of an intricately carved cane. He looked up, directly into my eyes, and I was almost undone by the intensity of the pain in his watery blue eyes. Tears ran down his face. He swallowed several times as though preparing to speak, but didn't. Daniel released my hand and knelt at the feet of the gentleman, saying only, "Father," as he wrapped his arms around him.

Ben and I stood motionless. I struggled to escape the sticky anguish of the old man, my head reeling in the power of his pain. His eyes never left mine. Finally, after endless moments, he said in a rusty voice, "You came. After all these years, you're here at last."

I simply nodded. No glib words rose to my lips. I felt nothing at all except his grief. He reached out his hand, and I stepped quickly back, stumbling into Ben who caught my shoulders and held me. I could not possibly hold more than what the old man was already giving me. He withdrew his hand, but not his gaze. Oddly, a smile peeked through his tears. "Ahhh," he said, "You have her gift." Then he displaced Daniel, reached into a pocket and pulled out a handkerchief, bright white in the gloom, and held it out to me. It took me a moment to realize that tears were coursing down my cheeks. I didn't know what gift he was referring to; I was overwhelmed by a grief that wasn't mine, and I was beginning to be afraid. But also, I really did need a handkerchief. I accepted it, and nodded my thanks, still unable to speak.

Daniel got to his feet. "We should go into the hall," he said, his voice rasping. Then he turned to me. "Emma, I would like you to meet my father, Walter Connor. He was Emma Rae's attorney, her friend, and, uh . . ."

"Just say it, for God's sake," Walter Connor snapped. "I loved her, deeply. I would have married her thirty-five years ago, if she would have accepted. I had to be content with what she was willing to give. And by God, every minute of it was a gift. Even the dreadful ones!"

There didn't seem much I could say to that. In fact, there didn't seem a whole lot I'd been able to say to any of this so far. Daniel helped his father to his feet, and we went out into the hall.

What a day that was! I hadn't realized how much I had isolated, insulated myself from others. To be in the midst of that crowd of people, all of them grieving to some extent, all with their stories of Emma Rae, all shocked by my resemblance to her, was overwhelming and exhausting for me. It seemed that everyone wanted to talk to me, even to touch me, and I really did not know how to handle it. I knew I'd secluded myself in the ten years since my divorce, but I was beginning to suspect I'd started long before that, that it had less to do with the pain of my demolished marriage and more to do with this, this affinity I had for the emotions of others, this inability to keep their feelings outside of myself. All day I felt barraged, besieged, and by the end of that long luncheon I felt battered and wrung out.

We were scheduled to go to Connor, Black and Connor after the luncheon to go over the details of the inheritance, and then on up to Emma Rae's property. We said goodbye to Ben. I had felt him watching over me throughout the day, but he was now headed back upcoast. I was loath to see him go, but felt uncomfortable voicing that. Daniel started leading me out of the building and to the car, but before we'd gotten far his father intervened. Walter took me gently by the elbow and steered me in the opposite direction, into an empty, out of the way room. With a sigh, Daniel followed. Walter guided me to a chair and eased me into it. I felt hollow. My eyes burned, and my hands were shaking. I'd hardly spoken all day, never knowing the right responses to all those people, yet my throat felt parched and scratchy.

Keeping his eyes on me, Walter spoke to Daniel. "I suggest, my boy, that you see if Mrs. Wingate has a room available again tonight, and that if she does, you get Emma to it as quickly as possible, brew her a cup of tea," here he paused and asked me, "You have your own tea from Emma Rae, yes?" and after I nodded he continued with Daniel, "And leave her alone until tomorrow. Business must wait."

Daniel agreed, although he didn't seem too pleased about it. Walter said to me, "Emma Rae used to look exactly as you do now, my dear, when she'd attended to too many people for too long. If she didn't allow herself to rest, she could become quite ill with the cares of others."

Although it took all my strength, I raised my eyes to his. "What, exactly, did Emma Rae do?"

He blinked in surprise. "So it's true. You really don't know anything about her."

"It is true. I never even knew she existed before Daniel called. I didn't even know I was named after anyone in particular."

He shook his head. "I find that very peculiar, even though it's what Emma Rae told me. No matter. She was a healer. She made very fine teas also, teas with, shall we say, unusual properties, custom-made for the needs of each of her clients. And she was, shall we say, a counselor. She counseled with people, helped them in that way also. She had very . . . special and specific skills. As you've seen, she was very well loved. I doubt there's a soul for 100 miles who wasn't helped by Emma Rae, and she had clients all over the world as well.

"But enough of that for now. You shall drop soon if you aren't taken care of. Daniel?"

Daniel had been across the room, talking quietly on his cell phone. He tucked it into his pocket and smiled at me. "Yes, Mrs. Wingate can have you again tonight, and even now she's putting the water on to boil. Shall we go?" He held out his hand to me.

I stood, turning to Walter. "Will I see you tomorrow?"

"I don't need to be there. Daniel has been handling the estate for years now. But would you like me there?"

I felt very young, very needy, and I tried to say of course not, I'll be fine. But instead I simply nodded and said, "Yes, please."

"All right, then. Shall we say 10:00? Will that work for you, Daniel?"

Daniel grinned. "I guess it'll have to now, won't it? Emma Rae Wright has been our company's first concern for decades. I see some things don't change, after all."

We turned to go, and then Walter spoke again. "Emma?'

I turned back.

"I trust that you will find that not all of the gifts you shared with Emma Rae are as . . . exhausting as the one you've experienced today."

I had no idea what he was talking about. And at that moment, I was too tired to care. Later, though, I would remember his words, and wonder.

Ahhh, Emma Rae's tea. At the first whiff of it, the exhaustion of the day began to recede. And by the time I was up in my room at the bed and breakfast, the black dress flung across the end of the bed and myself flung into the overstuffed chair in the corner, I could almost think again. All the feelings of all those people seemed to have drifted off. They simply wafted away on the steam rising from the thick ceramic mug that was filled with my very own blend of Emma Rae's tea.

*　　*　　*

Ben Rainey sat on his porch and looked across the highway, over the grassy bank and beyond, out to where the waves danced and played with the glistening sunshine. Emma. Unbelievable. Who could have imagined this?

He remembered the first time he'd seen Emma Rae after he moved back. It was shortly after he'd taken possession of his grandma's old house where it mildewed on the Northern California coast. He'd been a disillusioned young man who'd made and lost fortunes on Wall Street. Thankfully, he'd ended up in a much better position than many, and he'd gotten out of the game and returned here, to where he'd spent vacations growing up, one young pup of a big litter. His siblings were scattered around the country, his folks gone, but this was his place, and he loved it.

He'd been hiking, taking a break from bringing order out of chaos in the old house. There was a most amazing place in the woods up north, in the protected State lands. The Mystic Wood, they called it, the place where redwood trees forgot their straight and true nature and grew in the most bizarre shapes, carved by the land-breeze that raced over the hilltops and down to the ocean. It looked to him as if the souls of caribou had stopped there and inhabited the quiet trees, and he returned again and again to breathe in that sacred space.

That day he'd found Emma Rae on the ground at the foot of the most gigantic of the giant trees. She seemed to be sleeping, but roused sluggishly when he shook her, almost as though she'd been drugged. It took her some time, some water from the bottle on the ground beside her, and a bit of chocolate from his trail mix before she was coherent, and then she seemed skittish, looking around and starting at noises. Something had happened, that much was clear, but she seemed unharmed and she obviously didn't want to talk about it. Ben helped her up and back to her house which, it turned out, was just a couple of miles north of his.

He remembered the red of her long curls as they splayed around her on the ground, and her compact build, sturdy but very feminine. She had deep blue eyes, and most of the time they met his directly. He'd been unable to guess at her age. She only looked to be in her fifties or so, but that couldn't be right. He remembered her from years past. She was his grandmother's nearest neighbor and her good friend. And there was something about Emma Rae that seemed, well, old, regardless of how she looked. He couldn't define it, and he didn't try to. She had a wide smile and laughed easily, and by the time he'd delivered her to her door, they were already friends. And friends they had remained, good friends, and eventually business partners.

So it had caught him very much off guard to meet Emma, who looked like a twin to Emma Rae, while at the same time having a completely different, well, feel. Where Emma Rae's strong square hands were always busy, reaching out and mixing, fixing, preparing, conjuring, Emma's worked at her sides, the thumb tracing over and over her fingertips, revealing a nervous and withdrawn nature. She had no ready smile, no overt confidence, and bruised looking eyes that dropped too easily. Yet he was drawn to her immediately, irresistibly. He was, in brief, smitten.

Would he have to tell her about Emma Rae? Would it be his job to take her to the Mystic Wood? Did she even have to go? And what about the way Emma Rae had . . . gone? Was it his job to tell her the truth of that?

Ben sighed and dug his hands deep into his jeans pockets. Emma Rae had tried to prepare him for Emma's arrival. But nothing, *nothing*, had prepared him for this.

* * *

I sat in an upholstered armchair in Daniel's office at Connor, Black and Connor. Daniel's father sat beside me, and I was aware that if at any moment I needed someone to explain a sticky point, or even just to hold my hand, he was ready. Daniel sat facing us from behind a large walnut desk.

"I imagine you've got many questions," he began, "about Emma Rae herself and about the inheritance. I propose that I start with the details of the estate, and after that I'll try to answer any questions you have about either that, or about Emma Rae herself. I'm sure my father would be happy to answer any questions that I cannot. Is that acceptable?"

"Yes," I said simply. I did have questions, so many that they jumbled together into a big mess in my head. If Daniel could help tease the knots out into strings that made sense, I'd be grateful.

"Good. All right then. To begin with, thirty years ago Emma Rae began transferring her assets to you under the terms of her irrevocable trust, using discounted valuations and various exemptions."

"Thirty years?" I interrupted in surprise.

Daniel scanned the top document on his desk. "October 28, 1980, to be exact."

"That was right after my wedding!"

"Yes, that's correct," Walter interjected. "Emma Rae worried a lot about dying that year. She wanted to make sure that her property would come to you at her death without you having to worry about taxes or probate or any other inconvenience. It was quite a sophisticated estate plan and I couldn't understand why she was so concerned about it. Of course, I had no idea then that she had just turned eighty. Emma Rae never told anyone her age."

Gee, I wonder why.

Daniel cleared his throat. We looked back at him attentively, and he continued. "The real estate includes a house, a barn, three greenhouses, a large shed, and 19 acres of oceanfront property."

My jaw dropped. Nineteen acres of *oceanfront*? In *California*??! What must that be worth?

"In addition are all furnishings, vehicles, clothing, jewelry, household goods, etc. etc., valued at approximately $9.6 million. All of that is now yours under the terms of the trust."

My knuckles were white on the armrests of my chair. I breathed in slowly through my nose, and relaxed my hands on the exhale. I looked around the room. It looked exactly how I imagined an attorney's office should look. But this could not be real.

Walter reached over and patted my hand. "Are you all right, dear?" he said solicitously. "Would you like a cup of tea? Emma Rae made us a special blend just for occasions such as this."

I licked my very dry lips and swallowed, twice, before I could speak. "Yes, thank you, I think that would be good."

He got up and crossed the room, stuck his head out the door, and spoke quietly to Daniel's secretary before returning to his seat. "It will be just a few moments," he reassured me.

"Are you all right?" Daniel asked. "May I go on?"

"There's more?" I asked, my voice squeaking embarrassingly.

"A little," he affirmed.

I looked at Walter and croaked, "How 'bout that tea?"

The tea helped. So did a short walk around the small garden behind the attorneys' office. And another cup of tea. And a cookie. Daniel kept talking, and I truly tried to pay attention. Emma Rae had a thriving company, Two World Teas, which was now mine. Ben worked with her, and could help me with that. I remember Daniel talking about the cost of living in California, and property taxes. Did he have any idea that one week ago I'd struggled to pay the rent and had eaten ramen noodles several times that week, and three days ago I had quit my job? Now I had ocean front property and my own business. Unbelievable.

He stopped talking, finally, and sat back in his chair. "There's just one more thing," he said, giving a nod to his father.

Walter stood once again, and walked to a safe in the wall. He fiddled with it briefly, his back to me, then the heavy door

swing open, and he reached inside, taking out a manila envelope (seems I had one just like it in my suitcase), and a long,
polished wooden box. He brought them back, and handed the
envelope to me. "I believe this is a personal letter. You may read
it now if you like, but perhaps it would be a good idea for you
to read it in private, after you've had a little breathing space.
If it contains anything you'd like to discuss, either Daniel or I
would be delighted to assist you."

I nodded numbly. I seemed to be doing a lot of that these
days. I laid the envelope in my lap with the care I would've
given a live cobra.

Walter sat beside me again, and leaned toward me with
the compassion of a loving uncle. "I know this is a lot to take
in. And we're now finished with all legal matters and matters
of the estate." He rubbed his hand over his face in a gesture
reminiscent of one I'd seen Daniel make, then handed me the
wooden box. "This is personal now. I kept these for Emma Rae
as a favor, as she had a deep distrust of banking institutions.
She never told me the story behind these, and I never saw her
wear them," he said. "They've been in my possession for over
fifty years. And now they're yours."

My hands were actually shaking. What more could there
possibly be? I opened the box.

Never in my life had I ever seen anything like the jewelry
in the wooden box. It looked like something a European queen
might have worn in a far and distant past. Thick workings of
pale gold, glittering diamonds, and nine rectangular stones,
gems that I didn't recognize, formed a heavy, exquisite collar.
The longest, center stone was a full inch long and half an inch
wide; the single stones set in each of the two earrings were
only slightly smaller. Each large stone was framed by a crust
of diamonds. I dragged my eyes away from the set and stared
at Walter. "What kind of stones are these?" I asked.

"Alexandrites."

I held up the necklace. The stones, appearing bluish green at first, changed color in the light until, at certain angles, they actually looked magenta, almost raspberry. I'd never seen anything like them. "What is it worth?" I whispered.

He shook his head. "As far as I know, it's never been valued," he said, "although I can tell you that the gold is 24 Karat, and the diamonds and alexandrites are absolutely genuine. I learned enough to be able to satisfy my curiosity on that. But Emma Rae absolutely refused to allow me to have it valued. She didn't like to see it or talk about it. However," he added after a moment, "she did very specifically want you to have it."

That was enough for one day, I thought, more than enough. But apparently not. As I finally stood, rolling my shoulders and head to relieve tension, Walter touched my arm. "There's something I want to show you, if you think you can take one more shock."

I raised my eyebrows at him. I made a silent vow not to ever again ask, "What more could there possibly be?" As Daniel had warned me, Emma Rae seemed to have no end of surprises. Who was this woman? "All right," I agreed cautiously.

Walter led me down a short hall and into his own office. He took me directly to a large framed photograph that hung on one wall. When I first looked at it, the world seemed to tilt sideways, like when you're in a parked car and the one right next to it begins to move. For one weird, heart stopping moment I thought I was looking into a mirror.

It was uncanny. Unruly red curls tumbled down to tangle over her shoulders. Deep blue eyes laughed at the photographer. Pale freckles scattered like gold dust across the short, straight nose and strong cheekbones. It could have been a picture of me, except that this woman was full of life, full of laughter, brimming with some secret inner joy that I had only ever dreamed of.

"Wow," I breathed. "That explains a lot. When was this taken?"

Walter made a choking sound, paused, and tried again. "Two years ago."

I whipped my head around. "What?" That strange anger bubbled up again. "Why are you doing this to me?" I demanded furiously.

Then I noticed the tears falling once again down his worn and wrinkled cheeks. I saw a ghost of a smile whisper across his pale lips. "I know," he said, "It is impossible. But I took the picture myself. It was her birthday. Emma Rae absolutely loved her birthday. I never understood it. Until now, of course. Now it makes perfect sense."

"How can you believe that she was 111 years old? What makes you think that?" I asked.

He sighed, and we both looked back at the photo. "Emma Rae was a planner, extremely logical, analytical. She thought things out very carefully, never trusting anything to chance. Some years ago she gave me a sealed packet with strict instructions that it only be opened at her death. Naturally, I thought I would never see the contents." He paused, cleared his throat and continued.

"In the packet was a copy of her birth certificate, photos that went all the way back to the early 1900s, a lock of baby hair. One day, like it was all a lark, Emma Rae suggested that we go and get ourselves fingerprinted. 'Who knows,' she told me, 'it could come in useful one day.' She put those fingerprints in the envelope. She knew what she was doing. She knew what her intentions were. And beyond establishing her own identity, she also provided all the links to you. There is no mistake, there isn't even the shadow of a doubt. Impossible as it is to believe, those are the facts. Please trust me, Emma, I followed up very carefully before we contacted you. "

There was no way I could believe this insane story, but there was also no way to doubt this grieving old man. He had followed the chain of evidence, he was telling me. He had done his due diligence. That gorgeous, vibrant woman had been, indeed, my missing 111 year old great-grandmother.

Once again Daniel and I were in the car, riding silently. I tried to keep my hands relaxed as they rested on the smooth wooden jewelry box and the manila envelope that lay on my lap. Walter had suggested that I return the jewelry set to his safe, and I imagined I would at some point, but for now, I wanted to keep it with me. And I must have been adjusting to living in a state of perpetual astonishment, because I was able to appreciate the gorgeous coastal views as we drove north on Highway 1. Believe me when I tell you that the car commercials do not do it justice.

Daniel had again asked if I had questions, and once again I had put him off. I imagined I would have about a million once I'd had some time to myself, but I really did need the opportunity to assimilate all that had happened, all that was still happening. One thing only did I grasp fully. Life as I knew it was completely, irrevocably changed.

After about twenty minutes, Daniel broke the silence to gesture at a house on the right, across the highway from the ocean. "That's Ben Rainey's house," he said. "He's your nearest neighbor."

Ben. I pictured again the hazel eyes, the broad shoulders. I could do worse in a neighbor, I thought. "What does he do way up here?" I asked.

"He does a variety of things, I think, beyond his work with Two World Teas. Writes about conservation for magazines. Gives flying lessons. . . ."

"Flying lessons?"

"Yes," he said. "He's the one who taught Emma Rae to fly, close to twenty years ago, I guess. Those two were always up in the air. He helped her a lot in her gathering, also."

"Her gathering?" I prompted.

"For her teas. She has, *had*, extensive herb gardens on her property, you'll see. But she also gathered all kinds of stuff from all around. She loved going into the redwood forests, all along the beaches. . . . She could find stuff anywhere, and she always seemed to find uses for it. I used to worry that she'd poison herself or someone else, but she never did. She seemed to just know. It was uncanny, really." He made an odd noise, like a cross between a snort and a chuckle. "A lot of stuff about Emma Rae was uncanny, that's for damn sure."

"I'm beginning to get that impression," I said drily.

He gave me a quick glance, and a smile flitted across his face. "See, I could tell right off you were smart."

Hello! I turned my full attention on him. When his face softened like that, he was actually rather handsome. The smile lit up his eyes in the nicest way. I looked back out the window, suddenly warm. "How far is it to Emma Rae's house?"

"Just a few more minutes. As you can see, it's not too crowded up here. Most of this land is government owned, national trusts or state land, and there's also a lot that's been designated conservation lands. Emma Rae, and also Ben's grandparents, bought their land before a lot of that was set up."

"How long ago was that?" I asked.

"Well, it was before I was born. I think Emma Rae moved out here right after World War II . . . hm, wait a minute, that's not right." He shook his head. "I'd have to look it up, see what year she bought the land, at any rate. As you can imagine, a lot of Emma Rae's life is a mystery, and the timeline . . . well, let's just say it might not be too easy to know for sure. She looked the same since my dad met her, and that was back in the sixties I think, before my mom passed." He glanced at me again. "She passed in 1969."

"I'm sorry," I said, meaning it. "How old were you?"

"Thirteen. It was difficult, that's for sure, but Emma Rae was already a big part of our lives by then, like an aunt, and when my mom died she took over a lot of the mothering. That really helped a lot. She was always telling me stories about my mom, making sure that I'd remember her, I suppose, and letting me talk about her too. And when all else failed . . ."

"Let me guess," I interrupted, "A cup of tea."

He laughed, a nice, rich laugh. "You guessed it! As far back as I can remember, there was always Emma Rae and her tea."

He pointed to the right again. "And there it is: your very own little piece of paradise."

It didn't look like all that much, really. A big, two story house, like an old farmhouse back home. A huge faded barn was behind it, further back from the road, and between them were the greenhouses, long and low. The buildings were on a large cleared lot, but back a ways on all sides and behind, there were wooded areas. My heart began to race. This was incredible. This was *fantastic!* That was all mine, free and clear, *mine!* Maybe the house could use a coat of paint, maybe the barn had seen better days, but even so. My heart was singing so loudly I could hear it in my ears. I was a pioneer. I was a homesteader. This was my adventure. This was my land. I had come home.

Almost before Daniel had come to a full stop in front of the house, I was falling out of the car, as eager as I'd ever been for anything. I was seized with a passion I'd never dreamed of, and I was fit to burst with excitement. Never one to hurry, I was nonetheless actually running towards the house, up the steps, to peer through the etched glass window beside the solid front door. I tried the molded brass knob. Locked, of course.

I twisted my head to look back at Daniel, and bounced impatiently on my toes.

He crossed the yard with measured steps, almost teasing, I could swear. "What happened to you!?" he asked with a laugh. "I didn't know you had all that energy hiding in there."

"Hurry up!" I demanded as a giddy laugh rolled up from deep in my belly. What *was* happening? As he came up the porch steps, key already in his hand, I reached out and covered it with my own now-shaking hands. "Wait," I said, my voice breathless. He stopped cold, and we stared at each other for a long minute. I could feel the cold metal of the keys warming to our combined touch. I didn't know how to ask for what I wanted; I hadn't asked for what I wanted in many long years.

He figured it out, bless his heart. "You want to be alone for this?"

I nodded mutely.

He released the keys into my hand, and stepped back, looking up at the porch beams. "Tell you what," he said at last. "Why don't I just head back down the road a bit, stop in and see if maybe Ben's home, help myself to a cup of coffee. I'll come back in a bit, see if you need anything. Good luck getting service on your cell phone up here, but you've got my number, and you can use Emma Rae's phone if you need me sooner. All the keys are on the ring; I guess you can figure it out. How does that work for you?"

"Great," I said, wanting him gone *now*, "Really great. Thank you so much, Daniel, really."

He laughed again, turning away. "Have fun," he said over his shoulder. "You go on in, I'll set your bags on the porch before I go."

I was sliding the key into the lock before he reached the car. I paused a moment, holding anticipation like a birthday present, then I took a deep breath, pushed open the door, and crossed the threshold.

I walked into the foyer, and my heart almost stopped cold as, out of the corner of my eye, I caught movement. I whirled to my left, and there she was, Emma Rae. It was an eternal second before I realized that I was staring at myself in a large mirror that hung just inside the front door. Wow. Even as I sucked deep breaths into my gut and my heart slowed down, the jittery, spooked feeling remained. Under the mirror was a boot chest. I sank down onto it and sat for several long minutes, trying to calm myself. Even though I knew it was just my own reflection that had spooked me, that obviously Emma Rae wasn't here and I was most assuredly alone, I still had that prickly feeling between my shoulder blades that I was being watched. I allowed myself a brief, fervent wish that I hadn't chased Daniel away after all, but then I wrestled myself back into sanity. This was my house. I would not allow myself to start out by scaring myself like this. I gave myself a few more seconds to recover my equilibrium, and then I stood back up.

I looked at myself in the mirror again. Then I put the manila envelope on top of the chest, and opened the jewelry box that I was still gripping. Once again I was stunned by the brilliance of the gold, diamonds and alexandrites. The set didn't exactly match the flowered cotton sundress I was wearing, but I nonetheless clasped the heavy collar around my neck and replaced my small gold hoops with the huge earrings. Holy cow, that was something to see! My brain told me I looked absolutely ridiculous, but my heart whispered something else, something about how my blue eyes sparkled and my lips didn't look quite so pale and my red curls gleamed, something about possibility, and hope, and second chances. I nodded slowly at that strange creature in the mirror, picked up Emma Rae's envelope, and went on into the house.

It was definitely an older home, but it was beautifully maintained. The furnishings were a bit faded but of good quality, the windows were the modern, double hung kind. Everything was clean, orderly, comfortable. The big yellow kitchen was quite modern, probably completely updated within the last five years, and had a large walk-in pantry brimming with jewel-toned glass jars of home-canned goods. There was a dining area beside the kitchen, set into a huge bay window that overlooked the back yard and the gardens. I'd have fun exploring all that later. Besides the kitchen, dining area and a huge family/living room, there was an office, and a mudroom leading to the back door. Upstairs were two good sized bedrooms with nice, roomy closets and a shared bathroom, and a master suite with a walk-in closet, a full bath, and French doors leading out to a balcony that ran the length of the house. The balcony was furnished with a small outdoor table and chairs as well as a low, single bed, and from it I had a full and glorious panorama of the ocean. Back inside, I found a narrow staircase leading to the attic. What in heaven's name had Emma Rae needed with all this room? And what would I do with it all?

I headed up the stairs to the attic. I don't know what I was expecting, but I was somewhat disappointed that it looked so benign. Filtered light from the windows striped the plain wooden floor. Shelves, closed boxes and clothing racks were neatly organized. There was a large, dusty freestanding mirror, and an overstuffed chair with a little table beside it. There was a large wooden chest that looked like an old library card catalogue, with small drawers six across and twelve deep. I looked back at one of the sets of shelves, a five shelf bookcase. It was closely packed with books. I took a closer look.

There were notebooks and bound books in all sorts of colors and design. Dates were hand lettered on every spine. I pulled one out, flipped through it: page after page of handwriting, interspersed with beautiful pencil sketches. I returned it to the shelf and picked out another. It was the same. They were dairies, journals. Lots and lots and lots of them, shelved in chronological order. The book on the far left end of the bottom shelf was dated 1917, the year before Emma Rae left her family and her baby and disappeared. The last book on the right end of the top shelf was dated 2010. Last year. All of Emma Rae's missing years were right here at my fingertips. The answers to all the questions? I felt a strong urge to grab the first one, drop into that comfortable looking chair and just start reading, not stopping until I finished them all. At the same time I felt a certain kind of fear, like I felt whenever I approached an accident on the highway: what horrors might I accidentally encounter here? This could wait, I decided.

There must be one for this year, I thought. I wondered where that one was. I hadn't seen it in my first quick explorations. No doubt it would show up sooner or later.

I noticed how tired I was, and I felt the stiff paper of the envelope I still held. Another potential bomb. I'd dilly-dallied long enough. I headed down to the kitchen to brew myself a cup of Emma Rae's tea, then went back up to the balcony to find out what she had to say for herself.

My dearest Emma,
    Are you having fun yet?

You have got to be kidding me, I thought. The paper lay in my lap. I think I read it fifty-seven times. I looked at the front, I looked at the back, I checked the envelope. That was it. That was all she wrote.

I bet I sat there for fifteen minutes before I began to think about the question. Was I having fun yet? Hell, no, I wasn't having fun. My whole life had been taken, shaken, and turned upside down. What did she mean, *was I having fun yet*? That just pissed me off, that question. I was ready for some kind of an explanation about all this madness, and that's what I got?

I stood up, the offending paper gripped in my hand, and paced up and down the length of the balcony.

Was I having fun yet?

I stopped, leaned on the balcony rail, and stared across Highway 1 to the ocean. I couldn't see the beach; I assumed there was a sharp drop off somewhere. But I could hear the sound of the waves loud and clear, and I could see them dancing out forever until they met up with the blue, blue sky. I could smell it, the sharp salty smell of the sea that had so surprised me when I'd first smelled it two days ago. Five minutes, maybe less, and I could have my toes in that water, I could have my first baptism in the ocean.

Was I having fun yet?

To my right was the balcony bed. I could sleep out here if I wanted, the waves my lullaby, the moon my night light. If I didn't want, I had my choice of three bedrooms inside, not to mention numerous couches or chairs that could suffice in a pinch. On stormy nights I could sleep in my own big bedroom, in my own big bed, with a fire in my own big fireplace.

I went back into the house, dropping the letter on the bed, a gorgeous sleigh bed covered in an exquisite, handmade crazy quilt of midnight blue, burgundy and deep green velvets and silks. No, I wasn't having fun, that much I knew. But even more troubling was the question, *why* wasn't I having fun? I was in the midst of the most amazing adventure, and I was all stunned and numb and, for real? Annoyed? I hadn't even had to grieve to have this adventure. It was given to me by a complete and total stranger for whom I'd felt nothing. What the hell was wrong with me?

I caught my reflection in one of the many mirrors Emma Rae had hung all over the house. Who was that woman, I wondered, with her mussed up copper curls, her faded cotton sun dress, and a fortune in priceless gems around her neck and in her ears? And then it hit me, and it hit me hard: I could be anyone I wanted. Emma Rae must have invented her own self, right? She'd left everything she knew, and, well, who even knew what the "and" was? Look at this property, look at this *stuff*. And I hadn't even investigated the greenhouses, the barn . . .

I could be anyone I wanted. Which meant . . .

I could give up being miserable.

Wow. I sat down on the nearest chair. Now wasn't *that* something to think about?

Before going outside, I carefully returned the jewels to the wooden box and tucked it into the drawer of the bedside stand. Then I went out, wandering slowly through the gardens behind the house. Vegetables, and about a thousand different herbs. Back a ways were blueberry bushes and blackberry canes, further still a small orchard with apples, peaches, even citrus trees! Many of the vegetables were varieties I'd never seen before. However most of the plants were carefully labeled: about six different kinds of tomatoes, foot long burgundy beans and short string beans, round pale zucchini, long deep green zucchini, pattapan squash, so many different herbs. . . . It was incredible, the amount of work to keep this all so lush and healthy, let alone to have everything labeled so clearly. What on earth had Emma Rae done with all this produce? She certainly couldn't have eaten it all herself. Then I thought about the mudroom, and the deep pantry off the kitchen. Both had shelf upon shelf filled with jars of home-canned jams, jellies, preserved vegetables and fruits. Just thinking about it reminded me of Petie and her mom, and those long-ago days in their kitchen. Petie would love all this!

I was fascinated also by the way everything was laid out. Far different from the clean lines of vegetable rows I was familiar with, there was very little bare earth showing here. Herbs and low-growing flowers covered the ground under taller plants, which weren't laid out in straight lines but had a more organic flow. It was unusual to me, but I liked the relaxed feel of it. Bees, hummingbirds and butterflies obviously loved it; the whole place swarmed with gently humming life.

From the gardens I worked my way through the greenhouses. There wasn't a lot in two of them now, certainly not much I recognized. Some of the plants were far more exotic looking than anything I'd seen before. Again, however, what was there was neatly labeled. The third building, which I'd originally thought was another greenhouse, was different from the other two, more of a workshop. It was sunk down into the ground; three deep steps led down to the door. While the same long, low shape as the greenhouses, the wall and ceiling panels were glazed green. I assumed that would keep it much cooler so that it could be used year 'round. Braids of onions and garlic as well as bunches of dried herbs hung from the ceiling, the sides were lined with counters which held all sorts of tools and containers, there was a deep sink, and a bookshelf was crammed full of books on gardening, growing and using herbs, preserving, etcetera. I would definitely have to take a closer look at those soon, I told myself.

I was just leaving the workshop when I saw a red jeep pulling into the drive. I glanced at my watch. Good heavens, Daniel had been gone almost two hours; I'd barely noticed the time passing.

It took me a moment to recognize that my guest, casual in an old T-shirt and cargo shorts, was Ben. "Hey you," he called as he strode my way.

"Hey yourself." I ignored a flutter in the region of my heart.

"Daniel got called back to town. He tried to phone, but I guess you were out here. I told him I'd swing by to make sure you didn't need anything."

"I'm exploring," I smiled up at him. "Wanna come?"

He grinned back. "Sure. Although I have to warn you, I've seen it all before."

"Oh, re-e-eally?" I fired back at him, and he laughed. "I'm just headed to the barn," I told him.

"That's exciting," he said, "Hang on to your hat."

I thought he was joking, but as he dragged back the huge barn door, I reevaluated. Inside was a well used Ford pickup truck, a late model Honda CRV, and, exciting indeed, what seemed to be a two-seater airplane. It was little more than two seats suspended in a cage-like frame under light wings, all shiny and deep blue and silver. I caught my breath, and turned to Ben.

"She's a beauty, isn't she?" he asked, walking to the plane and running his hand along her top . . . wing?

"Is this . . . ?" I started, then stopped, uncomfortable with the question.

His hand dropped and he turned to look at me. "No," he said, "She was in her other one when she went down, her old ultralight one-seater."

"Oh."

We were silent for a long minute, then, "Emma."

"Hm?"

"You know Emma Rae and I were good friends, as well as business partners."

"Partners?"

"Well, I guess maybe not on paper. Emma Rae hated all the fuss involved in what she sarcastically called, 'doing things right.' She preferred to make up the rules as she went along, and as long as it seemed kosher to me, I was happy to do it her way.

So officially, no, we weren't really partners. The business was hers and she paid me. But in practical application, yes, we were"

Was he trying to tell me something more? "Do I need to pay you something, or buy something from you, or, um, what are you telling me?"

He laughed again. I liked it. "No, no, I'm not trying to tell you anything like that. It wasn't that kind of business. We made and sold tea, that's all. We grew ingredients here, we gathered plants from everywhere, we both did that work. Emma Rae did most of the work of actually making the blends, although I did help her with that from time to time. I did all the paperwork, bookkeeping, tedious inside work. We split the profits 50/50. If you decide to continue the business, I'll be glad to teach you all that I know. The recipes, now, that was part of her gift. When it came to that, I was just the worker, Emma Rae was the queen bee."

He looked at me quizzically. "What do you know about this stuff, about herbs and tea making and all?"

I shook my head. "Absolutely nothing. Wait, I had an aloe plant once, does that count for anything?"

"Oh, boy," he said.

I looked away from his bemused expression, back to the little plane. "What will happen to this, now?"

"That's up to you. Emma Rae hoped you'd fly it."

"What do you mean? How can you know that?"

He sighed. "Emma Rae talked about you a lot, Emma, about her hopes and dreams for you. She's been planning for you for years."

"How is that possible?" I asked. "I don't understand this at all! Why didn't we know about her? If she cared about me, why didn't I ever know about her?"

He walked around the plane, touching it here and there, not looking at me. "I don't know if I can explain all that. There is a lot to Emma Rae's story, and I doubt any one person has all the pieces even now. Plus, Emma Rae loved a mystery, a surprise, a game. I imagine you'll be finding pieces of this puzzle for the rest of your life. Well, if you decide to put it together, that is."

"What do you mean?" I asked again.

He faced me. "Emma Rae spent years setting this up, that's true. She planned things very carefully so they'd play out in certain ways. She made certain provisions for you, she's probably left you some clues, and she's left you some clear instructions. But everything she did really is unimportant now. Emma Rae is gone." He swallowed hard, then continued. "You don't have to play her game, Emma. You can walk away. You can sell everything and walk away, back to your life in Michigan, or to any other life you want."

"Is that what you think I should do?"

He smiled, a big, genuine smile that lit up his whole face. "It makes no difference what I think. The beauty of it is, you have choices. Lots and lots of choices. You can do anything you want."

I thought of the letter I'd left lying on Emma Rae's big bed. "Are you having fun yet?" she'd asked. I looked at that lit up face smiling down at me and I felt a funny lift under my rib cage. And I realized that right now, in this minute, I was definitely having fun.

"So," he asked softly, "What do you want, Emma?"

I slanted a look at the shiny little plane, then I looked up into Ben's deep hazel eyes, and I smiled right back at him. "I want to fly."

He grinned. "I can help you with that," he said.

Chapter 4

After Ben left, I went in to fix myself a cup of tea, ruefully shaking my head at myself. A mere week ago, I was a coffee person, 100%. Now I couldn't seem to get enough of Emma Rae's brew.

With steaming cup in hand, I went up to the attic for the first journal, starting date January of 1917, then went outside onto my balcony, and settled in. All right, Emma Rae, I thought, what have you got to say for yourself?

January 1917

I've met the most interesting girl! Sophia Mikhailskovich (is that not a funny name!), here in New York all the way from Russia! She is Russian royalty, related to the tzar! She speaks little English, and poorly, but we were able to make ourselves understood to one another. She is very kind and good, but I often notice that her eyes seem sad. I would be sad too, I know, if my whole country was at war with itself, if my government was completely turned around and my family was in grave danger. But she sets aside her sadness, she says, so that she is able to enjoy each day, because every day it is a miracle that she and her family are still alive and together, all but her one brother. She says that he stayed behind when they escaped, making sure that everything went smoothly for them. They do not know if he was able to escape or not, and every day she is afraid for him. How frightening that must be.

I met her in the park, and it seemed that we were fated to be instant friends. We walked together, and when we passed the stationer's shop, she asked if I kept a diary. She said she has been keeping one ever since she was a little girl. With the whole world in turmoil, she says, people need to keep a record of their lives. Someday, someone might learn something useful from the things we experience now. That was such a romantic notion that I went right in and bought a notebook so that I may record my life, also.

Even though New York is very exciting, I miss Pennsylvania, and our quiet home near Philadelphia. Sometimes I feel so frazzled here. Everyone is always in a hurry, and it is so noisy! They even have motorcars here, and whenever one goes by there is always such a ruckus, as the horses do not like them at all, and people stop to watch the marvelous machine. It seems to me that one looks much like another, and if I cannot ride in any, I do not need to see them going by all day.

Papa does not seem very happy here, either. He prefers the quieter Philadelphia office, where he makes all the decisions. Here someone else gives the orders, and Father does not like that at all. Here he is told what he has done wrong back home and how he needs to change things. I know that he resents that. But once this business is concluded, we will return to our quiet lives where Papa is the King. Mama likes the shops here, but even she is beginning to look tired. I hope we do not have to stay much longer. But as long as we are here, at least now I have my new friend to make the days go by more pleasantly. And perhaps I can help her to have more pleasant days, also, and keep her from being consumed with worry about her dear brother.

February 1917

Sophia is so excited! They have reason to believe that her brother did escape after all, and may soon be arriving here in New York. She speaks of nothing else. I hope for her sake that it is true. So much of the news from Europe is very grim indeed.

March 1917

    I am not very good at this writing business. It is just that either nothing is happening so why write at all, or too much is happening and I do not have time. I have been wanting so much to return to Pennsylvania, to my quiet garden and my old school friends. Yet now I do not want to return home, and it seems that at last we will! Everything is tumbling around inside of me. At last, Sophia's brother is here. He was shot with a bullet, and almost died on shipboard! But he has been here now for a week and the infection is gone and yesterday for the first day Sophia brought him with her to the park.

    What words can I use to express what I am feeling? As much as I knew immediately that Sophia and I would be friends, those feelings were trifling beside what I feel for Alexis. Who knows if he felt anything at all? Perchance the flush on his check was left from his fever. I had no fever before, but oh my heart, I am burning now. Though we could barely understand each other's words, I feel that my understanding of the entire world has opened up, new and astonishing.

Emma Rae may not have been very good at keeping up to date in her writing, but she was wonderful at capturing life in her drawings. Her pencil captured street scenes, architecture, individuals, bringing them to life with remarkable clarity. Her picture of Sophia showed a young woman with lovely, delicate bone structure and deeply haunted eyes. What had Sophia already experienced in her short life that had left her so marked? And the sketch on the opposite page, the young man . . . He could only be Alexis, though the drawing wasn't labeled. He looked so much like Sophia, with matching bone structure and a similar tension around the eyes. Yet there was a deeper glimmer in his eyes, echoed at the corners of his mouth, that spoke of humor, maybe even a mischievous nature. It was magnetic.

Incredible that Emma Rae had captured it with a few light strokes of pencil. I was held captivated by the image for long minutes before I was finally able to snap myself away from that impish expression and turn the page.

April 1917

I feel as though I have received a stay of execution: Father has been told we cannot return home yet after all. How my heart sings! Though truth be told, if he knew why I smile so, he would take me home at once! Every chance I get I steal away. With Alexis it is even worse. He is a prince, I am no one. No one, that is, but the woman who loves him with every beat of her heart, with every particle of her being. His mother is planning even now to marry him to some other Russian émigré, a beautiful dark countess whom he has known since he was born. He assures me he cannot bear it. I know that I cannot. What are we to do?

May 1917

My heart is breaking! At long last, the time has come for us to return home to Pennsylvania. No and no and no! How can I leave my Alexis? But this is not our only trouble; his marriage is arranged! And Alexis says that he must marry her, that this is his duty. He says that we must still be together, forever he says, and yet he plans to marry another. How can this be? What world has he come from, that he could even suggest such a thing? And he says that I am the one who is unreasonable, that I know nothing of the real world. In one moment he calls me a simple farm girl, stubborn and naive, in the next he is gathering me in his arms and promising that his love for me is endless. Sophia tells me that what he says is true, that he must marry the dark countess, yet all can still be well for us. They are the ones who do not understand. Such a thing is impossible to me. *Perhaps this is the way it is in their barbarian Russia, but this is not how it can be for me, not ever. Oh what am I to do?*

August 1917

The summer has both sped by and dragged. I am so happy to be here in my home, far from the madness of New York, and as I tend the garden and help my mother harvest and preserve, I feel such a deep contentment, and the days fly by on bright wings. To have my fingers back in the good Earth, to breathe in once again the scent of growing things, is to return to joy.

And yet this time away from Alexis wrenches me to my very soul. Through Sophia he begs me to return, but how can I when his plans to marry remain in place? Even now they are arranging the marriage to take place at Christmas, one more thing to add to the festivities of the season. As much as I love him, as much as I had hoped that he would see things in a different way, I understand now that this will never be. And I have begun to heal, I think, from that deep wound. I have begun to accept that I will remain a simple farm girl, that this great love I have for Alexis was a page in my life's book that has been turned.

September 1917

The days grow shorter, and at night I sit upon the swing on our back porch and breathe in the sweet, cool air. I try to quiet my thoughts, I try to hush the mad racing of my heart, but I cannot. Will I ever know peace again? It will not be possible after all, to leave behind this desperate love. I know now that Alexis was right to call me naive, but not in the way that he meant. I was naive to believe his sweet words and ceremonies, to allow myself to be swept away on his romantic fantasies. I was naive to allow him to hold me as I did, on that last night before we left New York. I was naive to let him love me, for now I am pregnant. I have told no one, and as yet I have been able *to hide my growing middle, but soon I can hide nothing. What am I to do? My only solace is to think that now Alexis must marry me in truth, for I carry his child. Surely his hard-hearted mother cannot deny us now. I must find a way to return to New York, and it must be soon. His wedding day approaches.*

I dropped the journal to my lap. I'd been enjoying this adventure as though it were fiction, as though it had nothing to do with me, and of course the pregnancy was no surprise by this point. But suddenly I realized, this must be my grandfather she was pregnant with, this must be Grandpa Henry. Had I ever heard a word about his father? All I knew was the story that Emma Rae had married young and lost her husband in the war. Somehow, this didn't sound like the same story. Was it possible? Was Grandpa Henry's father a Russian prince?

These were the thoughts that played in my mind. But behind them were deeper questions, agonized questions that had no answers, that for years I had tried to suppress and ignore. I kept thinking my own pain was behind me, left in the dust of my past, only to have it dredged up again and again. And now, yet again. This poor, innocent country girl, in one brief moment, had changed her life forever, had started a new life in an apparently tragic chain of events that linked all the way to the present day. While I still struggled with my own tragedy, my childlessness, the cut to my soul that never seemed to heal. I had been pregnant once, a million years ago, but had lost the baby at four months. I'd never conceived again. Mitch had refused to go to the doctor about it. "If it's supposed to happen, it will," he always said. It was only years later that I discovered that he'd gone to the doctor all right, right after I'd gotten pregnant. He'd taken himself right on in and had a vasectomy, and by the time I learned of it, I was forty years old and he was divorcing me for some other woman.

Emma Rae had one night of passion, and, like so many other young girls who had no desire for children, she'd conceived.

Well, no one ever said life was fair. I sighed, and let my soul bleed for a little minute. Then I went and fixed myself another cup of tea, and remembered happy days from long before Mitch. I remembered playing out in Petie's garden, chasing each other around with worms and screams and laughter. I remembered the smile on Petie's mom's face as she watered and weeded, shaking her head over our antics. I sat back and picked up the notebook.

January 1918

It is done. By now Alexis must be married. And I, heavy with his child, am sequestered at my Aunt's, miles from the nearest neighbor. Every day I am bigger, rounder, and I waddle like an overweight goose. I am a disgrace, of course, and my father and my mother may never forgive me for the shame I have brought to them. But I admit to no regrets, for a surprising joy has grown in me in these long months, a love for this child that makes the love I once felt for Alexis pale by comparison. Oh what a liar I am! I love Alexis as much as I ever did! But even so, I love this child still more. How I long to hold this baby in my arms, to sing it the lullabies I heard at my mother's breast.

July 1918

What am I to do? My life is unbearable! My darling Henry is four months old, and he brings me joy beyond imagining. But my father is so cold to me now; he will never forgive me. He will not speak to me, he will not even look at me! Certainly he pays no attention to Henry at all. My mother is little better. They have circulated a story that I am married, that my husband has gone to fight in the war. Of course, this imaginary husband will die in the conflict. But I am confident that my father's animosity will not die. I was certain that, once he saw his grandson, so full of giggles and bubbles and smiles, his icy heart would melt, and even if he could not forgive, perhaps he would forget a little and allow himself to feel kindness towards the babe. But it is not to be. How can he keep his heart so cold? Where is the love he used to have for me? Where is the tenderness my mother once had?

I cannot continue to live like this. I will take my Henry, and I will go to New York and present him to his father. Alexis must acknowledge him; he must help us. How I will get the money for such a trip I know not. Perhaps Sophia will help me. Her letters are a rare pleasure to me still, and I know her heart is full of sympathy for my situation. But how can I ask such a favor?

Is it possible that my dear Aunt, who cared for me so lovingly during my pregnancy, could advance me the money? She would have kept us with her, but Father insisted on bringing me back, I think with the sole purpose of punishing me day and night for my "mistake."

How is it possible that anyone could continue to think that it was a mistake, if it brought me my baby, my beloved, my Henry?

September 1918

Six months, and my little treasure grows more dear each day. Each day that passes I put all my energies toward finding a way to get to New York, to take Henry to his father. Surely Alexis will help us. But I cannot even visit my aunt; Father and Mother watch my every move. I cannot continue to live in this manner. Some days I despair. But despair will not help Henry.

April 1919

Can it be that two years have passed since I first met Alexis? To think, I believed that our love would last forever. Oh how foolish I was, how young! What a thoughtless, careless girl I was then.

I have returned to New York at last. With Sophia's help I did manage to meet Alexis. She had not told him I would be there. He did not recognize me at first. Am I so changed? But for Henry, I approached with a boldness I did not feel, and at last Alexis knew me. He cannot deny that Henry is his son; the beautiful dark eyes are just the same, as is the deep dimple just to the left of his full lips. Perhaps I saw love still deep in those eyes, perhaps it was more pity. It does not matter. He will not claim us. I am undone. How can I raise my son, the light of my existence?

This last night in New York, a maid came to my room. Sophia had come to speak with me. She had been sent from Alexis. His suggestion was that I stay here in New York, where he will care for me and for Henry. This is what he suggested to me before, before we made Henry, that I live a secret life with him. It is no more palatable to me now. Sophia and I talked late into the night, but she could not convince me. It is impossible. I will not compound my errors by becoming a kept woman. At long last Sophia understood that I would never agree. She admitted then that Alexis had told her I would remain firm. He had given her a large sum of money to help us. When she left, we clung to each other like sisters; I fear we will never meet again.

May 1919
If I have to live like this any longer, I fear I will take my own life. I am treated like a slave in my own home. One thing only has improved: while I was away, it seems my Father and Mother came to know the love they have for little Henry, and now he is the cherished one. Nothing is too good for my little man now. But now they keep all the care of him; they keep my own son out of my hungry arms! It is they who feed him

and play with him and teach him to walk and to speak, and I have the cooking and cleaning and the tending of the gardens and animals. They even keep him in their room at night. If I object, they flail me with cruel words and threaten to send me away without him. I would have been better off to stay with Alexis and live a harlot's life; at least I could have held my son in my arms.

July 1919

    I cannot continue any longer. Henry is a king here; he will be well taken care of. I leave tonight, if I can slip away without being seen. I have kept the money Alexis gave me. With it, I will return to him. I know not if he will have me. But any other life is better than the life I am living now, tortured every moment by circumstances I cannot control.

    Goodbye my little man, my Henry. I will come back for you one day, when I can keep you and take care of you in a little house of our own. I would take you with me now if I could, but even your sleep is watched over by the jealous eye of your grandfather. It will be a small miracle if even I am able to escape. But I must try, for if I stay another day, I fear that I will do myself grave harm. The escape I choose now is temporary, my little love, which I must believe is better.

    God's blessing be upon you, my son. I will come back for you, my darling, I promise. I promise!

I woke early the next morning, groggy from a restless night's sleep. I'd dreamed sad dreams of Emma Rae, dreams in which she was running, always running, and I tried to help her but could never reach her until finally somehow we traded stories and I was the one running away, and she tried and tried to get to me. I was tightly wrapped in my sheets when I woke up, and almost more tired than I'd been when I'd finally stopped reading Emma Rae's journal and gone to bed.

This was certainly a different story from the one my father had been told. The drawings she had made of baby Henry, pages and pages of sketches, seemed to rise up off the pages, so powerful were they, so eloquent of the love she had for him. I was eager to tell Dad and Mom about it, but decided to wait a few days, and see what else the journals might reveal. Besides, I had so many things to think about, and I thought that today, my first day alone since I arrived in California, would be a good day for thinking. I intended to explore much more diligently today, to take my time and open boxes and cupboards and drawers. Of course I wanted to get back to Emma Rae's story also, but that could be done at mealtimes and in the evening. There was so much to do, so much to learn!

And of course there was the larger question: was I staying? I wanted to, I knew, even though the thought of it was actually quite terrifying. I'd be leaving all my friends and family far, far behind and starting a whole new life in a sparsely populated area. Would I die of boredom? How would I meet people or make friends? Mendocino County was not exactly a metropolitan area, and Emma Rae's property was twenty minutes from the nearest town.

Not to mention, how would I earn a living? Was the tea business really enough to support me? It wasn't like I had great job skills, and I didn't imagine there were a whole lot of positions around here just waiting for me to show up with my retail resume. I didn't know what taxes were on the property, either, but I'd have to come up with it somehow, and keep coming up with it if I hoped to make my home here.

I explored in the kitchen as I ate toast made from the stale half-loaf of bread I found in the bread box. I was definitely going to have to get to a store soon, though there was enough home-canned food in the pantry to feed the whole county for a year, as long as they didn't demand perishables. I found keys on a hook by the back door; I figured these were to the car and truck out in the barn. I rummaged through a junk drawer and found over a hundred dollars folded up tight in an Altoids tin. Hmm.

I looked more closely through the pantry. Whole peaches, spiced peaches, apple sauce, cinnamon apples, green beans, whole tomatoes, diced tomatoes, tomato paste, tomato sauce, salsa, tomato juice . . . Emma Rae sure liked her tomatoes! She also had jars of homemade chocolate sauce and fudge sauce, and bottles of several different kinds of wines and fruit cordials. My long gone piece of toast wasn't enough to keep me from salivating hungrily as I read labels. I picked up a box of graham crackers; it felt odd, somehow, and I peered inside. Holy cow! It was crammed full of five and ten and twenty dollar bills! I poured them out on the kitchen island and counted almost $600. Well, the idea of exploring every nook and cranny of Emma Rae's house was getting more interesting! I investigated the rest of the pantry shelves a little more closely, but only found food. Even with the lure of boxes full of cash, I was too impatient right then to spend more time in this little room. I was ready to move on to something else anyway.

I headed out to the garden. I was amazed all over again by the seeming chaos of the beds, but the plants were thriving and producing abundantly. I broke off a twig of rosemary and breathed in the heady aroma. I helped myself to a bright orange tomato the size of a marble, and gasped as the flavor exploded in my mouth. Several more of the tiny tomatoes followed, and then some purplish ones that were the size of large grapes and which had a deeper, more complex flavor: so delicious! I took a bite out of something round and crunchy with a prickly, yellowish skin. It seemed to be a rather odd cucumber, slightly lemony. I had a hand full of what appeared to be eighteen inch long maroon beans when I heard a car in the drive, and looked up to see Ben climbing out of his jeep and striding towards me.

"The plunder begins!" he greeted me.

I laughed, wondering if I'd dripped tomato juice down my shirt. "I tried, I really tried to resist!" I lied, then changed the subject quickly. "What are you doing here so bright and early?" After all, a good offense is a great defense.

"It's a workday. I came to work."

I must have looked a little caught off guard, because he quickly reassured me, "Don't worry, I won't bother you."

I shook my head at him. "I wasn't worrying. But what are you going to be doing?"

"This and that. Checking over the gardens, though they usually don't really need much besides watering. That's the beauty of the system."

"How so?"

He gestured over the beds. "We've spent years working on this, getting the plantings just right. It's partly companion planting, partly permaculture, all an adventure." He laughed at the confused look on my face and went on. "Besides the vegetables, we've planted things that attract beneficials like bees and butterflies. All the low plants, the herbs and clover and whatnot, protect the soil and provide shade and protection from the sun. They also add a variety of nutrients back into the soil. Traditional planting tries to keep the soil around the crops bare, believing that 'weeds'" (he gestured the little quote signs) "attract bugs and plant-eating animals and steal the necessary nutrition and choke off the crops. If you select the ground covers with care, they do the exact opposite. And as for choking off the plants? Look around you at nature. Very little grows up from bare ground and stays in bare ground. The natural way of things is for something to grow in every bit of dirt. The way we've laid it out is more self-sustaining and much less work, not to mention less costly in the long run. We don't need to water as much since the moisture evaporates more slowly than it does from bare soil. And when the system is working right, there's no need for chemical fertilizers or insecticides."

He stopped and grinned. "Sorry. I can go on and on about this."

"No, it's okay. I've never heard anything like this, and it's pretty interesting, actually. Get me a cup of coffee and I could listen for hours!"

"Oh no, a coffee drinker!" he laughed, throwing up his hands as if to ward me off, "I knew it, you're an imposter! No relative of Emma Rae's could be a coffee drinker!"

I sighed a loud, exaggerated sigh. "I was afraid of that when I couldn't find a coffee maker. . . ."

He took pity on me and turned me towards the house. "If you make enough for me, too, I'll show you where she hides the coffeepot," he said. "Out of the kindness of her heart, she kept it for me." Then he looked all around and lowered his voice to a whisper, "And every now and then, even Emma Rae liked a cup of coffee."

We went inside and he directed me to the freezer for the coffee. "As seldom as she used it, Emma Rae always kept it in the freezer. But any *real* coffee drinker does too. Keeps it fresher."

I dug around in the packed freezer till I found a coffee bag. I unrolled the top and stuck in the spoon Ben had handed me, but, "What? Oh, wow! Not again!" I laughed. I'd scooped out money.

Ben turned around to look and then started laughing. "Again?" he asked. "Already discovered another of Emma Rae's quirks, have you?"

"This is the third time today," I affirmed, emptying the bag onto the counter.

"Well," he said, "Get used to it. Emma Rae treated money like a squirrel treats nuts. She did not trust banks, that's for sure. I convinced her to use one for business, but she made me do all the banking. In any case, I imagine if you live here the rest of your life, you still won't find all of her stashes." Then an odd look crossed his handsome face for just a second, but it was gone just as fast.

"What?" I asked.

He shook his head and turned away, "Nothing" he said, his voice sounding false to me. But then he turned right back, his face lit up, "Hey, what do you say we go flying today?"

"Today? In that?" I gestured vaguely towards the barn.

"No, no, the one in the barn, well, that's for you to learn in, that's yours. I thought to take you up in mine first, just to give you a taste, to whet your appetite."

I wanted to, I really did, but I thought of Emma Rae coming down into the ocean. "Is it safe?"

A grim look came and went, then he nodded. "As safe as anything else in this crazy world. The weather is great for it today, and I just went over my bird with a fine tooth comb. We'll do a real easy flight, stay low and slow. What do you think?"

My heart was racing at the thought. I can be anyone I want here, I reminded myself. No one here knows what a coward I am. I can do this. I looked up into Ben's eager face and gave a sharp nod. "Let's do it!"

Nothing in my life had prepared me for that, for flying in what Ben told me was a light sport aircraft. This is the lightest imaginable plane, with seats that are barely more than aluminum baskets hanging below feather-light wings. It rose and soared, lifted and swooped, until I was almost insane with the joy of it. Of course it wasn't the full freedom of flying that I had experienced so often in my dreams, but it was closer than anything I'd ever believed in. Poor Ben had to practically slap my hands away to keep my itching fingers off the controls, and he took steps to make sure I wouldn't try out Emma Rae's little plane on my own, without his lessons and supervision. I supposed I could take legal action against him for it, but I was honest enough, with myself at any rate, to recognize that it wasn't just the plane ride that had my heart soaring. There was just something about that man! I hadn't felt that lightness of spirit in many, many years, since long before the bitter end of my marriage.

After the flight, which started and ended on a long, flat area behind Ben's house, he took me back to Emma Rae's. I wanted to invite him in for lunch, but I didn't even have enough bread left for sandwiches. Also, I didn't want to seem too forward. I had never gotten back into the game after my divorce; I had wallowed in my loneliness and hadn't even considered dating. I thought it would be wise for me to move very slowly now. So I thanked him for the ride, and left him working while I took the Honda and headed to town for groceries. In the store, I noticed some sidelong glances, but I ignored them, changing direction when necessary to avoid speaking to anyone, shopping quickly and rushing away home.

That afternoon I brewed up a pot of Emma Rae's good tea, poured it over a glass of ice, and headed up to the attic with the tea and a handful of sugar cookies. As I climbed the steps, carrying the aromatic tea, I thought of all the fun Petie and I had playing up in the attic when we were little girls: lying on the dusty floor reading Nancy Drew mysteries, wearing my parents' old clothes, of camping out in piles of blankets on cold winter nights, making scary flashlight faces at each other and laughing till our sides ached. What treasures might I find in this attic, I wondered.

Second to the shelf of journals, I was most curious about the card catalogue chests. I went to the first one and pulled out a drawer. In it were little file cards with names in alphabetical order, and between the cards were packages of, what else? Tea. I pulled out one of the cards. "Rose Phillips," it said, and under that, "Struggles: Discouraged, lonely. Misses her mom. Has a hard time believing that good things will happen to her. Desires: Belief in a happy future." On the back of the card was a recipe, for the tea, I guessed. Some of the ingredients were familiar, others had odd names that I'd never heard of, such as "Bluestalk: three small young leaves," and "Furtongue: 4" twig, chopped small." I opened the bag and sniffed at the dry leaves. A feeling of hope stole over me, and I suddenly felt so close to my mom, as though she was here beside me in the attic rather than halfway across the country. I was smiling as I resealed the bag, tucked it and the card back in their places, and pulled out another card. "Jason Provost. Struggles: Anger, unforgiveness. Desires: Peace, even temper, ability to forgive." It, too, had a recipe on the back. I breathed in his tea, a long, deep breath. I thought about Mitch, my husband of twenty-one years, on the day I found out he had been cheating on me. I thought of the look on his face as he calmly informed me that he no longer loved me, he was leaving me and marrying his mistress of three years. I thought of the twist to his mouth when he told me he'd had a vasectomy years before, and I'd been too stupid, he said, to ever figure it out. A howling wind of fury washed over me, a familiar and bitter wind. It roared with a vengeance for long minutes, then slowly gentled, and at last whispered off like a quiet evening breeze until it was simply gone, leaving me with empty memories, memories that no longer raised anger or bitterness. In fact, I felt instead an almost overwhelming relief that I could now get on with my life, that the miserable days as Mitch's wife were behind me now, far, far behind me

Wow. I carefully put the bag and the card away and closed the little drawer. That was some powerful stuff there. I opened drawer after drawer; each drawer was stuffed with the cards and their accompanying teas. There must have been hundreds. On a whim, I looked in the Ws, and there it was: "Emma Rae Wright: Struggles: Depression, sense of futility, sad memories, inability to let go of past." No desires were listed. Was this for Emma Rae, or for me? I sniffed it, and the familiar scent lit my mind with memories of walking through corn fields on sunshiny days, laughing through the rows at Petie, dodging toads and the occasional snake. I turned it over to see the recipe. Among the ingredients was "mist from a sunlit cloud." Hmmm. Now how do you gather that?

Chapter 5

I didn't like to admit it, but sometimes the old house down-right spooked me. So often I felt like I was being watched, and the back of my neck would creep. All those mirrors: I kept catching my reflection out of the corner of my eyes, and I'd whip around, heart jumpstarting, just to see myself looking at me out of scared eyes. The mirror in the foyer and the freestanding one in the attic were the worst. And honestly? I was ready to be done with being scared all the time. For years I'd lived with uneasy fear, always feeling like the ground under my feet could give way at any moment. And guess what: it did. After that I'd insulated myself so that nothing like that would ever happen to me again, but even shutting myself off from relationships and opportunities didn't stop me from being afraid. That's how I'd gotten to be such a homebody, as I called myself. It wasn't that I loved being home in my comfortable little nest. Let's face it, it may have been little, but it sure wasn't all that comfortable. No, I was simply trying to avoid another round of misery.

Of course that hadn't really worked so well for me. Now I was perking up again, sticking my nose out of the nest, taking a look around at how, just maybe, things could be different. I'd been given this incredible, golden opportunity to rewrite my life, and I was actually eager to do it, which was the biggest surprise of all.

But I was also scared. Of course I was scared because of all the changes, who wouldn't be? But behind all that was this spooky feeling of being watched. Creepy. If I couldn't be comfortable in my own house, it was going to be a lot tougher to create this great new life for myself.

I started looking through the tea drawers again, this time with a new mission. I read the cards until I found this one. "Mary Jameson: Struggles: afraid of everything. Desires: everyday courage." I borrowed a little from her stash, and went to brew myself something new.

Cup in hand, I headed out the back door. Ben's Jeep was still in the drive, and I wanted to talk to him, to set up a time for my flying lessons to start, I told myself. But really, I just wanted to be with him, to talk with him, to hear his warm voice and see his sexy smile.

He was in the first greenhouse, his hands working the dirt at the roots of a tall, bizarre looking vine. He looked up with a smile. "Hey."

"Hey yourself," I smiled back. "Thanks again for that ride. Wow," I laughed again just thinking about it, "that was so amazing. When can you teach me to fly on my own?"

"Ready to be done with me already, are you?" he teased, faking a hurt expression.

I flushed to my roots. "Uh, yeah, right, that's exactly what I had in mind." To turn the topic, I motioned at the weird plant he was working with. "What is that thing?"

He frowned at the vine for a minute. "This is one of the, um, more exotic plants Emma Rae found in her wandering."

"It's exotic all right," I agreed. "What's it for?"

"Well, we're still working on that. It's actually pretty exciting. It seems to make the properties of some of our other plants more potent. If I'm able to cultivate it, my life could become a whole lot easier, because I could use less of a lot of other herbs by adding a little bit of this to the mix."

"Sounds useful. I found Emma Rae's tea chest in the attic, with all the customers' names and recipes and stuff."

He looked up sharply. "What are you talking about?"

I took a step back at his intensity. "That chest in the attic. . . ."

"I don't know what you're talking about. I've never been up there."

"Oh! Well, there's a big wooden chest full of little drawers. They're all full of cards with people's names and problems and their tea recipes and some tea."

He leaned hard against the counter and all the air seemed to flow out of him. He rubbed his forehead, leaving a smear of dirt. He seemed to be talking to the floor. "Can I see it?"

I took him up to the attic, and he opened the tightly packed drawers just as I had, one after another, reading the cards and occasionally breathing in the aroma of a tea. I stood quietly, feeling again that we were being watched, but it didn't feel bad or scary this time. It felt kind of comforting.

After a while he stood still, a bag of tea in one hand, the little card in his other. "You have no idea what this means, Emma. I didn't know what I was going to do. Emma Rae developed all of these recipes, she made the teas. When she left, I thought I'd lost all of that. I didn't know how I was going to tell people. All these people? They depend on this. Some of them can barely get through a day without it."

He turned to look at me. "Emma Rae was a very unique lady, and she loved her games and her mysteries. At times she could be incredibly exasperating, and she was the personification of the word 'stubborn.' But she was a true healer, and she had the most incredible gift of knowing exactly what a person needed. So she'd make up a tea, just for them. And whatever the person's problem, with the help of that tea, they'd start coping better, start making better decisions, start making the changes they needed to make to have a better life.

"I thought all that went with her when she left. I never knew about this. I didn't know what I was going to do. Maybe

I can't make anything new for anyone, but at least all of these people will still have their tea."

He sank into the chair, apparently exhausted. I thought about how I'd come to depend on my tea in just a few short days, and how I'd borrowed from Mary Jameson's stash to calm my fears. It had worked. It was incredible.

"Ben," I said, and he looked up. He still had that smear of dirt across his forehead, and it made him look so young. I wanted to brush it off, but Mary Jameson's tea wasn't that strong. "This stuff," I gestured at the chest, "maybe it gives us everything we need to make tea for anybody."

"How so?"

"Well, we can analyze the recipes, can't we? We pull out all the recipes that deal with fear, and we cross reference them and that way we can figure out what she used for fear. Right? Same with anger, hopelessness, whatever. There've gotta be hundreds of different recipes here. At the very least, that ought to be enough to get us steered in the right direction, yes?"

He stared at me for so long I started to get nervous. Was my idea that stupid? It had just come to me, it seemed logical to me, but what did I really know about any of this anyway? I was just about to apologize for my idiotic suggestion when he stood up, pulled me into his arms, and hugged me so hard I thought I'd squeak. I could actually feel tension draining out of his body, and I wrapped my arms around him in support. This had to be the longest hug of my whole entire life. Before it was done, he said softly into my hair, "You did say 'we,' didn't you?"

I smiled into the collar of his shirt. "Yes. I said 'we.'"

*   *   *

Ben stood at his porch railing, looking across Highway One at the ocean. His blood hummed in his veins like a tonic of joy and relief, like he'd just had one of Emma Rae's more potent blends. He'd been frustrated with her many, many times, but these last few days since her . . . *passing*, he'd been beyond that. He'd thought she left him with nothing more than dust, nothing more than the day-to-day growing, gathering and preserving of things he only partially understood. He thought she'd left all the people she'd ever helped stranded, too. He sighed. He could almost hear her voice on the air, brimming with mischief: "You know me better than that."

It was true, he did. But he hadn't seen Emma coming. He pictured his own recipe card; what might it say? "Ben Rainey: gets bogged down in minutiae, doesn't see the big picture, cynical, doesn't know how to trust." All true, even after twenty years of working with Emma Rae. Who could have imagined that Emma, shoulders slumped in defeat and face lined with sadness, would spit out the solution just like that? Who besides Emma Rae, that is, the old gypsy! In just two days Ben could see Emma changing, opening up, believing in new possibilities. Why was he still surprised? He'd seen it over and over again, Emma Rae's elixir, that potent blend of her tea and her mischief and her love, bringing life back to barren hearts.

He had to admit, though, it had never before mattered to him like it did now. Emma Rae had taken herself off to her next adventure, but she had not, in fact, left him alone to deal with the fallout. She had brought him Emma. And Emma was blossoming before his awestruck eyes. Emma Rae's magic was still alive and well in the world.

And what's more, Emma seemed to have struck, just like that, on a very workable solution. Just knowing that there was some tea stored for their current clients, complete with recipes, had been relief enough. But now he, *they*, had so much more to work with. And what's more, Emma had seemed ready to start that very instant. Was it just a moment's interest, or was it possible that she would take up where Emma Rae left off? Could she have Emma Rae's healing discernment? Could she go where Emma Rae had gone?

His phone rang, and he went inside to answer.

"Ben? It's Emma." She sounded breathless, like she was laughing. "I hate to bother you, but I was wondering, could you come back over?"

"Sure, is everything okay?"

"Yes, yes, I just . . ." she broke off, and yes, he could swear she was laughing. Had she snapped already? "You have just got to see this, that's all."

"Okay, sure, I'm on my way."

*   *   *

I pulled a bottle of homemade wine out of the pantry. Who knew if it was any good, but I didn't care. This called for something stronger than tea. I also pulled out the packet of dark chocolate I'd bought in town, and some crackers and a wedge of delicious looking cheese, some kind I'd never heard of before. For a little hick town, they sure knew how to stock the goodies. I hummed a little tune, startling myself. When was the last time I'd done that? Oh who cares, I thought, this is the new me, and I went back to humming.

In only a few minutes, he was knocking at the front door. Just hearing his hurried steps had started me laughing again, and I danced to the door, made a face at the mirror, and opened to Ben.

"You are not gonna believe this!" I greeted him, grabbing his hand and tugging him across the threshold. "C'mon."

Without giving him a chance to say a word, I led him through the house and up the two flights to the attic. I had pulled out a card table and folding chair that I'd found in a corner, and set them up by the chest. I'd been excited by my idea of cross referencing the tea recipes and thought I'd get started right away. A notebook and pen lay on the table, and the contents of several drawers were laid out neatly. Ben raised his eyebrows, but I waved him past all that and pointed into the mostly empty drawers. He peered in. His breath caught briefly, and then he, too, started laughing. "You have got to be kidding me!" he said. "May I?" as his hand hovered over the first drawer.

"Be my guest," I laughed back, and he reached in.

At the bottom of the drawer was a stack of bills, all hundreds. There were twenty of them. Same thing in the next drawer. And the next. "Are they in every drawer?" he asked.

"I haven't checked them all, but I checked some in every row, and all of the whole top and bottom rows. Seems consistent."

He raised his eyebrows at me again. "How many drawers are there?"

I couldn't seem to stop laughing. "Seventy two."

"Oh my Lord. Emma, that's $144,000!"

I threw my hands in the air and danced in a little circle. "I guess I don't have to sweat the taxes this year!" I crowed.

"I guess not!"

It was incredible. I had a home. I had a business. I had money. And maybe, just maybe, I had a potential romance. Would wonders never cease?

I pulled a sweater out of the closet by the front door, wrapping it snug around my shoulders as I headed out into the cool night. I was nervous to be going anywhere alone in the dark, but I could no longer resist the tug of the relentless ocean. I'd been busy and preoccupied with so many concerns ever since I got here, and I'd ignored that pull, but I could do so no longer. I crossed the highway and a stretch of tall grass, walking carefully until I found the edge of the bluff. To my right I saw the posts that framed the top atop of a long wooden staircase that led to the beach below. My heartbeat sped up as I descended. I'd never met an ocean up close and personal before, and I admit I was intimidated. In Michigan I'd lived a mere three blocks from Lake Huron, but I had never felt a pull to the lake. This endless sea called with frightening insistence. But as I neared the bottom of the steps, the strange intensity of the ocean's call filled me, no longer with that irresistible fear, but with a blood-banging excitement. I jumped from the next to last step, toed off my sneakers, and raced across the sand into the surf.

A shock of cold hit me with the first wave, and right behind it a second roared in, soaking me to my hips. As the water rushed back away, the suck at my legs staggered me, and again fright raced through my veins as I realized that this ocean, this playful surf, was extremely dangerous. With more caution, I began a teasing dance at the water's edge, chasing the bubbling tide as it sucked out, racing away ahead of it as it roared back up the beach. Out and away we danced, back in and up we ran, back and away again. Over and over the icy water drenched my legs, sometimes roaring almost to my waist, but somehow I wasn't cold, and I gasped and laughed with exhilaration. This was a living, breathing monster, this ocean, and I filled my lungs with her watery exhalations and knew myself to be lost in a love I'd never imagined.

Once upon a time, when I was very young, I used to sing to myself. Now, unexpected and unanticipated, I was singing a wild and wordless song to this ocean and her denizens, a siren song full of longing, though I did not know what I was so longing for. And even as the longing grew until I could barely contain it, the ache filling every particle of my being, I felt, as well, a wildly growing joy, a sense that this, *this* was what I'd been looking for. Had I been looking? I didn't even know. But now, it seemed, I had *found*, and even in the finding I longed for more, and more, and more.

I don't know how long I played there at the world's edge; time had no meaning there that night. What I do know is that when I got back to the house I simply collapsed on my bed, too exhausted to do anything more. And when I woke the next morning, my hair stiff from salt spray and my eyes heavy from lack of sleep, my throat was hoarse from the singing and the salt, and the sea had taken up residence deep within my spirit. I jumped from the bed, ran down the stairs, swung open the door to yell a crazed woman's hello to the ocean. Yes, she was still out there, her song, her call to me, just as strong as it was the day before. I smiled with my whole being as I turned back into the house, and, as often happened, I caught my reflection in the mirror.

Emma Rae.

My heart stuttered, stalled, caught and beat again. It was just me, of course, what else? But there had been something there, in just that split second, an expression wild and smug and knowing that I had never worn, like my own edges had blurred and overlapped with another image, an image so almost, but not quite, mine.

Just that quickly it was gone. Gone? No, it had never been there, *of course*. As I turned away I glanced back once, a sliding sidelong glance. But after all, what did I think I'd see?

Too much was happening too fast. Nothing had happened in my life for so long, and nothing good for even longer. Now my life had taken on the characteristics of a whirling dervish, and my thoughts struggled to keep up. I'd tamped down my emotions for so long, and now they had blasted through Pandora's box with a vengeance. Was I losing my mind? What did I think had happened at the beach last night? What did I think I saw in the mirror?

I told myself I was simply exhausted from so much change so suddenly, and I was without my mom and dad, without Petie, and had no one to talk to, no one to help me defrag all this input. My thoughts were spiraling insanely, but that didn't mean I was insane. I headed up to the attic. Surely there must be a tea for this, I thought.

"Jordan McAllister: Struggles: runaway thoughts, mania, overwhelming dreams. Desires: a calm mind and the ability to slow down racing thoughts" was my selection. Not that my dreams were overwhelming . . . well, unless unrealized or forgotten dreams were unexpectedly stirred up. Hmmm. But in any case, I definitely had runaway thoughts. And after all, what harm could it do?

As I waited for the water to heat, I cleaned up the little mess I had left in the kitchen after Ben left last night, just a few crumbs and the partially empty bottle of wine. It had been pretty good, actually. I opened the bottle and breathed in the fruity scent. Over the bottle top, I saw the bag of tea lying on the counter. I thought of mulled spiced wine.

What about wine mulled with Emma Rae's teas? What might that be like? What if I isolated herbs that stimulated feelings of love, and heated wine spiced with those herbs? Would I be serving a love potion?

What if I served a tea-spiced wine at a party? What if, say, I wanted to present a concept to people who might not think it was such a good plan, and I spiced the wine with herbs that supported openness to new ideas. Could I manipulate people with these herbs? And forgetting the wine, for just a moment, wasn't that what Emma Rae had been doing: manipulating people to feel certain ways? I assumed the people who drank her tea, those who had their own blends, were fully aware of what she was doing, and of the results they could expect. But they weren't always, I knew. She had sent me tea without telling me what it was for. Had she manipulated me? Had she manipulated others without their knowledge?

And could I?

Did I want to?

Suddenly it seemed that I had a lot more on my hands than just a bunch of herbal recipes. I had felt the effects of these teas. In fact, already I relied on them. Was this, in fact, such a good thing?

I went back to the mirror by the front door, and looked at my reflection. "Emma Rae," I said softly, "Who were you, and what were you up to?"

I knew it was just my over stimulated imagination, but I could have sworn my reflection had an expression that I didn't, just the tiniest glimmer of mischief around the eyes.

Yeah. Right.

May 1920

This is my life now. I have a small apartment, clean and pretty with room outside for a tiny bit of garden. I have money enough to dress well, and some jewels that Alexis has given me. From time to time we go out together, but more often he comes to me and we stay in our little world, just the two of us. It is a good arrangement for him. As for me, I am so lonely here. Once upon a time I had a family that loved me, and good friends, girls I had known since I was born. Now I have only Alexis, when it is convenient for him. I am shunned by my neighbors and by Alexis' family, friends and business associates. I had thought at least to have Sophia as a friend, but no, it is not acceptable. Sophia must be a sister to Alexis' wife now, not a friend to his mistress.

Every week I write to my beloved Henry. My arms ache to hold him, my lips to kiss his little face. I send money, I send trinkets to delight a tiny boy. But my parents never reply. I hear nothing.

March 1921

I have been growing herbs in my window. I remember what I learned from my aunt, the many uses of these plants, for food and for healing. First I seasoned my breads, and I began taking them to my neighbors. I knew they looked down their long noses at me; it is no secret here in this quarter who I am. But I hoped that my baking might soften hard hearts. At first it seemed to make no difference, but what else did I have to occupy the long days? So I baked, more than I could ever eat, and I shared.

I think that they did not want to eat my bread. If it had not been unforgiveably rude, I think some of my neighbors would have thrown it back in my face. Perhaps they threw it in the rubbish the minute my back was turned. It did not matter to me. I only wanted to preserve my sanity, to occupy my time in a way that did not feel entirely without purpose. And perhaps even the hardest heart can only resist warm herbed bread for so long. And this much I know: once the first bite has been taken, the feast is sure to follow.

And so it happened. Soon they would greet me at the door, happy to see my covered basket at least. When the winter came, I began making thick stews, once again making full use of my thriving herb garden. As people all over the city became ill with influenza and other winter illnesses, those who ate my cooking remained well. As the season progressed, those who became ill began to send for me, to request the foods I made.

I began to notice that, as I cooked for this or that person, I would have a sense of what herbs to put in the food. I learned to always follow that sense. Soon I would go to the market to search out different plants, following this deep inner knowledge. It seemed to know far more than I. At times I would be drawn to some new plant and would add it to my basket. Always, *within the day I would know who this herb was for, and I would add it to whatever I was preparing for them.*

And so, in these few short months I have gained a new kind of notoriety. I am still the fallen woman, the paramour of a wealthy married man. That will never change. But now I have a usefulness, now I provide something these righteous people need, and so I am treated with more civility and, from time to time, even a kind of wary respect.

Beyond that, though, I have a new excitement coursing through my veins. What is this gift that is springing to life in me, this knowledge that guides me in helping others? I understand my aunt better now, my mother's sister, she who cared for me during my pregnancy. She lived far out from our small town, yet people came to her, and never left empty-handed. I was so deep in my own problems at the time I did not care to think about her life, but now I remember details and I see that she, too, must have this kind of knowledge, and be respected for it. And feared for it. For it is frightening, and yet it draws me deeper and deeper in. I cannot stop it now, and I do not want to. Finally I have some sort of purpose.

Chapter 6

I was up in the attic, carefully making notes on Emma Rae's teas. In a notebook I copied out the information from each card: person's name, struggles, desires, and the recipe for his or her special tea blend. In addition, I wrote out a large chart, trying to separate ingredients and purpose. This was a much more complex task. I was beginning to think I needed some highly sophisticated computer program for this; I believed my idea was a good one, but the doing of it might be beyond my abilities. After all, what did I know of herbs beyond parsley, sage, rosemary and thyme?

Then I remembered Walter's words after Emma Rae's service: "You have her gift." I hadn't known what he meant then, in fact I still didn't. But if I had one of her gifts, whatever they were, maybe I had others as well. I went through the house and out to the herb garden. For a few minutes I just walked quietly on the meandering paths, asking myself, "What are my struggles? What are my desires?"

My struggles came to mind far too easily: loneliness, depression, isolation, anxiety, fear of rejection, lack of purpose. These had been my constant companions for many years; some of them had been with me since childhood. My desires were much harder to know. And why is that? I wondered. How is it that I don't even know what I want?

That thought stopped me cold in the middle of a step. It was as though a deep fog was in my mind, obscuring my mental vision. If I didn't even know what I wanted, how was I ever going to get it? I was stunned by that revelation.

And just like that, as if guided by someone, I swung around, took seven steps back, and reached down to a small, furry plant that was completely unfamiliar to me. I broke off a sprig and, without even thinking, popped it into my mouth.

Eeeew! It tasted horrible! But even as I grimaced at the strong flavor, desires that were even stronger rose up in my mind: I want to love, and I want to be loved; I want to be useful; I want to understand Emma Rae; *I want to fly.*

Well, okay, fine. I knew what to do about that last one. I looked around for some peppermint to offset the bad taste in my mouth, and headed off to find Ben.

I found him in the workshop, stringing up herbs for drying. His back was to the door, and I stood unnoticed. A bitter taste lingered on my tongue. I watched Ben, his arms raised above his broad shoulders, strong hands tying up the herbs. *I want Ben.* That flush I'd been feeling so much lately washed over me, rising from the soles of my feet to the roots of my hair in a burning wave, then falling back and leaving me chilled and prickly, restless with desire.

He tied off the string and turned, startled. "Emma! I didn't know you were there. Is everything . . . are you all right?"

Concern flashed across his face and I felt the heat rise again, this time embarrassment. I knew I must've been ten shades of red. I gave a shaky laugh and scrambled in my flustered brain for an explanation. "Uh, yeah, I'm fine, I, um, just ate something strange."

He reached out and touched my arm, and the heat rose yet again. For Heaven's sake, this was ridiculous! "Not one of Emma Rae's herbs?"

The flush receded, leaving me feeling downright weak kneed. "Yeah, something from the herb garden."

"Emma, you want to be really careful about Emma Rae's herbs. Some of them are quite potent."

Now he tells me. "Well, is there a book or something I can study so I don't accidentally kill myself?"

He grinned at that. "Well I don't think she's got anything that'll outright kill you." He gestured to the shelves. "Help yourself to her books." His brows lowered briefly. "But some of her plants probably won't be listed in the books."

"Oh? Why is that?"

He looked away, and I got the very clear impression that he was, well, that he was hiding something from me. About Emma Rae's herbs? That didn't make sense. I must be imagining things, I thought. Again. Sheesh, I really must be losing it.

"Some of her plants come from, uh, let's just say exotic locales. They aren't what you could call well known."

"Really. Then how did Emma Rae know about them?"

He began working again, brushing together another bunch of herbs from a pile on the table. Was he avoiding looking at me? "Emma Rae had what you might call really good instincts. She seemed to just know things about plants and their healing properties, like they spoke to her or something. I never understood it. It was really uncanny. You've seen her recipes, you know they go way beyond stuff like helping someone sleep."

I noticed he hadn't answered my question, but I just nodded. "Yeah, I've been reading her journals. She wrote something about that."

"Her journals?"

I nodded. "They're up in the attic, you know, tons of them. They go all the way back to 1917. I've just started reading them."

"She kept journals since 1917? You mean like diaries?"

I caught the note in his voice then, saw the intense look on his face. "Yes," I answered. "In fact, I've been meaning to ask you about that. There isn't a current one. Would you know where it might be?"

He shook his head slowly, thoughtfully. "I didn't know about them." His eyes didn't meet mine. "Can I read them?"

"Ben?" His eyes came up then, but I could still feel that hesitation. "What's going on here?"

He looked away again. "What do you mean?"

Time seemed to shift for me, and suddenly I was back ten years, fifteen, twenty, back again with my husband, talking to him and seeing this exact same body language, this same unwillingness to meet my eyes, the same partial turn away, oh so subtle. All those years I'd chosen not to see it, I'd ignored the drag on my heart calling me to *wake up*! And eventually I'd fallen so deeply asleep to that deep inner knowledge that when he came to me and told me he was leaving me, I was caught completely off guard. I'd had no idea he'd been having an affair. But here, now, a door in my mind opened and I knew in that instant that I had chosen not to know. And furthermore, I also knew, with full and sudden conviction, that he'd been having affairs since the beginning. He'd only told me about the last one, the one he chose to leave me for. But now, here, so many years later, I understood everything. I even understood that I had blinded myself. Here, now, somehow, the blinders had been blown off.

I think I actually staggered. I had Ben's full attention then, as he caught me. "Are you all right? Do you need to sit down?"

I looked around and saw a high stool. "Yes, please, can I sit there?" My voice was rough.

Still holding onto me with one hand, he dragged the stool over with the other, and helped me up onto it. "Can I get you something? Water? Tea?"

My mind was racing. There was water right here, that wouldn't do. And tea? No thank you, not just now, I needed my own faculties just now, free of any of Emma Rae's influence.

"You know, I think I could use a cup of coffee. I hate to ask, but . . ."

"No, it's no problem. I'm happy to make it for you. Will you be all right here for a few minutes?"

"Yes, I just, yeah, just let me sit a minute. I'm okay."

As soon as he was gone, I walked myself slowly out of the workshop to a bench outside. I didn't know what herbs he was working with, but I was beginning to be highly suspicious of them all. I needed the light breeze to clear my mind. I needed to look at what I had just seen in myself.

Because it was shocking. It was, quite literally, life changing. In that instant, seeing Ben prevaricate, it was as though a hidden door deep inside of me had blown open, and what I saw inside had me reeling. Sometime long, long ago, I had closed my eyes to the things I instinctively knew. I had hardened my heart against things that I thought might hurt me, I had turned away from my own innate knowledge. I had blinded myself. As clearly as I had just seen that I did it all throughout my marriage, I had also seen that I'd started doing it long before I was married.

I had no idea what would happen now. How would this affect my life? As I sat with this knowledge, it seemed as though my heart was expanding, growing, filling me in a new way, like it was a plant that had been dormant for a very long time and now, suddenly, was bursting into full and glorious bloom. I felt tingly, I felt a humming all through my body. I felt alive in a completely unfamiliar way.

Wow. It was crazy. It was incredible. I felt brand new, or rather, like a stifling grey blanket had been over me for decades, and now, quite suddenly, it was gone. Now, in an instant, I was seeing, hearing, smelling, *feeling* cleanly for the first time since I was a tiny child.

Ben returned with coffee for both of us, and sat beside me on the bench. "Feeling better?"

I sipped the coffee. Ahhhhh, that was good. I hadn't known how much I was missing it. Rather than answering Ben's question, I looked directly at him and asked one of my own. "What aren't you telling me?"

His eyebrows shot up and his chin dropped.

He stared at me for a very long moment. Then, without taking his eyes off mine, he carefully set his coffee down on the bench. "Wow," he breathed. "I left Emma in the workshop and came back to Emma Rae in the garden."

I waited. I had all the time in the world. All the time in two worlds? a tiny voice said in my head, but I ignored it as nonsense. I let this moment stretch. How can I explain the power I felt as I returned to my true self, the self that I'd turned my back on so long ago? This much I knew already: I would know when people were not being honest, when they lied or when they were hiding things. I would know. Always. And that was some kind of power.

It could have been a minute, that we stared at each other; it could have been an hour. I remember drinking my coffee, holding his gaze over the rim of my cup. And finally, finally, he smiled into my eyes, and it was as though the sun broke through. He took my hand and stood up, pulling me with him. "Come on," he said. "Let's go flying."

Somehow I knew he wasn't stalling me. It seemed I'd passed some sort of test. I had a feeling my real education was about to begin.

*   *   *

Holy shit, Ben thought, Emma Rae had been right. In spite of his intense and unexpected feelings for Emma, he'd seen from the first that she couldn't take over for Emma Rae. Emma's eyes held deep and chronic bruising, symptoms of a crushed spirit. She had a timidity about her, an uncertainty. She didn't trust herself; naturally she didn't trust other people. She seemed easily confused, and even more easily overwhelmed. How, Ben wondered, could he ever tell her the truth? She couldn't possibly handle it.

He'd known he was right about her. As soon as he'd met her, he'd struggled with despair, knowing with certainty that all of Emma Rae's elaborate schemes would come to nothing. Even yesterday, when she'd shown him all that money, when she'd been full of light and laughter over Emma Rae's eccentric behavior, he'd still been sure that she simply didn't have the personality, the spirit, to inherit everything that Emma Rae had left for her.

When he left her in the workshop, staggered and reeling, weak with shock, he didn't know what was happening. He'd seen the calculation in her eyes as she requested coffee, but he hadn't believed it, hadn't credited it. But when he came back, when she took a drink of the coffee, looked through his eyes and right to his center, when she challenged him for the truth, his world had gone back to True. North was North again. Emma Rae had been right after all. This woman, *this* woman, was Emma Rae's rightful successor. What had happened in that short space of time he might never know. What he did know, however, was that Emma Rae had taught him, and now it was time for him to teach Emma. She wasn't going to believe it; no doubt her brain was going to put up quite a fight. Oh, well, so had his, back 20 or so years ago. They'd get through it.

And so now, let it begin. He would take her first to the door, where he had found Emma Rae so many years ago.

As he led her to the plane, his heart felt like it could fly them there all by itself. He couldn't stop smiling.

*   *   *

Oh how I love flying! Even just walking toward the plane, I couldn't keep the giddy grin off my face. When would he teach me to fly my own little plane? When could I go up by myself? But I didn't question him. I knew he had something on his mind right now and I was going to leave him to it. I'd read something about breathing to calm the mind and settle the spirit, so I tried it now. I breathed deep into my belly, letting my tummy relax and bulge like a puppy's, and then I released the breath again slowly, slowly. I did it again, and again, and as I did, my spinning thoughts settled and quieted. Hmmm. Handy skill to have. I had to keep reminding myself, but by the time we reached the little two-seater, I was surprisingly calm. I felt able to let Ben script today's flying adventure.

As we climbed into the suspended seats, Ben told me, "We're going to go up the coast a ways, into the Yellen State Forest. I should be able to find a stretch of beach where we can land—where there aren't too many people—and then we're going to take a hike. Okay?"

I'd changed into jeans and sneakers before we left Emma Rae's, so I simply nodded.

Funny thing about going up in a light sport aircraft: as high as we ever go, somehow my heart always seems to rise higher. The everyday boundaries of my mind slip away, fall below perhaps, and my thoughts become so much . . . *bigger* than when I have my feet on the ground, more expansive. All the petty stuff that I allow to bug me floats away.

On that day, all my worries about being watched in the house slid away. My concerns over working with Ben in Emma Rae's tea business, Two World Teas, flew off on the wind. The fears I had about leaving my old life behind to take up this strange new life dissipated. Of course they would return to me when I set my feet back on solid ground, but while I was in the air, none of it mattered. All that mattered was the joy that rose in me like a tide as we leaned out over the ocean and skimmed above the flirting waves.

We came down on a wide, empty beach. To our right the land rose and became wooded. We pulled the plane far up on the beach, away from the hungry tide. Ben handed me one of two water bottles, and we started walking inland. There seemed no need to talk, not yet anyway. In just a few minutes we were off the beach and following a rutted dirt road. We passed an occasional tent set back a ways, and nodded to a few people we saw, but for the most part we had the quiet woods to ourselves. Ben had a backpack slung over one shoulder and a pocket knife in one hand, and every now and then he stopped to cut off a plant, bag it, and put it in the backpack. We barely spoke. I was experiencing something unusual, a strange feeling, and I played it through my mind and my body curiously. It was a little startling when I identified it as contentment. How was it that contentment was so unfamiliar? I refused to pursue that line of thought; I chose to simply enjoy.

After about fifteen minutes, Ben grinned at me and gestured up a steep slope that cut off from the road we were following. "It gets a bit more challenging here."

"Okay," I smiled back. It certainly did get more challenging. Let's face it, I'd been a pretty committed couch potato for years. I hoped I wasn't about to be completely humiliated by my poor physical condition.

Thankfully, Ben kept the pace slow and helped me often. It was cool and shady under the trees, but still I was panting and sweating in no time. We stopped often to swig from our water bottles. I made a pact with myself that, the next time I climbed this path, I wouldn't need anyone's help. And I *would* climb this path again. We were deep under massive redwood trees, and the feeling of quiet peace under these giants was intoxicating. Their scent cleared my sinuses and left me feeling charged and ready for adventure.

And then we were there; we'd arrived at our destination, a place called the Mystic Wood. My breath caught in astonishment. Though the name seemed trite and Disneylike to me, it was, in fact, an accurate descriptor. We were in a grove of trees unlike any I'd ever seen or imagined. The very air seemed ancient, sacred. Ben assured me that these were redwoods, but that they were unlike any other redwoods on the planet. Back about five hundred years ago, when these trees were just babies, the land breezes roared over the hilltops toward the sea, breaking off the tops of the saplings. They regrew from where they had broken off, sprouting arms sideways that then curved and headed back skyward. Over the centuries the trees had grown huge, and in bizarre shapes. Some looked as though they were the embodiment of caribou spirits. It was eerie, beautiful, strange, moving. We walked through the woods, our steps almost silent on the thickly carpeted forest floor. He led me to the largest tree of all. Or, well, trees? It seemed made up of several massive trunks close together, branches growing out in all directions. Some places I was sure I could squeeze between the trunks if I tried. If I'd had access to such a tree when I was a kid, I would have made it into the grandest tree fort of all time. We walked all around it, then halfway again, ending up at the backside.

Ben looked up into the branches. "My house used to be my grandma's," he said. "When I was a little boy, my family used to visit her in the summers. Grandma's best friend was her neighbor, Emma Rae. I barely remember from those days. And I'd forgotten all about her by the time I moved back here twenty years ago. I had just gone through a nasty divorce and all I really cared about was avoiding people and recovering. I never saw her. I used to hike back in here when I was feeling really bad. This place always helped me get my perspective back. And one day I found her here. This is where we really met for the first time." With a toe, Ben scuffed the ground in front of the giant, displacing inches deep detritus, then smoothing it over again. "This is where I found her," he said, his voiced hush.

I looked from the forest floor to his face. "What, here?"

Again he moved his foot. "Right here. She was lying on the ground right here."

I looked all around but said nothing, waiting for him to continue.

"At first I thought she was sleeping, but that made no sense. Then that she was hurt, but she didn't appear to be. I spoke but she didn't respond. Finally I shook her, and then she came to. She was dazed, like she'd fainted or something, and I'm not sure she even realized I was there at first. It took her a few minutes to regain coherence."

"What had happened to her?" I prompted when he paused.

"She wouldn't tell me. She just kept looking around, like she was looking for something. I gave her some water, and after a while she let me walk her back out. We recognized each other, of course, after the first few minutes." He laughed. "I'll never forget the look on her face when she saw my plane! I hadn't realized she'd driven in, I guess I wasn't thinking too straight. And when she saw the plane, she didn't tell me until I'd flown her all the way home. I had to bring her back to get her truck the next day," he laughed. "That was just like her, too. She saw something she wanted, and she went for it. Next thing I knew, she was buying her own plane and I was teaching her to fly it. Anyway, that's how I got to know your Emma Rae. It was a pretty good foundation for a great friendship, I guess."

"What had happened that day, did you ever find out?"

He looked at me before answering, and I knew he was deciding whether or not to tell me the truth. I set my mind that I would not let him get away with a half answer. He must've seen it on my face, because he decided. "Emma," he said, "I don't imagine you're going to believe me. And I guess I don't care too much whether you do or not, because I'm going to tell you the truth as I know it. What you do with that is up to you."

"Fair enough."

"Emma Rae used to come here all the time. Not just here in these deep woods, but all around here. All kinds of useful plants grow in this whole area, and she was always gathering things. But she loved it in here, just like I always have, so whenever she was nearby, she'd come on in to 'commune with the trees,' as she put it."

"One day years earlier, she told me, she decided to climb this old tree." I started to interrupt, but he stopped me. "I know, I know, but Emma Rae was a tree climber from way back, and when I met her she was still at it. In fact, she never did stop climbing trees. In any case, that day she wanted to climb this one, even though the lowest branches are too high. So she decided to wedge herself between the trunks and try to get up that way, like the Grinch in the chimney in 'How the Grinch Stole Christmas,' I guess."

He shook his head and chuckled, then he went on. "The way she told it, she squeezed herself in there," he pointed to the widest spot, "and then something really strange happened, like she was being pulled or dragged or something, even though no one was around, and she heard a loud rushing noise, like a storm wind, and then she felt like she was falling, but it was just a big jerk, like in a dream, you know? And she was somewhere else."

He stopped. I didn't understand what he was saying and I waited for him to continue, but he didn't. I said, "What do you mean, 'she was somewhere else'?"

He didn't answer directly. "Do you believe in other worlds?" he asked.

"What? Oh come on, really?"

He laughed. "I know, right?" he said. "But no, really, do you believe in other worlds?"

I narrowed my eyes at him. His eyes were still lit with laughter, but I could tell he was serious. "I'm not sure I understand what you're asking. Are you about to tell me that Emma Rae fell into another world? Like Alice down the rabbit hole?"

"Well, um, yes."

I don't know what possessed me. That was just about the dumbest thing I'd ever heard, and I couldn't believe he was going to stand there and expect me to believe that shit. I'd read the Narnia books, I knew that supposed doors to supposed other worlds are supposedly unpredictable, no doubt so that you couldn't disprove them just because they weren't there. Yeah, right. But I really didn't even think, I just kinda flung myself into that break in the tree trunks, pushing against the rough bark while Ben yelled, "Emma, NO!"

*   *   *

"Emma, NO!"

But it was too late. What had happened to the girl he'd met three days ago? Oh, he knew where she'd gone, but what had *happened* to her? That confused, depressed woman had completely disappeared, well, yes, but even *before* she completely disappeared! Never, never, never had he imagined that instead of arguing, or calling him a lunatic or a liar, she'd simply *go through the door.* As he stood, hands limp at his sides, staring at the place he used to stare at when Emma Rae did this, he was filled with admiration and respect. She had simply gone through. He couldn't believe it. In twenty years, he had never once had the nerve to even slide his hand between the trunks, not after he knew what could happen. Or rather, what *would* happen. Emma Rae had never once *not* been able to go through, not when Ben was with her, anyway. And now Emma was gone. Unbelievable. This was not a complication he had anticipated, and anticipating complications was supposed to be his strong suit. It was one of the main reasons he'd been indispensable to Emma Rae.

What if she didn't come back? What would he do? How could he explain her disappearance? But beyond explanations, how would he *survive* her disappearance? Saying goodbye to Emma Rae had been hard enough, but Emma? Oh, no, he couldn't lose her. Cliché as it was, it was still true; he had been waiting for her his whole life, and he'd never even known it. If she didn't come back? Well, hell, he'd go in himself, plain and simple.

But not yet. She'd gone in like that for a reason, though they may or may not ever know what that reason was. That other world called who it called, whether he liked it or not. And this time it had called Emma. Well, fine. But it had damn well better send her back soon, or he was going in after her.

*   *   *

The sound of Ben's voice was drowned in a wind so fierce I thought my hair would be pulled right out of my head. Just like he'd said, I felt like I was being pushed and pulled every which way at once, and then *whoosh*, just like that I was falling and bam! I hit the ground on all fours. As fast as I could I whirled around with my hands out—do not let the door close! There it was, the tree was right behind me, looking just like it had a minute ago. But nothing else looked the same. I was in a meadow, it seemed, full of wildflowers. There was a sweet, fresh breeze, a breeze with no salt tang in it. It seemed later in the day, with an evening coolness.

I peered through the space between the trunks. I just saw more meadow. It was true. I was in another world. I sat back against the tree. I felt like I'd been run over by a steamroller, my muscles pounded to rubber. I felt spacey and as if I had a metal band wrapped tightly around my head. I had no interest in exploring. No way. Not now. My main interest right now was in *not* throwing up. It was enough to know that it was real. There was no way on Earth, or, well, wherever I was, that I was going to walk away from this tree and risk getting lost in this new world. After all, things had just started getting really interesting in my old world! As soon as I caught my breath, I was going right back through. Just as soon as I caught my breath.

I felt a strange humming under my right hand, so faint I barely noticed. My palm was spread over little white flowers, something like miniature daisies with tiny, brilliant purple eyes. When I raised my hand I lost that humming feeling; when I put my hand back down on the flowers, it started again. Looking around I saw that I was sitting surrounded by the tiny things. They grew right up close to the truck of the tree. I put my other hand down on them, and sure enough, the same humming started, almost like it was my own blood rising up in my own body. I liked the way it felt, like new possibilities, like new life. I ran my hand across the tops, as far as I could reach, and raised a palm covered with thick, purple dust. I sniffed it gingerly. It had a spicy smell, something exotic, sharp. I breathed more deeply, filling my nose with the heady, tangy perfume. . . .

I came to with a start. It was almost too dark to see. How long had I been, uh, asleep? Off a ways I could see stars, but the tree I was under successfully blocked the sky overhead. I remembered where I was, and how I'd gotten here. If time passed at the same rate in both worlds (really? Did I really believe I'd passed into another world?). Ben would be beside himself by now. Or, wait, he knew all about this. Maybe he'd brought along a book or something in that backpack of his. In any case, although my head was clear now and my stomach settled, there was still no way I was going exploring here, not at night. It was time to be getting back to my side of the tree. Hopefully. Feeling my way in the deep gloom, I wedged myself back between the trunks until, ugh! that pushing/pulling/roaring began again. I barely had time to think, "there has got to be a better way!" when I was staggering and falling once again.

"Emma! Emma, are you all right!?"

Ben was on his knees beside me, gathering me up into his arms. As before, my head was pounding and I felt downright woozy, but not so woozy that I couldn't appreciate the strength of his broad chest. Hmmm, I could get used to this.

"Emma!"

I forced my head back so I could see him. His handsome face was creased in worry. I smiled past the rolling surf in my brain. "Hi," I breathed.

I felt the tension drain out of his body and he wrapped his arms more tightly around me. "Please don't ever do that again," he said, his voice rough.

I spoke into his shirt front. "Isn't that why you brought me here?"

"No! No, I just meant to tell you."

"I never would have believed you otherwise."

He squeezed tighter. "I know. I don't care. I just don't want you to ever do that again."

I smiled against his broad chest. At the moment, I didn't care if I never did one other thing besides curl cradled in this man's arms. The pounding in my head was easing off and I was experiencing a sense of wellbeing that was rather astounding for a girl who'd just squeezed herself in and out of her own reality. I stayed still and let him hold me. I stayed still and let myself enjoy him holding me.

After awhile, though, it seemed time to move. I stirred, and Ben instantly relaxed his grip. The dizziness was gone. The headache was gone. The wellbeing? That was still there. And, beneath it all like an underground stream, I could still feel that almost imperceptible humming. I breathed deeply. I still had the scent of that purple dust in my nostrils. Ben released me, got to his feet, and helped me stand. "You okay?"

"Yes. Thank you. Do you have anything edible in that pack? I'm starving."

He burst out laughing. "Oh lord, that's rich! The woman returns from another world and her first words are 'gee, I'm hungry'!"

"Well I am! It's hungry business, this popping off to Never Never Land and back!"

He pulled a bag out of his pack. "I hope you like trail mix."

"I do now," I affirmed and helped myself to peanuts, cashews, raisins and—ahhh, Heaven!—dark chocolate chunks.

Chapter 7

Fortunately it wasn't as late here, since we still had to hike back to the plane, and then fly back to Ben's house, all of which was much better accomplished in daylight. Again, we didn't talk much as we walked. I, for one, had an awful lot to think about, and not all of it concerned the disconcerting knowledge that I was now living cheek to cheek with a different world, and could apparently go for a visit anytime I chose. My much more immediate concern was this man walking briskly ahead of me, and the way he'd said my name and held me. I'd gotten a very clear message. And somehow, that message was more interesting to me than the other concerns of the day. I couldn't keep the smile off my face, and I was glad that Ben led the way, that the path here wasn't wide enough for us to walk side by side.

"So, about tasting unknown herbs," Ben began once we were back on the wider grassy road. "A lot of the plants Emma used in her teas are from 'across the border' as she liked to say. So you want to be very careful when you're working with them. They can have rather, well, unexpected results."

I could still feel that lovely humming in my body. Was it getting stronger? Apparently eating unknown flora wasn't the only way to get 'unexpected results', but Ben probably didn't need to know about that. "Yeah? Like what?"

"For starters, you need to know that Emma Rae had some kind of amazing instincts about plants, even those that she'd never encountered before."

"Okay," I affirmed, "She wrote about that."

"Right. So, she never used anything that made her sick or might hurt anyone. But one time she had a terrible cold, and she had a new batch of stuff she'd gathered, and she went right to this one, knowing it would help her. I'll never forget it; it looked like silk tassels knotted together at one end, you know, like a bunch of long pine needles?"

I nodded and he went on, "Except these were super soft, more like silk threads. And they were almost more blue than green. Anyway, she just grabbed a handful and ate them, just like that. I hated when she did stuff like that, and sometimes I think she was careless that way just to get me, just to tease. Anyway, she swallowed it down and then . . ."

He stopped talking, and I looked up at him. He was shaking his head and laughing, harder and harder. Finally he got control, and he gasped out, "She turned blue! I mean it, the color just rose up on her face like she was blushing, except it was blue, like she wasn't breathing, except she *was* breathing, she was *fine!*"

"No! For real? No way!"

"Yes, for real. I'm not kidding! And it wasn't just her face, it was all over. It was unbelievable, but I took pictures; I'll show you if I can find them. It was a long time ago, and after that she was a lot more careful."

"How long was she blue?" I wasn't sure I was buying any of this story, but I was willing to play along.

"Oh, well, it was like, what, three days? She couldn't even go to town for milk and eggs, she had to send me. Served her right, I thought."

"Did it help her cold?" I asked, curious.

He looked startled that I'd thought to ask that. "Hm, you know, I don't even remember. It was all about the blue at the time, you know? I was pretty upset, but I also couldn't stop laughing every time I saw her like that. But Emma Rae was always like that, spontaneous, careless . . . she preferred to call it care*free*, but she worried me a lot. I never knew what she'd pull next."

"Well," I said drily, "she can't have been all that careless if she survived for 111 years, right?"

"You'd think," he answered, "but Emma Rae seemed to have some kind of charm over her that kept her safe. She had to have, right? I mean, look at the pictures. She never even aged. She was even safe from time."

"Guess the charm ran out," I said.

And there it was again, that sudden knowledge. Ben didn't answer, but I knew he'd had something to say.

September 1922

"Stop writing. Stop sending things. You are dead to us. You left the child with us. He is ours now."

These are the words my father wrote to me. For three years I have allowed myself to believe that, even though they never responded, there was softness in their hearts, and one day we could be reunited; one day I could once again hold my son. But today I received these heartless words from my own Father. I have written every week. I have sent money. I have sent gifts. Now at last I have had a response. My little boy, my little Henry, is lost to me.

This is what I am thinking. But I show the letter to Alexis, and he is so angry, more angry than I have ever seen him. "That is enough!" he shouts. "Who is this man, that he thinks he can keep my son from me?"

I look up at him, astonished. I know how he loves me, he makes it clear in every way possible. But this rage over his son? I never expected it. He has asked about the boy from time to time, and often enough he has held me in his arms as I wept for my lost son. But that he thinks of having Henry here with us? I never imagined.

"But what can we do?" I asked him.

"Do?" His face is crimson with fury. "Write to that man, your father. Tell him to expect us. Tell him that I, Alexis Alexander Mikhailskovich, am coming for my son."

I have never before written a letter with such haste. I am delirious with joy. To think that soon I will hold my son in my arms again. To think that we will be together, not the perfect family, not the family of my dreams, that much is true. Yet we are family nonetheless, and soon we shall all be together. Even as I write this, Alexis has gone to make arrangements for our journey.

Here followed page after page of Emma Rae's beautiful pencil sketches. Alexis appeared several times, reading a book, laughing, gazing off into the distance. With just a few lines, she captured his strong chin, deep set eyes, the wave of hair over his high forehead. Was he worth all she had lost for him? I wondered.

Between the portraits were highly detailed drawings of plants, flowers, birds, hills and trees and other travelers. Without words, Emma Rae had so clearly captured that journey, as she traveled towards her dearly beloved son after those long, agonizing years of separation.

But when she returned to words at last, her spiky writing tore across the page, blotted and smeared.

Oh, cruel! How is it possible? After long days of travel, Alexis and I arrived at the home of my parents, only to discover that they have gone! They have taken my son, my Henry, and have disappeared! The neighbors know nothing, only that three days ago, with no word to anyone, they packed up their household goods and drove away. We went to speak with my aunt, and to my dismay we learned that she died of influenza two winters ago. We went into Philadelphia, to my father's place of business. They know nothing, only that my father has not come to work at all this week.

They must have gone the very moment they received my letter! How could they do this, how can my own mother and father keep my son from me like this? Further inquiries revealed the depth of their commitment to keep my Henry as their own: the day they left, my father sold the property, the house, the animals, everything. They are gone. They left no information with anyone. Alexis has all but bribed everyone he has spoken to. It is all for nothing. Henry is lost to me forever.

Holy cow. They stole my grandfather. Dad would never believe it. What kind of people did something like that? And afterwards, why couldn't they just have told Henry that his mom died? Why did they make up their horrible stories, tell him that his mother never came back, didn't want him? How much damage had that done to him? And after him, to my dad? Maybe even to me? How would things have been different if my grandfather hadn't been raised to bitterness? Would my dad be different? Would I?

Of course I would never know the answers to these questions. What was done was done. But at least I could set the record straight. But what kind of tea, I wondered, would I have to blend for my dad to believe it?

Back home in Michigan I had been pretty much bored to tears, and too apathetic, or depressed, to do anything about it. When I wasn't working, I was numbing myself with books and TV and movies. It drove Petie mad, and she had tried and tried to get me up and out of my crappy apartment, but it all seemed like just too damn much effort. I slept as much as I could, just so each day had fewer hours I'd have to find a way to fill.

Out here I almost hated to go to bed. There were so many things I was interested in. There were the obvious things, like learning to fly, taking over a business I knew nothing about, reading up on my eccentric ancestress and, oh yeah, discovering a parallel universe down the road. But beyond that, there were other things, smaller things that surprised me. I started wanting to cook, I mean real food, not just slapping together a peanut butter or grilled cheese sandwich when I was hungry. I wanted to invite people into my house, make a big dinner, serve sun tea.

And I wanted to dig in the dirt. Way back in the early days of my ill-fated marriage, we used to host parties, have people over, talk and laugh and play card games. I would cook, he would do the clean up. We used to have so much fun. And the most fun of all was in the late summer, when a lot of the food I prepared had come straight out of our garden. Back then, I had loved growing things, and I'd had a way of putting them together into amazing meals, meals our friends had raved about.

Even before that, growing up with Petie, preserving stuff from her mom's garden had been so much fun for us. Petie still did that with her Mom, though the garden was a lot smaller these days. But I hadn't joined them in many, many years.

Those old urges were stampeding each other now to get to the top of my "must do" list. I'd get up early, often while it was still dim and misty outside, and I'd head across the road to wake up to the roar of the tide. I'd run right in to that freezing spray and play up and down the beach, singing nonsense with my whole heart, until hunger or sanity drove me back inside to the coffee pot and frying pan. I'd cook up an omelet big enough for three, eat about half of it, fridge the rest and head out to the garden with my tea. Usually I drank my own blend, but some days I experimented with others. I loved Emma Rae's gardens. While I didn't understand this whole permaculture thing, and many of Emma Rae's plants were unknown to me, I still just had to get my hands in the dirt. I'd make my best guess at what might be weeds, and I'd start digging.

The morning after my New World Experience, Ben found me sitting on my heels, shaking my head and laughing.

"What's up?"

I tossed a dirt encrusted can at him. I'd just dug it out from under a humongous dandelion (I knew that was a weed . . . wasn't it?).

He looked inside and joined right in laughing. What else? The rusty thing was crammed full of money. Oh, I did love living at Emma Rae's house!

"Want some tea, or coffee?" I asked, struggling to my feet. My knees, ankles, hips, shoulders all protested at once. Sheesh, fifty was a bitch. But even as I shifted around, trying to ease the stiffness, my hand reached out to a bright green plant, pinched off a bunch of leaves, and I popped them in my mouth without thinking.

"Emma!" Ben said, grabbing my hand.

"What?"

"What did you just eat?"

"What did, what?" I hadn't even noticed I did it, but the evidence was still in my mouth. Mmm, it was pretty tasty, too. "Um, er, I, uh, I don't know," I confessed.

"Emma, you can't keep doing that!" he exclaimed. I swallowed my mouthful, and was about to agree with him when a most delicious warmth spread through my whole body, and the stiffness in my joints simply melted away.

"WOW! What was that stuff?"

"That's what I just asked you," he pointed out.

"Oh, well, I have no idea. But it's a helluva lot better than aspirin! We ought to bottle that stuff!" The warmth was dissipating, but I still felt like my joints had just been lubricated with hot oil. I leaned over and read the little tag under the brilliant green foliage. "Heartleaf. Oh, yeah, look at those leaves. Kind of an obvious name, isn't it? Is this one of the plants from," I lowered my voice to a spooky whisper, "*the other side?*"

Ben actually rolled his eyes. "Yes, as a matter of fact, it is. We always named them for their most obvious attribute, so it was as easy as possible. But Emma, really, you've got to be careful with them. Or any plant, for that matter. It isn't safe to just eat them like that."

I nodded. "I know, Ben, and I really do agree with you. I don't know why I keep doing that. It's not like I'm the sort of person who forages, you know? This is very unlike me. But the thing is, well, it's hard to explain."

"Please try."

"Well, my head doesn't know anything about any of this stuff. We both know I'm about as ignorant about herbs and plants and tea and all that as you can be. But *something* in me seems to know *all* about it. And that something is, I don't know, I guess *guiding* is the right word, but how flaky is that? Anyway it just seems to do its own thing, and its own thing seems to be just what I need in that moment. Does that make any sense?"

He sighed. "Only because I worked with Emma Rae for so many years. I thought she was scary. But you . . ." he shook his head. "Just please be careful."

"I know, right? I wouldn't want to wind up blue!" I absently turned away, walked down the path for about 20 paces, stopped by a pale yellow plant, and picked a few leaves. I took them back to him. "Here," I said, "this will make you feel better."

His eyes widened in disbelief. "Did you hear anything I just said?"

"I did, Ben, I really, really did! And you are absolutely right! But if you just eat this, you really will feel so much better about everything. I promise!"

"Oh boy," he said, shaking his head again. "I can see how this is gonna go."

And then, to my surprise and delight, he ate the pale leaves. I was so proud of him! Then I felt a moment's unholy terror, a rush of fear that I'd lost my mind, had no idea what I was doing and had just poisoned the man of my dreams. But I watched as the lines on his face smoothed out, the tension eased out of his shoulders, and a little smile lit up his face. Then his eyes darkened, and giving me no warning whatsoever, he dropped his head and kissed me, square on the lips.

And then he kissed me again.

And then I kissed him back, and he was ready for me, and then, oh yes! and then my hands were in his hair and his tongue touched my bottom lip and oh my merciful heavens! Haaawow!

Shock staggered us both, and it was over as quickly as it started. Our clothes had not, in fact, ignited and burned to ash in the heat of those few moments. We stared at each other, our eyes wide open in the most delicious astonishment.

Without a word, I turned away, walked down the path for about 20 paces, stopped by the pale yellow plant, and picked a few leaves. I took them back to him. "Here," I said, "How'd you like to try that again?"

*   *   *

Ben sat in his jeep, hands gripping the steering wheel, going nowhere. This was not good, not good at all. Either that, or it *was* good, good beyond his wildest imagining. Which was it? How to know? In just these few short days it was evident that Emma had gifts beyond Emma Rae's, and Emma had only just begun to awaken. Talk about a sleeping giant! How would he be able to teach her when her natural talents were so extreme? What might she *not* know?

Emma Rae had never offered him fresh, raw plants. He knew that she had eaten them from time to time, but certainly not with the careless confidence Emma used. Three times in two days! And right on every time, apparently. Those leaves she'd given him: no way could she have anticipated that! Or could she? She had seemed as startled as he was. And, oh yes, just as pleased, that much was obvious.

That was another way she was so very different from Emma Rae. Emma Rae had a slyness, sometimes she was almost sneaky, at times downright devious. Emma was transparent; she hid nothing.

What was their relationship going to be like? Did she have any idea that he, too, had certain gifts? He hadn't been using them lately, that was true. He'd been lax, assuming too much about Emma from his first impression. But she was changing very quickly, and her acceptance of the changes was astounding. And unlike Emma Rae, Emma was no chatterbox. She saw, she understood, so much. But she didn't talk it all out as Emma Rae always had. She just filed it all away behind those deep blue eyes and thought about it all on her own.

Ben wanted her to talk to him. He wanted to answer her questions, to hear her thoughts, to find new answers together with her. She didn't know yet what his role had been in Two World Teas. She didn't know what hers was supposed to be. He'd thought they'd have had that talk by now, but she asked almost no questions. Instead she absorbed information at lightning speed, investigated on her own, and invited him to . . . to what? He thought about it, about what she wanted from him. And when the word formed in his mind, it rocked him to his core. Emma wanted to play. And she was inviting him to play, too.

Well there was no doubt about it, that would certainly change the way he approached coming to work every day!

*   *   *

I was just having so darn much fun! I couldn't remember ever feeling like this before, like each day was more fun than the last, like there were exciting things to do and see and think and learn, more than I'd ever have time for.

But there was one thing I definitely was going to have time for. Petie had to come out here. I did not want to go one more day without my best friend. This was just way too much fun for me not to be sharing it with the friend who had stuck by me all these long years when my life sucked. I'd only talked to her once since I'd gotten to California, just to tell her about the inheritance. And there was plenty more to tell her. I didn't plan to tell her everything, oh no way. But she'd be nuts over all the stuff about Emma Rae and Alexis and baby Henry, and about this crazy tea business, and she would love the gardens, and of course the ocean, my very own amazing piece of the big blue sea. And the Mystic Wood? She was gonna love that (though not all of it, of course!). Back when Petie was still married, she and The Rat used to travel some, and she missed that, I knew. Well, she was about to come into some first class travel, that was for sure!

"Hello."

"Petie sweetie, it's me!"

"Well glory be, the hippies let you get to a phone after all?"

"Oh very funny. You just would not believe how insanely busy I have been."

"'Insanely busy?' Girl, this is Petie you're talking to. You are not a 'busy' type of person, you know what I'm saying?"

I laughed. It was true, once upon a time. "Well honey, don't go telling that to the hippies! I am reinventing myself out here, and I think maybe 'busy' is gonna be my new middle name."

"Oh, *hell*, no! Not in one million years!"

I couldn't blame her for being skeptical. If I'd had a minute to think about it, I would've been skeptical too. "Well, don't take my word for it. How soon can you get some time off work?"

"What are you talking about?"

"Petie, it is just too crazy out here. I need you to come on out for a while and keep me company."

There was a little silence. Then, "But when are you coming home?"

More silence. "Well, the thing is, I don't think I am. Not to stay, anyway."

My heart thudded hard while I waited for her to speak again. Finally, "Well, I can't say I'm surprised. What's to come back to old Michigan for, right?"

I wanted so much to defend my decision, but I knew I didn't need to. I did, however, want her to know how much better I was already. "Nothing but you, babe. And if I play my cards right, maybe I can talk you into a permanent change of scenery, right?"

Again with the long quiet moment. "Emma, it's California. How could I afford California? I love the idea, but honey, I don't see how I can afford a plane ticket out there right now, and you know I don't get vacation pay. How can I even come for a visit, let alone move there?"

I grinned into the phone. "I hear your concerns," I said in a mock-serious tone of voice, "but there is just so much stuff you don't know yet that might have some bearing on the issues at hand."

"Such as?"

I heard it, that curiosity. It was a start. And the rest? Oh, yeah, this would not be difficult. It might take some time, but I was determined to get my best friend out here.

"Well, as you said, this is hippie country. And I've got gardens out the wazoo, not to mention a huge pantry full of stuff

Emma Rae canned. The house and all are mine, free and clear, no mortgage. And there's plenty of room for you here, trust me on that."

"That sounds great, of course, but you already told me you didn't even know how you were going to pay the taxes on the place. You haven't exactly got a job either, you know."

"Like hell I don't! I own my own company!"

"A tea company, right? Just how profitable is that?"

Well, gee whiz, when she put it that way, I realized I had no idea how profitable it was. How profitable could a big wooden chest full of tea really be? And was the company supporting Ben, too? Guess I'd have to look into that, but for now, I would misdirect. "Oh, it's not just *any* tea company, believe me! But the taxes and all are taken care of, no worries."

"No worries? Just how did that happen?"

"Petie sweetie, Emma Rae had some very endearing qualities, let me tell you. And one of my favorites so far is . . ." I let it hang, trying to hook her.

She bit: "Yes?"

I burst out laughing all over again at Emma Rae's audacious nature as I told Petie, "She hid money all over the place!"

"What are you talking about? How much money?"

"About $150,000 so far, and counting!"

"*No way!*"

"Yes, way! It's cra-a-azy! Just this morning I dug up a can outta the garden that had, like, three hundred some dollars in it!"

"You have got to be kidding me!"

"I swear it on my favorite fuzzy pajamas, girlfriend, and I am gonna use a tiny little bit of all that lovely crazy cash to buy you and me a road trip from Michigan to my very own little piece of paradise, you hear me?"

She was laughing now too. "All right, okay, fine. But only on one condition."

"What's that?"

"You let me do the weeding while I'm there."

My days were falling into a routine. Most days I was awake before the sun was out of bed, and I'd dance across the road to the ocean, playing and singing until the light spilled over the waves and hunger drove me back to the house. After breakfast I'd go out and work in the gardens, learning the names of plants, getting familiar with their growth habits. I learned that if I cupped my hand above the roots, or maybe fingered the leaves, the plants would tell me their secrets. Some I tasted. Some I rubbed on my skin. All had useful attributes and I loved learning about them. I remembered gardens from my past, how I'd always felt so alive in them, so hyper-sensitive to smell and sight and the breath of the air and the warmth of the sun. When had I stopped going outdoors and appreciating the green and growing? And why? But no matter, because now I was out every day. I could practically feel my soul expanding as I wandered among the plants and let them teach me what they wanted me to learn.

Most mornings Ben would come over to work. He'd show me how to dry the plants so they remained potent, how to process and mix and package them. He taught me about permaculture, about making the most out of every inch of space and every available plant. There was so much to learn, and I needed to learn all of it.

He was also training me about the business itself, Two World Teas. He'd bring orders in from our P.O. box in town, and I'd go up to the attic and find the clients' tea and pack some for shipping. As I shipped the prepared blends, I took the recipes to Ben, and he'd guide me in making more. I was surprised by the prices we charged, but Ben explained how each client had talked at great length with Emma Rae until she had gotten their blend exactly right. Of course we also had ingredients that were available nowhere else in our world, at least as far as we were aware, and that made the teas more valuable still. If the tea is not appropriately priced, Ben told me, some customers don't value it, and it goes to waste, sitting unused at the back of a cupboard. Emma Rae used to get furious with customers who didn't drink the teas she'd worked so diligently to perfect, he told me. In her anger she raised the prices, declaring that if she was going to waste her time, she would for darn sure be well compensated for it. Much to her surprise, once it was priced at what she considered an outrageous amount, her customers became much more consistent in drinking it regularly.

In the afternoon we had flying lessons. This was my favorite part of the day, even better than waking the sun. It wasn't really hard, learning to fly my lovely little silver and blue plane. In fact, it was very straightforward and intuitive. But Ben had so much to teach me about wind speed, reading and interpreting the instruments, and learning to read the weather. He was a great teacher, passionate and patient. Of course, just to be flying was beyond incredible, and I never tired of it.

In the evenings I read Emma Rae's journals, went back down to the beach, baked, or sometimes just sat on the porch and watched the sunset, thinking about what a charmed life I was leading now, so very different from the dark and dreary life I'd lived before. It didn't occur to me that I was actually more isolated, more insulated now than I'd ever been back home. I didn't yet understand that, although my circumstances had changed remarkably, I was still the same woman who had cut herself off from so many things before. But that wake-up call was coming.

Saturday afternoon I took Emma Rae's Honda and headed into town. Once upon a time I had loved baking bread. I remembered the feel of the dough under my hands, its elasticity and life, its responsiveness to my kneading, the pungent smell of the awakening yeast. It was time to start baking bread again.

So there I was in that well stocked little grocery store, debating different types of flour, when I heard a gasp behind me and a voice inquiring, "Emma Rae?"

I turned to see a tall, gaunt woman looking at me with wide, astonished eyes, and in that instant I was hit by a wave of grief and confusion mixed with hope and joy. I was staggered. I tried to answer, but my voice was caught back by the tide of emotion. What was happening? She stepped toward me, to embrace me, I think, and I reared back, stumbling into the shelves behind me.

"Emma Rae?" she said again, uncertain now, and I had a moment to recover.

"No," I said breathlessly, "I'm Emma, her great-granddaughter."

A second wave hit me, this time of raw grief, almost despair. I gripped the edge of the shelf that was digging into my hip, afraid I might fall under the onslaught of emotions. What was happening?

"Oh, I'm so sorry," the woman said, attempting to recover herself. "You look so much like her, I, I . . ."

"I know," I nodded foolishly, "It's, it's uncanny, isn't it?"

And then, to my extreme discomfort, the woman began weeping, and I stood, pinned to the shelves of flour and sugar and canned milk by her anguish. I couldn't think, I couldn't move; I could only barely stand in the waves washing over me.

"What am I going to do now?" the woman asked hoarsely, demanding something of me that I didn't have to give, something I didn't know anything about.

It was all I could do to keep from falling. I couldn't find any words for her. And after an eternity when she stood weeping before me, she finally turned away, shoulders hunched and trembling.

I myself was so shaken that I didn't move for long minutes. I felt the bite of the shelf in my hip, but I didn't yet have the strength to move. I had no idea what had just happened, and I was terrified. As the powerful emotions began to drain away and I once again was able to breathe, I took great gasping gulps of air.

As soon as I was able, I left the store without buying anything. I went at once to Emma Rae's car, locking myself in and then just sitting, my head resting on the steering wheel, trying to recover. When I stopped shaking, I started the car and drove back to Emma Rae's.

As I entered the house, I caught her in the mirror by the front door. "What are you doing to me?" I asked. Her eyes were full of sympathy. Or maybe that was just me.

Chapter 8

I admit, I wore them at the most inappropriate times. One morning I wore them when I made the breakfast biscuits. The afternoon before that I wore them while I picked tomatoes. Returning home from the grocery store that day, shell-shocked and empty handed, I put them on: Alexis' alexandrites. They flashed and changed colors at me, warm and alive. Even though it was a hot and sunny day, I wrapped myself in a heavy sweater. I still felt raw, exposed, so I dug a scarf out of the chest in the foyer and wrapped it around my neck. I went out to the herb beds and walked until something sang to me, and then I snipped off a heavily leafed twig, took it into the kitchen and shredded the leaves into a glass pan. I poured a sweet white wine over the leaves and turned on the burner. Slowly, slowly I brought it just to a simmer, then I poured some into a cup and went out to the porch, curling up in one of the chairs.

Ben found me there.

"What happened?" he asked.

I still could barely speak. I didn't even try. I was shocked to my core, and though the herbed wine was helping, it wasn't enough.

I saw something pass behind his eyes. "Is there more wine?" he asked.

I nodded.

"Is it safe for me to drink?"

I looked up at him, startled. What did he know? I thought about him, and I thought about the herb, and I thought about the wine. "Yes."

He came back out with a full mug, and pulled another chair up close to mine.

"Emma," he said, "please tell me what happened."

I shook my head. "I don't think it was real," I said, knowing I was lying.

He snorted. "It was real, whatever it was!"

"What do you know about it?" I snarled.

He put one hand on my knee and ducked his head to catch my eye. "Emma? You are not delusional. If you think something weird happened, please trust me when I tell you that something weird must have happened. You're living in a strange place, where strange things have been known to happen. And you have a bit of the strange in you as well, you know."

I pulled away from him. "What do you mean? What are you talking about?"

He sighed. "Really? You really want me to spell it out for you? You know what I'm talking about."

It was my turn to sigh. "What aren't you telling me, Ben?"

He chuckled. "Oh, Lord, Emma, that could fill a book or two! We've only just begun this journey, you and I. It will take some time."

Who was this man? Even as upset as I was, my spirit danced in his presence. Come to think of it, who, or what, was I?

I told him what had happened, and was rewarded with yet another sigh.

"Well, I was afraid of that," he said. "You've got what might be called an uncommon degree of empathy. Emma Rae had it, too."

"Is that what you call it?" I said with just a touch of sarcasm, thinking about the flood of emotions that had paralyzed me in a grocery store aisle. "An 'uncommon degree' of empathy?"

He grinned ruefully. "Emma Rae taught herself how to deal with it. You're going to have to, too."

"How do I do that?"

He sat back in his chair. "There are a variety of ways. I'm guessing you've already tried some of them."

"What do you mean?"

"Isolating yourself? Shutting the world out? Isn't that what you did in Michigan?"

I sat up and stared at him. "How do you know what I did in Michigan?"

"Here we go!" he said to the sky, then looked back at me. "Emma, you aren't the only one with, shall we say, fine tuned perception. I see a lot that you've never spoken about. There's a lot you don't say, and that tells me things, too. You don't talk about your friends or your job, you seem in no hurry to go back to Michigan, you spend all day every day quite content to be by yourself. You are not behaving in a way that speaks of a rich and satisfying life back home."

I stared at him with my mouth open. Of all the nerve! How dare he . . . ! I shut my mouth. He was right, of course. It seemed kind of stupid to get all offended when he was right. The jerk. I sat back in my chair, took a good healthy pull at my wine. Oh, yeah, that was a nice combination, that wine with that herb. Now if I added just a little. . . .

"Emma?"

I looked up, into laughing hazel eyes.

"Could we stay focused here?"

Good question. I grinned back. "But you've got to admit, the wine is lovely, right?"

He took a drink, and his eyes softened. "What did you put in it?"

I shrugged my shoulders. "I dunno."

He sighed, then took another sip. "Emma Rae never used herbs in wine this way, or in her cooking. I don't know why. For her it was always just in the tea."

"She used to," I said, "back in New York. Think of the possibilities."

"I will, Emma, but not this minute. Right now we need to talk about what happened at the store."

"Do we have to?"

"Do you want to be able to go out it public ever again?"

"Oh."

"Right."

I was finally starting to warm up, come back to life. I unwrapped the scarf, and Ben's eyes dropped to my neck and widened in astonishment. "What is that!?"

I reached up. I'd forgotten I was wearing the alexandrites. I grinned, tossed my hair back and laughed at him, "What, this old thing?"

He dropped his head into his hands. "Oh, Emma Rae," he groaned, "what have you done to me?"

The first step, Ben explained to me, was to learn to center myself. It's all about energy; everybody's got it. Strong emotions are strong energy, and I, according to him, was very susceptible to other people's energy. It's like we're all baskets sitting in a lake, he said. Some baskets are woven so tightly that no water seeps in and no water seeps out. Other baskets are so loosely woven that the water all mixes, flowing in and out with every current. The trick, he said, was to learn to tighten the weave on my basket so other people's water couldn't flow in without my permission. As an added bonus, if my weave was tight enough, I wouldn't be constantly leaking, either. If I was always leaking energy, I would never have enough for myself, he explained.

Then he talked to me about breathing. Oh, sure, I breathed all the time, I could do this.

Yeah, right. Who would've guessed we're all doing it wrong? And yet we keep on living in spite of it.

"Emma?"

Oh, yeah, I *wanted* to learn this stuff. I forgot. That whole never-being-able-to-shop-again thing really would be a drag. I corralled my thoughts and tried to focus.

I honestly never knew what a difference it could make, just slowing down my breathing, letting my ribs expand and my belly relax so the air could go all the way down behind my navel. I figured I was ahead of the curve, since I'd already tried this once or twice. But I forgot how hard it could be to do it more than twice in a row without getting completely distracted, only to notice a few minutes later that my stomach was all tight again and my shoulders were back up around my ears and my forehead was all creased up. I guess maybe I wasn't so damn smart after all. Maybe, just maybe, this might be helpful to me.

Ben was patient, sitting beside me, doing his own steady breathing, bringing me back to it again and again as I struggled with the shallow habits of a lifetime. After a bit, I did start to get the rhythm of it. And as I did, my thoughts smoothed out, began flowing like a wide river instead of piling all up on top of each other. I didn't understand why this crazy emotion thing was happening to me all of a sudden now. But as my thoughts stilled, I remembered all the way back to grade school, how I would always feel what my friends were feeling. Even if they tried to hide what was going on, I'd feel it so strongly.

And later on, in my marriage, I would feel what was going on with Mitch. When he was happy, having a good day, feeling loving, I responded with equal fervor. Then came years when he got angrier and angrier, drank more and more, left home early and worked late. During the long days I went about my business calmly, able to be detached from his chaos. But as soon as he walked in the door, I'd start to spiral in the strength of his out-of-control emotions. And even after that, once he'd removed himself from me emotionally and become remote and silent, I still felt the turmoil whenever he was near me. He wouldn't speak of it; he denied it was there, but whenever he was home, his turbulence rocked whatever calm I was able to achieve during his absence.

When he finally came to me, admitted his affair, told me he was leaving me for someone else, it was actually such a relief. It was devastating in many ways, yes, but I was also more relieved than I cared to admit.

By that time I'd already been closing up to others for a long time. Only Petie refused to let me shut her out of my life. I'd been there with her during her own horrible marriage and divorce, she wasn't leaving me alone with mine. But after Mitch, I never wanted to date again. I didn't like going out. Now, breathing slowly and deeply in, and out, in, and out, for the first time I began to understand why.

But had it ever been so strong as it had been this time, at the grocery?

I felt my breathing quicken at the memory, I felt fear slipping past my guard. I couldn't let that happen again! I couldn't. . . .

"Emma," Ben breathed my name.

Oh, yeah, right. I forgot. In two three four, out two three four. Consciously, deliberately, I allowed peace to return.

Ben took me back to the market for flour and yeast. The first time I'd come, rushing in and out, I hadn't been approached by anyone. This time, several people did come up and speak with me. Two of them had been to Emma Rae's service and so had already gotten over the shock of our uncanny resemblance. The third person was headed off by Ben, and then introduced carefully. I felt like an idiot, like some kind of an invalid, but it was decidedly uncomfortable, the way these people seemed to be expecting something from me, even knowing I was just Emma. I said as much to Ben.

He slanted me a grim look. "First of all, you are not *just* Emma. You are not less than Emma Rae on any level. You just are *not* Emma Rae. Soon enough people will stop thinking of you as though you are. Secondly, yes, of course it's uncomfortable. To be approached like this by total strangers who seem to think you're an old friend? That's got to be unnerving."

"It is!" I affirmed with a sigh.

"Well, as I'm sure you've figured out, Emma Rae was loved by many people; she helped most of the people around here. If anyone was sick, she went to them. If they were having any sort of problems, Emma Rae was there for them. I imagine they think that, since you look just like her, you must be just like her. But she lived here with these folks for over fifty years. She chose to be family for them. It was her way.

"But you get to choose your own way. You don't have to be influenced by the expectations of others. In fact, you shouldn't be. It's important that you make your own way, for your own reasons."

"That's easy for you to say," I snapped back. "I'm living in Emma Rae's house, learning Emma Rae's business and Emma Rae's ways, flying Emma Rae's plane and hanging out with Emma Rae's partner. All by the plan of Miss Emma Rae herself, not my own."

He walked me right out of the store, leaving our cart in the aisle, and led me to a bench outside, where he sat me down and plopped down beside me. "Emma," he said firmly, "It may be true that Emma Rae planned all this for you. But you do not have to do one single thing you don't choose to do. You aren't beholden to her or anybody. It's true you didn't ask for this. But you are not a victim, not of Emma Rae's plans or of the blessings she's left you. You can walk away at any moment. It is your choice, and your choice only, whether you live according to what you think she wanted or according to what you want."

I did not appreciate being chastised. "Are you done?" I asked through clenched teeth.

"Not quite," he said. "I also want to say that the sooner you stop thinking of all this—*stuff*—as Emma Rae's, the better. Emma Rae is gone. She's not coming back. It is *your* house, *your* business, *your* plane, *your* partner. To do with whatever you choose."

I stared at him in silence for a minute. Finally he said, "*Now* I'm done."

But I had nothing else to say just then. *My* partner? To do with whatever I chose? Now that was a deliciously distracting thought!

Oh for pity's sake. There was just no doubt about it; I must have adult onset ADD! Being deliberately provoking, I looked him right in the eyes and IN two three four, OUT two three four, IN two three four. . . .

Oh, yeah, I saw the heat rise. If we hadn't been sitting right out in front of God and everybody, that would've gotten me another smooch, no doubt! Instead, we just burst out laughing our silly heads off, and went back in to pay for my groceries.

Ben carried the groceries into the kitchen for me, then headed home. What a nice man he was. I ran up the stairs to change into a different shirt and wash my hands and face before I mixed up the bread dough. There on the table beside my bed was that damn letter. I grabbed it and shoved it into the drawer of the bedside stand. "Dagnabbit, Emma Rae, give it a rest!" I grumbled into the drawer just before I slammed it shut. But inside my head I was thinking about that delicious, playful heat that kept flaring up between Ben and me. I thought about baking bread again, after all these years. I thought about my bubbling ideas for mixing herbs with wine. I thought about flying. I wouldn't admit it to that pushy Emma Rae, but oh, yeah, I was having fun all right!

I laid out the flour, yeast, and salt on the counter. Keep it simple and basic, I told myself, you haven't made bread in years. But then I was at the fridge, pulling out butter, milk and an egg. I took a quick run out to the gardens. Connection, honesty, trust: those were the words in my mind as I picked a little bit of this, a little pinch of that before going back into the house. Ben was coming for dinner. I heated the milk on the stove top, added a thick chunk of butter and cracked in the egg. Not too warm, just enough to soften the butter. Honey? no. This would be a rich bread, but not sweet, not with those herbs.

In fact, hm, yes, this would be perfect for bacon, tomato and cheese sandwiches. Oh, this was California, I'd better slice up some avocado to layer on top. Not the fanciest dinner menu, but oh, well, on this bread, and with the luscious, thick pepper bacon I had, it would be delicious, and light enough for a summer evening. I hummed as I sprinkled the yeast into the warm milk mixture and set it aside for a minute to wake up, to begin its lightning fast reproduction, to bubble up and fill the kitchen with its unmistakable beery scent. It had, indeed, been far too long since I had given myself this pleasure, this heady combination of touch, sight, smell, and the almost forgotten sound of my own cheerful humming. Why had I stopped baking bread? Silly, that's what. I'd denied myself so many of the things that gave me simple pleasure. Well, don't worry about the why, I told myself. Just start doing them again.

As I mixed flour into the bubbling yeast mixture, I gave myself over to the celebration of the senses known as making bread from scratch. Lovely.

June 1931

> *I am leaving Alexis. I am leaving New York. Though I have many people now who come to me for my potions and cures, I know that I will never have true friends here, and I am tired of*

being so very, very alone. This world is changing in so many ways, but one thing has not changed, and that is the way people look at me. My heart has never stopped bleeding for my darling Henry, and though he has continued to be kind and patient, Alexis has never understood this. He thinks it would be different if I had had other children. He also has not understood that I would never allow myself to have another child in these circumstances. He thinks his love, his responsibility for us, would be enough. But it is not even enough for me. It cannot make me respectable.

He has tried to find Henry. But it was not to be. And I have done everything in my power to be content in this half life that I have lived these ten years. That too is not to be. Alexis has his wife, his children, his many business concerns. It is time for me to go, to find something worth living for.

He comes tonight for the last time. I am preparing his favorite meal, and one last time I will lie in his arms. Tomorrow I, like so many before me, will begin the long journey West. I don't even know where I am going. I only know that it is time to go.

My heart is breaking for Alexis. He begged, he pleaded with me to change my mind. He told me again and again that he has never loved his wife, that he has never loved anyone but me, and of course I believe him, but what good is that? No more now than it ever was. He gave me money, he insisted I keep all the jewels he has given me over the years. How can I possibly travel the country with such riches, I asked. Does he not know the state of things?

He could not stop weeping. He had one last gift for me, he said, and he brought into the apartment the oldest, shabbiest valise I had ever seen. Out of it he brought horrible, threadbare dresses. "Wear these," he said, "Use this valise. When you get where you are going, write to me and I will have all of your lovely things sent. Please allow me to do this for you my love, please allow me!"

How could I refuse? He has always been so thoughtful. But he was not finished yet. "My beloved, in my heart you are my wife; it has always been you." Once more he reached into that shabby valise. He showed me that it has two bottoms, a false bottom that looks real but covers a secret compartment beneath. From that compartment he removed a flat wooden box. "Please take these. They have been in my family for generations, and it is right that you, my only love, should have them." These things he gave me, they are jewels fit for the tzar! I have never even dreamed of such stones as these. Alexandrites, he told me, after all the Alexanders of Russia, and more diamonds than there are stars in the skies. What am I to do with such as these, I who have no name? I tried to argue, to refuse, but he placed such gentle hands over mine, "No, do not argue with me! For the rest of my days I will be looking for our son. I know that you will too. Perhaps one day we will find him. He must know that he has a father who acknowledges him. He must know who I am and that I am proud of my son. Take these for him, if not for yourself."

I almost changed my intentions then! Who could leave such a man? But I know I must, for I can no longer live his life. I must find my own path now. And so now, today, now that he has left me for the last time, now as the sun rises on this city once again, I dress in rags, and I take up the most threadbare valise ever seen, and I carry a king's ransom in jewels, and at last I begin my own adventure.

The next day I found a compass on one of the shelves in the attic. I picked it up and looked over at the standing mirror. It was just me looking back at me. This time. I'd never given much thought to ghosts, but if ever a house wanted to convince me they were real, this one did, yet I didn't get spooky, eerie feelings from the house. I didn't feel in any way threatened. In fact, it seemed more like guidance than anything. But what kind of guidance? From someone, or something, that had my best interests in mind?

The nagging refrain from the letter, "Are you having fun yet?" pricked at the edges of my mind. I turned the old fashioned compass, weighty and beautiful, over and over in my hands. Then I went down to Emma Rae's office and booted up the computer. I googled "Yellen State Park" and "Mystic Wood." In minutes, I was on my way.

It was certainly a greater challenge to get there by road. Whoever was in charge of this area wasn't putting up big billboards to direct the flow of traffic. In fact, I'd say the locals were going out of their way to keep their little gem hidden to all but the most determined. Well, that would be me. Once I finally found the road in, it didn't get any easier. Barely wider than my truck, twisting and turning tighter than a boomerang, lots of wide open space way too close to the left side of the truck and a rough wall to the right, the road had me sweating and praying that no one wanted to come out while I was going in. On the seat beside me was a backpack I'd found in the mudroom. In it was the compass and plenty of plastic bags, a small but deadly sharp pair of clippers (I knew all too well just how sharp), a bottle of water with a twig of some energizing herb in it (I really needed to learn the names of these plants), and a sandwich made of the leftover bread (even better than I'd imagined) and two kinds of cheese. At the last minute I'd thrown in a thick bar of dark chocolate and a flashlight. I felt prepared for any emergency.

I had way too much time on that crazy road to debate the wisdom of my plan, but I could barely spare the attention. Just a moment of distraction and I could regret it big time. By the time I was finally headed back down to sea level, my shoulders felt permanently affixed to my earlobes, and my head was pounding. Oh, oops, forgetting to breathe again, Emma.

Once I was back on the level, I almost immediately recognized the place where the path to the Mystic Wood twisted up a steep hillside. I drove a ways till I could park the truck off to the side, grabbed my backpack, and hiked into my own adventure.

There was no getting lost on that trail, as it was as clearly defined as it was narrow. I encountered no one. The sunshine changed from filtered to missing as I went deeper and deeper into the redwoods. I had to concentrate on that whole breathing thing, because I was increasingly nervous about this idea. Really, Emma? You're really going all by yourself to explore that other world? No white stones to shine up my path back in the moonlight, not even any bread crumbs? I shrugged off the voice of caution. If I'd wanted to hear it, I would've told Ben my plans.

And there it was, the giant, the guardian of the door between the worlds. Or at least, between these two worlds. If I could believe in even one other, I guess I'd have to be open to the possibility of infinite worlds. Wow. Mind-boggling.

I approached the giant, leaned against the rough bark, breathed. I was inches away from insanity, and I was determined to ground myself quite thoroughly on this side. I'd never done anything this absolutely asinine before, and I needed to be quite ready.

I crawled through.

The wind, the push, the drag and pull: sheesh, would this ever get any easier? Pop! I staggered out on the other side, and reached back for the tree to keep myself from falling. Even as my head whirled and my breath came in gasps, I smelled again the sharp bubbly tang of the purple and white flowers, and a sense of joy and childlike fun infused me. I felt the smile rise up from deep in my soul, and I closed my eyes and rested back against the giant.

What took you so long?

I laughed as the words danced through my head. I didn't know who put them there, but I understood the question "Irrelevant!" I said loudly to the crisp, sparkling air. "I'm here now!"

As I look back on that afternoon, I always feel an overwhelming sense of relief. What kind of fool was I? I could have walked into any time, any place, into disaster beyond anything that had ever happened in my own world, and yet I went with the same kind of innocence with which I approached the ocean every morning, playing and dancing at the edge of a power that was vastly beyond my own, and yet always feeling safe. Wasn't I way too old for that kind of naive conviction of my own immortality? And yet it has never yet let me down, that innocent joy. Maybe I had stored it up, unused, in the previous 50 years, and now it overflowed, pouring out of me in an irresistible flood. Whatever the case, after a lifetime of hiding, of depression and isolation and nameless anxiety, once I arrived in Emma Rae's house, I stepped away from those old fears and ran headlong into the unknown, learning with each unconsidered step how to laugh, how to love, how to live.

That afternoon was spent in a glorious daze. Let me say at once that I believe that breathing the purple pollen of that world changes a person. I know it changed me. Before my first visit to that world, my veins ran blood just like everyone else's. But from the moment I first lifted my pollen washed hands and breathed in the life of that other world, I swear my veins ran champagne, and I'm not talking Asti Spumante. To this day, in quiet moments, I feel it bubbling, humming, singing through my veins.

But back to that day, the day when I chose my path as a traveler between two worlds, as a healer, as Emma Rae's rightful heir.

The first thing I did after greeting that world was to sink down and get a second infusion of "the purple thrill," as I came to call it in my own mind. I didn't bother to bring it up on my hand; this time I sank to my hands and knees and put my face right into the little white flowers, shaking my head like a dog and breathing as deeply as I could. For those of you with allergies, I apologize for this description. But believe me when I tell you this was nothing like the pollens we know and hate. I couldn't even feel it in my nostrils. It was more like breathing air that is so shiny and silky that it causes a sharply heightened awareness, an awakening in all the senses.

As soon as I had breathed my fill, I became aware of the music of unknown birds, of a wind that sang a different song from the wind I knew, of the hum of unseen life. I realized at once that if I wasn't very careful, I could lose myself in that strange euphoria and wander that world forever in the manner of an opium addict who loses touch with reality so completely that he simply fades away to death.

That thought brought me up short. I wiped my face on my shirt, brushing away any remaining pollen. I was lightheaded, but I stood up anyway, knowing now that I needed to keep from breathing any more of it. I rooted through my backpack, but then thought that maybe I shouldn't drink my water or eat the bread, since both had herbs from this other world in them. I peeled the cheese out from the sandwich and ate that, grounding myself in my own world, after which I popped a huge chunk of the dark chocolate in my mouth, and let it melt as I checked my compass for coordinates.

In that world, I discovered over time, the giant always showed at North on my compass. It is a good lesson for me to always remember: my own true North is always in my own world.

I started that first exploration by just standing at the foot of the giant, breathing, and listening. Even the smell of that other world is different, fresher somehow. The breezes sing songs that spin a little differently through air that is almost shiny, it's so clean and bright. I heard no ocean, the constant background music that I'd begun to take for granted back on the other side. But after a moment I heard another water sound, the chatter of a stream. I started walking, kicking up tiny purple puffs with every step. Even so, my head cleared of the euphoric buzz and I settled in to an eager curiosity. After several minutes, the level ground began sloping downward, and a few minutes later I came to the sharp bank of a brook. The brook was several feet wide, and as clear as the air as it splashed its way along a rocky bed. I noticed lots of plants growing along the bank, many unfamiliar kinds. I took off my shoes and socks to wade. The water was shockingly cold, so cold I could only stand in it for a brief minute before my bones starting aching. I stepped out, then knelt down and put my hands in the water, splashing it over my face and gasping with the cold. Again I acted before thought could stop me; I filled my hands and drank deeply.

I rocked back on my heels. Even now, I've never found the words to accurately describe what it feels like to drink the water from that other world. The best I can say is that the water, like everything else over there, seems vibrant, sparkling with life, *younger*. And when I drank it, that vitality washed through me, energized me, until I felt as though I, too, was sparkling. I bent back to the stream and drank, and drank, and drank. Then I poured out the water I'd brought with me, and filled the bottle from the stream. That stuff was amazing!

I didn't go much farther that day; I kept the giant in my sights all afternoon. I followed the course of the stream for a ways, and walked back through the meadow slowly, feeling a different sun on my shoulders and a different breeze on my face. I meant to gather plants; that was what I was there for, I'd told myself. But on that first day, after washing in that crystal stream, I simply walked and looked and breathed, acclimating to a new place, one that, over time, would become as familiar to me as a close friend's house.

When I felt a change in the air that told me evening was arriving, I walked briskly back to the giant, though it was farther than I thought. It was deep dusk before I got back to the huge tree. I took a deep breath, prepared for the chaos, and headed home.

Ben was sitting on my porch when I pulled in. My heart started racing. I was excited to see him, but at the same time I knew he'd be furious if he knew where I'd gone, and all alone, too. I didn't want to lie to him if he asked. I didn't want to deal with him angry. My mind was chattering away like a monkey as I walked toward the house, and I tried to slow down my breathing and wear a normal expression.

"Hey you," I called out cheerfully. "Waiting for some tea? You could have helped yourself."

He smiled, but I could see that it was an effort. "Well, now, some tea would be lovely. And I never walk into a lady's house until she invites me to do so."

I passed him to open the door, and grinned up over my shoulder at him. "Well, come right on in, then. Don't be a stranger. Hot or iced?"

"Iced, if you've got it ready."

"Made some up this morning," I affirmed, filling two glasses with ice and tea.

He followed me back out to the porch and we sat quietly, sipping our tea, enjoying the cooling evening. As before, this "time zone" seemed several hours behind, and our day was just now leaning toward dusk. I wondered if that was consistent; could it be depended on?

"Emma," he said after a bit.

"Mm hm?"

"There's something you should know about me."

I looked up into serious eyes. "What's that?"

He took another sip of tea and looked out toward the ocean as if gathering his thoughts. "Ever since I can remember, I've known things that there was no logical way for me to know."

"What do you mean? What kind of things?"

"For instance, I knew when and how my dad died. It was just before I graduated from college. He was in a car accident. I was sleeping at the time, but I had a dream—or a vision—and I saw the whole thing. I was already packing to come home by the time I got the call. It had happened exactly as I saw it."

"Wow, that must have been terrible!" I said. "I am so sorry."

"Thank you. It was terrible, and a lot of bad times came after. But it was a long time ago. The point is, I have that kind of knowledge about a lot of things. And my work with Emma Rae, well, it fine-tuned it in a lot of ways."

Was he telling me he was psychic? Clairvoyant? Up until a week ago, I would never have believed such a thing, but my world view had changed quite a bit recently. Or was that "worlds view?" Either way. "How so?"

"My mom, my brothers, my sisters . . . I always have a general idea of where they are and what they're doing. It's just kind of an awareness, in the same way I'm aware of birds nearby, or the ocean. It's background for me. While working with Emma Rae, I learned how to focus in on it, to the point where I can actually get a vision of exactly where they are, what's going on, what they're seeing and hearing."

"Wow," I said again. "Isn't that kind of . . . invasive?"

He nodded. "It can be. I almost never do it, only if I get a strong pull that makes me pay attention. My mom and my sisters have it too, though not as strongly as I do. From time to time we actually communicate that way on purpose, though anything more than just a touch, so to speak, can be exhausting."

"What about your brothers?"

He shook his head. "They've got nothing like it, at least not that they've ever admitted. They both really freaked out about it when my dad died, and after that we've never spoken about it again."

"Yeah, I imagine that would have freaked me out, too," I acknowledged.

"I figured it might," he said. "That's why I've been hesitant to tell you."

I searched his face. "Why are you telling me now, then?"

Again he studied the distant waves, drank his tea. "I had the same kind of connection with Emma Rae," he finally said. "It wasn't automatic like it was with my family. It happened after we, well, we shared an herb-related, uh, event, many years ago, and I guess our minds linked. Afterwards, as far as I could tell, nothing was different for her. But ever since then, I had that link with her, just like with my family."

"Dude, that is crazy!"

He laughed, "Oh ho, you're starting to sound like a Californian!"

"I know, right!?" I laughed back. But then I went quiet again, waiting for him to continue.

"Okay, so, I'm telling you this now for two reasons. The first is that, well," he cleared his throat, shifted in his chair, then brought his eyes to mine, "I really care about you, Emma. I like to think our friendship is going to grow into a romance, into a lifetime. I know it's early days yet, but, well, there it is. And if that's going to happen, then you need to know this about me up front. It can be a very uncomfortable thing."

My heart was pounding. Holy kamoley! Now it was my turn to shift in my seat and clear my throat. I wasn't sure how to respond until I recognized that I wanted all that, too, so I'd better be prepared to be just as honest. "Wow, well, okay! It's been almost a week, right? But you know, I've been thinking the same thing." I flushed with heat and took a deep drink of tea, avoiding his eyes now. What the heck! Wasn't I kind of old to be responding like a teenager?

He was grinning like he was back in high school too, though, so I didn't feel so bad. "Okay then! Well!" he said, sounding very self satisfied.

We sat there for another little bit, both of us gazing out at the sky, now turning rosy as the sun neared the horizon. My tea was gone, and I wasn't sure what to do with my hands, or what else to say. But then I remembered that there was more. "You said there were two reasons?"

He started, brought back to the moment. "Yes, right." He looked uncomfortable again. "Well, the second thing is that I have that same kind of connection with you."

He said it so fast and low I didn't catch it at first, but then my brain processed it and I was left staring at him with my mouth open. "You, you what? What do you mean?"

"I always know where you are, too. And, to some extent, what you're doing, how you're feeling."

"What do you mean?" I said again, although of course I knew what he meant. But let's face it. It's one thing when someone tells you they can read people's minds. It's another when they tell you they can read *your* mind! I got all uncomfortable and twitchy.

"It's a lot like when you feel what's going on with other people emotionally," he explained.

"Yeah?" I challenged, "Except?"

He shrugged. "Except it's pretty much all the time. As I said, I don't focus on it, I don't look into your thoughts or anything."

"But you could?"

"I don't know. I haven't tried."

I sat there in a stew. I didn't want to ask him to try, but I wanted to know if he could. I felt incredibly vulnerable and violated, even though I believed that he hadn't actually done anything wrong. Too much, too much change!

Are you having fun? whispered through my thoughts. No! I yelled back silently. *Why not?* the whisper came again. And then, *How* could *this be fun for you?*

The whisper had distracted me, and I let myself play with the question. Well, it might be kinda fun if I could look into *his* thoughts.

Let me just say that, in retrospect, I see that I tried to do exactly what I would have been furious about if he'd tried to do it to me. But at that moment I didn't even let myself think. As I had at the giant tree, I simply barreled ahead.

There was nothing, just my own breathing and my own suspended thoughts as I pushed my mind toward Ben and tried to hear something that didn't belong in my head.

Wait. I felt it then, and all I can tell you is that what I felt was so clearly not me because, well, because it was so very *masculine*, so *other* in its very essence. And it wasn't like I heard any thoughts or anything. I just knew that I'd crossed through a door. Once again, I'd stepped into a completely different world.

Bam! I felt like I'd been shoved, and had a door slammed in my face. My eyes flew open and so did my mouth, and I was staring at Ben with the same look of shock on my face that he had on his. "Hey!" he said. Boy, did he look mad. My mind felt disoriented, splintered. He grabbed my arm, and yelled at me, his face deep red, "Emma! Good God, you have got to stop doing things without thinking! You could get hurt!"

I pulled out of his grip. I wanted to be furious right back at him, but I knew so completely that his anger wasn't because I'd tried to invade his head, but because he was afraid for me, really, really afraid. And from the ringing in my head, I knew he had reason to be. Wisely, I didn't even try to defend myself.

He rubbed his face, ran his hands through his hair. "I'm not going to talk about this any more right now," he said through clenched jaws. "But I am going to finish telling you what I started." He took two long, slow breaths before continuing. "There is one time when I don't feel you. It's when you go into the other world. When you go through the door, I lose you. It was the same with Emma Rae. And it scares the shit out of me. Anything could happen to you over there, and I'd never know." He ran his hand through his hair again. "But holy shit Emma, what difference does it make? You do crazy shit like other people drive. You don't even think. You're a menace to yourself."

Without another word, he got up and walked off the porch, down the driveway, climbed in his jeep and drove away. He didn't look back once.

Chapter 9

Boy did my head ache. And my brains felt scrambled. I'd never had a door slammed inside my head before, and I did not like the results, not one little bit. I didn't think Ben had meant to hurt me; I figured he'd just been startled, and his natural defenses defended. I couldn't blame him for that, and I couldn't blame him for being mad at me. He was right, I did keep doing things that were incredibly foolish. Like popping off into a whole different world without telling anybody. Like eating the plants all the time. How many plants are out there that are poisonous, or hallucinogenic, or whatever? But I just walked around cramming stuff in my mouth without even thinking.

But I *knew*, I argued with myself, somehow I just knew what the plants were for, and that they were safe. I wasn't risking anything.

Yeah right, self argued back, one week you've been this new brilliant intuitive person and you are so 100% perfectly tuned to the natural order of things—in two worlds!—that you're never at risk of making a mistake?

Oh please just shut up! a third voice yelled. Sheesh!

That did it, for awhile anyway.

I had to settle my head. I had to make peace with Ben. I buttered a thick slice of bread, the bread that I'd made with herbs for connection, honesty, trust. I poured a glass of white wine, one that I'd concocted for peace and contentment. I went out on my balcony, set my chair facing the direction of Ben's house, and slowed my breathing down, way down, eating the delicious bread and sipping the wine. And I opened my mind, slowly and carefully, just a bit, holding Ben's name in my heart as I issued a very non-aggressive invitation, like someone who opens a door just a crack, hoping a breeze might come in.

I startled awake, instantly aware that I wasn't alone. It was full dark out, and the stars lit the sky like tossed brilliants. Ben sat in the chair beside me, a glass of wine in his hand.

You woke me, I said silently.

Yes.

How long have you been here?

Since you called. Almost an hour.

I'm sorry.

"I know," he said. "Please, Emma, please let me teach you properly."

"I'll try, Ben, I really will."

"Emma. . . ."

"It's just that I've never been this person before, this spontaneous person, this never-look-before-you-leap girl. I don't know how to rein her in, because I've never had to. I never know what she'll do next."

"Nice try, Emma," he said, "but that's not good enough."

"What do you mean?"

He leaned forward to take my hand, and turned my chair to face him. "This girl you're talking about? That's you. You aren't a victim of some demon possession or something. You are still responsible for what you do, even if what you do is something you've never done before."

I had to think about that for a minute. Did I think I was a victim? Had I been thinking that I was a victim all along, all those years when I was in hiding? It made sense. That would explain why I didn't try to change anything, why I simply curled up on the couch, and why now, I simply went with the flow and took on this new persona without really thinking things through.

But Ben was right. I wasn't a victim. I never had been, even if I'd acted like one. Sheesh, that was a whole different perspective. Again. This Ben character, he had some pretty good insights.

"Yes, Ben," I said, tightening my grip on his hand. "I will let you teach me."

I dreamed about flying again that night. But in this dream I was a kite, a brilliantly colored kite with long, colorful tails. I soared and danced upon the air, tugging now and then on the string that tethered me to the earth. I resisted that string, I resisted its guidance and its strength. I fought it, snapping away from it again and again until at last I ripped free. For brief seconds I laughed triumphantly as I raced higher than ever on a breeze. But suddenly the breeze became a wind, harsh and buffeting, battering me up and down, back and forth. I didn't understand this wind, I didn't know how to ride it! It ripped me to shreds, tearing through my bright colors until, screaming, I plummeted to the Earth far below. I awoke with a jump, sitting upright in bed, still screaming.

I quieted my racing heart. I didn't have to be a genius to get the symbolism. Rolling over and punching my pillow, I complained to the air, "I get it, I get it! I said yes, didn't I?" But though I complained, I took the message to heart. Ben would be my tether. I didn't have to allow it; I could fight, and I would win. But would the winning be worth it?

March 1958

What a day I have had! I was collecting plants in the Yellen State Park, and as usual I went up into the Mystic Wood. There is not much to collect there, under those trees, but redwood makes a nice oil and in any case, I have always loved the feel in there, almost otherworldly, more so than I could possibly have imagined, in fact! There is a giant tree deep into the grove, the biggest one there, that I have always been drawn to. So I made my way to it. I was tired (perhaps I am getting too old for such gallivantings), and planned to rest under the tree, but for some reason today I decided to climb up into those huge branches. It has multiple trunks, and I planned to use them for leverage to climb high enough to reach the branches. So I was wedging myself between the two biggest trunks when all of a sudden . . . Well, I do not even know how to describe what happened. There I was in the deep quiet of the Redwood forest and it was as though all at once I was falling into absolute chaos! And I was falling! I hit the ground and I do not know, perhaps I lost consciousness. But when I regained awareness, I was on the ground under the tree, yet it was definitely not the ground I was expecting! I was not in a grove; there were not any other trees, only this one familiar giant in the middle of a large, sunny meadow. It was extremely disorienting!

For a moment I wondered if I had died somehow, if I had arrived in Heaven. I looked around for the light I have heard about, or for my dearly departed coming to welcome me, or some such. There was nothing like that. I walked all around the tree, however other than the tree itself, the whole of the Mystic Wood had simply disappeared, leaving me in an entirely unfamiliar place. I was not feeling very well; my head was ringing and my stomach was upset, so I sat for a short while, leaning against the tree. I wanted to explore, as soon as I had recovered my breath, yet I admit I was afraid. If I walked away from the tree, would it disappear? Would I be lost forever in this place? I thought of Walter and Mary, my dearest friends. I thought of my neighbor, Ramona. How would it affect them, if I simply disappeared? I thought about all my friends, and the people who come to me for help. Was I willing to risk all of that? I had left everything before, more than once, in my 58 years. Did I want to do it again?

I closed my eyes, trying to get my head to stop spinning. When I opened them, I was astonished to see a man sitting cross legged in front of me. I had heard nothing! He was stunningly beautiful; his hair looked like melted copper, and it was long and tied back. His skin was bronze, and even though he was sitting, I could see that he was tall, and his shoulders were broad and strong looking. His clothing was unusual.

Oddly enough, I was not afraid at all. Rather, I was drawn to him, as though he were water and I had not had a drink in many days. He smiled at me and I thought I would swoon! How silly is that, at my age?

We really could not talk at all. I did not understand a word he said. And after a time, the light began to fade, so I knew I needed to see if I could climb back through that tree. I tried to explain it, and I tried to tell him I would return if I was able. I do not know if he understood or not. But in any case, I will assuredly go back if I can. Not only is there an abundance of plant life there that I have never seen before, but that man? Oh, my! If it was not quite insane, I would believe that I am head over heels in love, for the first time since Alexis!

"Oh my" is right! Did Emma Rae have a love affair with someone from the other world? Her journals just got better and better!

I'd been in California for a week, and I no longer had any doubt that I was coming to live here permanently. Not only did it simply make sense, given the circumstances, but I loved the whole set-up: the house by the ocean, the gardens and greenhouses and my little plane and Ben. . . . Oh, yeah, I'd be crazy to leave all this to go back to the gloom and depression that had been my life for the last ten years. Many more than ten, if I was honest.

So I had a lot to do. All of Emma Rae's things were still exactly where they'd been the day she took her last flight. In the master bedroom alone were her slippers, kicked off into a closet full of her clothes, a chest of drawers and a dresser, the bedside table with her books and a notebook and two pens. I'd barely moved anything, or if I had, I'd put it back, like I was a conscientious visitor. But all I had been visiting was my own new life, and it was time for me to claim it.

I called Daniel.

"Well, hello! I was going to call you this morning. How are you getting along?" he asked, his voice expressing pleasure to hear from me.

"Great! I love this place!"

"You're staying then?"

I laughed. "Did you really have any doubt?"

I could hear his chuckle. "It would have stretched credibility, I admit."

"So I was wondering if you had any ideas about what I should do with all Emma Rae's things. Her clothes and stuff?"

There was a silence. I had to remember that Daniel had loved her, she'd been a second mother to him, and she was so recently gone. Finally he said, his voice betraying no emotion, "Anything you don't want you could pack up for St. Vincent DePaul, or there's a thrift store in Boast Point."

I hesitated, then, "Do you think your dad might want to go through anything? Or do you? I really haven't even started the process yet, and I don't know what I intend to keep and what I'm going to get rid of. But if there's anything you wanted, something that has meaning for you . . ."

He let out a breath. "At the moment, I can't think of any-thing. I'll ask my dad if you'd like me to."

"That would be great. Thanks."

He went on, "If you'd like help going through things, I could come up for an afternoon this week. And I imagine my dad would be interested in seeing what's in that attic."

I suddenly realized there were, in fact, things I would not be willing to give up. I wasn't ready to have her journals up for inspection, especially by Walter. As much as he had loved her, learning about Rhein could only cause him pain. And, of course, I mustn't let anyone know about Rhein's world.

Also there was the tea chest. Other than that, I didn't know what surprises she might have left for me.

If he heard my hesitation, he ignored it. "Also, my dad gave me some photo albums he thought you might like to look at. He's always loved taking pictures, and he's got lots and lots of Emma Rae. He'd probably love to sit down with you and go through them, just to reminisce.

"I'd like that. But maybe not this week? I'd love your help sometime, though. And I was hoping you and your dad could come for dinner one night after I get back from Michigan. My friend Petie is coming back with me, and we can have a din-ner party."

"Company already?" he laughed. "That sounds great! And I have confidence that I'm safe in saying Dad would love to come too. I know he's been hoping you'd get in touch. He feels, well, we both feel that you're family. I'm so pleased that you've decided to stay."

We arranged an afternoon for him to come, and then I said, "Okay, great. Now, what were you calling about?"

He chuckled. "I'm guessing you don't know what day it is today?"

I admit, keeping track of the days had been a big challenge for me since I got to Emma Rae's. "Um, Sunday? No, wait, Monday, right? Yeah, Monday!"

He laughed. "Ni-i-ice. Yes, it's Monday. It's also the Fourth of July. Dad and I wondered if you'd like to come into town and be our guest for the festival and fireworks tonight."

"Festival? Fireworks?" That was enticing.

I could still hear the laugh in his voice. "Yes, there's a big barbecue on the beach, some of the best food you'll ever eat. The fruit cobblers alone are worth selling your soul for, and the ribs are almost that good. That's not even to mention 25 different kinds of potato salad and baked beans that've cooked for days in sunken fire pits. Trust me when I tell you there's no better eating this side of Heaven."

Okay, now I was interested! "Wow, all that and fireworks, too? How can I refuse?"

"Great! You want me to pick you up?"

"Not necessary. I'll bring myself if you'll just tell me where to meet you. Do I need to bring anything?"

He paused, then, "Emma Rae used to bring a huge cooler of her special iced tea. Have you found any of her tea?"

If he only knew! "Some, yeah. I'll take a look and see if I can figure something out." I don't know why I didn't just tell him.

"That'd be great, but it doesn't really matter. You're a guest. You don't need to bring anything but yourself."

After we hung up, I instantly started having second thoughts. I thought about the way people responded to me, and the way I responded to them. I thought about the whispers at the funeral, and the weeping woman at the grocery store. But if I was really going to make my home out here, I'd have to start going out in public sometime. I didn't want to go back into hiding. And anyway, I'd already committed to going. I'd just have to wear a giant hat and Audrey Hepburn sunglasses, and remember to keep breathing.

I headed up to the attic to see if I could find a drawer with Fourth of July Tea. Well, what do you know? Not, in fact, under Fourth of July, but under Iced Tea: "Perfect for events, especially family reunions, instills a sense of innocence and wonder and is great for keeping old antagonisms from flaring up." Hmm, all that and it tastes good, too? Emma Rae really was a miracle worker.

As I pulled the larger than normal packet out of the drawer, I read through the recipe. Looked pretty good, but . . . I thought about adding a pinch of this or that to the mix. Just yesterday I'd taken a nibble of something that had brought a rush of sheer joy coursing through me, startling me and making me burst out in laughter. Ben, working several feet away, grinned and shook his head, but opened his mouth willingly enough when I held out a leaf. I could tell by the expressions that crossed his sunflushed face that he'd had a similar response, and we shared a delighted laugh for no apparent reason. After that, it was quite natural to share a kiss, too, for no apparent reason. I smiled just thinking about it now, and felt a flush of my own rising. Oh, yes, the perfect addition to Iced Tea for a Crowd.

Thank God for my mother! I owed her big time. Not only had she insisted on taking me shopping and buying the funeral dress for me, but she'd made sure I bought some new summer things as well. It was nice having new shorts and girly tops. The bright summer dress, though, that was perfect for a Fourth of July festival, showing off the new, glowing tan that I had from my many hours in the garden, and making me feel pretty and festive. I slipped on my snazzy new sandals and sent another blessing winging her way. Digging through Emma Rae's closet,

I found a white lace shawl to drape around my shoulders later when the air cooled.

I wrestled the huge cooler out to the Honda. The tea, with my subtle additions, was delicious! I'd had to hold myself back, or there wouldn't have been enough left to share. And at the last minute I'd thrown together a few dozen zucchini muffins, moist and spicy, studded with pecan chunks and juicy golden raisins. Now as the late afternoon breezes began to whisper, I climbed behind the wheel and headed south toward Boast Point, looking forward to seeing Daniel and Walter, and wondering if Ben would be there.

At the edge of town I stopped at a little shop that had flags flying briskly, and bought a giant sun hat with trailing ribbons, and big, dark sunglasses. I was ready.

I was still a block away from the place where Daniel had instructed me to meet him, leaning my arm out the window and driving slowly, wondering where in all this madness I would park, and how was I going to get to wherever I was going with that heavy cooler of iced tea and that big bag of muffins? Already I was smelling the sweet spicy tang of the best kind of barbecue, and my mouth was watering.

"Emma!"

I heard the shout and swiveled my attention to the other side of the street. Daniel was hurrying towards me, holding his hand out to stop traffic as he crossed to me. Not that the traffic was moving much anyway, but still . . .

"Chinese fire drill!" he shouted, and, startled, I slammed the Honda into park, jumped out and ran around to the passenger side as he slid right into the driver's seat. "Good reflexes!" he laughed as he put the car back into gear and, having barely caused a blip in the slow traffic, eased us on down the road. "If I hadn't recognized the car, I certainly would never have recognized you!" he laughed. "But I saw it coming, figured it must be you driving, and decided that this was the easiest way to get us where we're going."

"Smart man," I said, grinning over at him. He was wearing a polo shirt and dress shorts, much more casual than I'd seen him before. "I was a little concerned because I brought a big cooler of tea."

"Oh! Did you find Emma Rae's iced tea?"

I nodded. "But beware," I cautioned, "I made a few tiny changes."

He looked at me, startled. "Did you now?"

I nodded again, still grinning. What would the general populace think? Would they even notice any difference? "Don't worry, I just added a thing or two to her original."

He looked like he was biting his tongue to keep from saying something. "What?" I invited.

He lost the battle with himself. "What possessed you to do that?"

My eyebrows shot up. "Why wouldn't I?"

"Well," he looked uncomfortable, "It's just that Emma Rae had been bringing that same tea to every town festival for, well, forever."

I felt his discomfort, and reminded myself that his grief was still fresh. "I know. I think, however, that the little changes I made will be appreciated, if they're even noticed."

He gave me a sharp look. "Do you?" he asked, clearly not believing me.

I shrugged. I didn't really think it was his business what I did, but I didn't need to get worked up about it. And there was no use arguing. "Might as well try it for yourself. If you don't like it, you don't need to drink it."

"I'm sorry, Emma," he said, "I didn't mean anything by it."

I turned toward him in the seat. "Don't sweat it, Daniel. I know you're missing Emma Rae, and I imagine you thought this would be a little bit of her, still here. But I truly think that the little additions I made will be useful, especially because of you all missing her so much."

He slanted another look at me, this time more considering. "Is that so? Why would you think that?" It didn't come across as offensive this time, but curious.

"We-e-ell," I answered slowly, remembering what Walter had said about me having the same gifts as Emma Rae, "it seems I have inherited more from Emma Rae than her physical possessions."

He thought about that for a minute as he maneuvered the Honda around a tight corner, between pedestrians, and into a parking space that seemed to have been saved for him. "Okay," he said at last, "I look forward to trying some. And right about now," he added, turning off the car and leaning back into the seat with a big sigh, "I am more than ready."

I carried the bag of muffins while Daniel hefted the cooler as if it were empty, and carried it down the hill towards a grassy area above the beach. Long tables were set up for food, and blankets and beach chairs were set up in groupings all around. On the beach people were swimming, playing volleyball, chasing around and screaming and generally carrying on. As Daniel and I walked toward the tables, I saw Walter getting up from a low chair and coming to greet us. He was wearing a bright plaid shirt and madras shorts. I laughed under my breath to Daniel, "Don't tell me, your dad's a golfer?"

"Behave yourself," he whispered back, and then Walter was folding me into a warm hug. Not knowing what else to do, I hugged him back, rather stiffly. Long after the 3 seconds it took me to be done with that hug, Walter hung on tight. And after a few more seconds, all the tension seemed to drain out of my body and I sighed, releasing myself to the unfamiliar pleasure of being held with genuine affection.

"There," Walter whispered in my ear, "That wasn't so bad, was it?"

I pulled away, to see his big friendly smile, and I returned it quite naturally. What a nice man, I remember thinking.

"I see you've brought Emma Rae's cooler," he said eagerly. "Does it, by chance, hold Emma Rae's famous iced tea?"

Thinking of the uncomfortable conversation with Daniel, I simply smiled and said gently, "Well, it is full of tea."

"Wonderful! Let's have a glass, shall we?" he said cheerfully, and in a moment he'd procured plastic cups and poured for all three of us. I watched over the rim of my cup to see their reactions.

When Daniel lifted his cup, his face was tense and creased. I watched as the lines smoothed out, as his shoulders relaxed. Good, I thought. Perfect.

Walter seemed already poised to be pleased. As he drank, his eyebrows twitched in momentary surprise, and then his eyes closed in what looked like pure bliss. Ye-e-es.

"My dear, that is lovely!" Walter said, turning back to the cooler. Had he drained his glass already? His eyes twinkled at me over his shoulder as he poured. "I see you've improved on an already excellent concoction!"

"I have to agree," Daniel joined in. "I would not have thought it possible."

"Can I ask what you added?" Walter inquired, "or will you prove to be as secretive about such things as Emma Rae was?"

My heart was singing at their praises, and I could barely keep from laughing in pleasure. I realized, though, that Emma Rae had good reason to be cagey. The herbs I'd added wouldn't be found in any herb book on this side of the giant. "Oh, I believe I'll take my cue from Emma Rae," I said, looking as coy as possible. "After all, a woman needs her mysteries."

I felt silly acting that way; it wasn't like me at all. But Walter just patted my shoulder fondly. "Well done, my dear. And now, I must warn you, you will soon be famous in your own right."

I frowned. "Do you really think people will notice?"

"Perhaps not," he said. "You can always hope."

Daniel took my arm gently. "Tell you what, let's walk the beach for a bit. People can come get their tea while we're gone. And with the hat and sunglasses you're wearing, we should be safe for a bit. You can get used to the crowd that way."

I looked up at him nervously. "Will that help?"

He shrugged. "No idea. You can tell me later."

"Oh, thanks a bunch!" But people were starting to move in our direction, and he steered me away, not so quickly as to be obvious, but in moments we were well away from the tables.

"Emma Rae used to love these festivals," he told me as we walked, "but even so, they were draining for her. She and I used to walk along the beach every little while, away from the crowds. I'm happy to render you the same service." His smile took any sting from the words.

"I appreciate that. I'm not used to crowds, really. I was never comfortable in big groups of people."

"I understand. It's because of your extreme empathy, I imagine. That's what it was for Emma Rae, anyway."

"I never understood it before. I don't think I even realized why I preferred to be alone most of the time. I used to love having people over for dinner parties, back when I was first married. But I haven't done anything like that for a long time."

He grinned down at me. "Sounds like you're ready to start again, though, right? Having Dad and me over when your friend gets here?"

I nodded. "Petie, yes! I can't wait to see her! She is gonna love this place!"

We talked for a while, and then we turned back toward the picnic area. A big wave rolled in, crashing onto the shore and causing screams of delight among the kids on the beach, and a blast of wind plucked the hat right off my head.

A race ensued among several kids as they scrambled to catch it before it went into the ocean. A little boy was the victor, and he raced it over to me, screeching to a halt as he held it out with a yell of triumph. I smiled to thank him, and the expression on his face changed from glee to shock. "Emma Rae?" he gasped, forgetting to let go of the hat.

I felt the shock hit me like sea spray. All the other kids stood, turned into living statues as they stared at me. I gasped, caught my breath. Daniel's hand on my elbow steadied me. I took a deep breath, another. Cleared my throat. Breathed again. Then I took off my giant sunglasses and forced a smile, squatting down to eye level with the boy. "No, just Emma. Who are you?"

Still hanging on to the hat, his eyes huge, he said in a trembling voice, "You're not Emma Rae?"

I shook my head. "No, I'm not Emma Rae. I look like her, I know."

He nodded, his mouth open. "You look exactly like her!" he declared in a very firm voice.

"Well, I'll have to take your word for it," I tried to sound cheerful, "because I never met her."

Another boy stepped forward, leaned into my face. I fought not to pull backwards. "If you never met her, how do you know you look like her?"

I gave up on the hat, letting it go. "Because people keep telling me. She was my great-grandma, but I never knew her."

A tiny little girl stepped up. I sighed, and sat down on the sand, feeling Daniel's hand on my shoulder "Why didn't you know her? We all knew her."

By this time a small crowd of children was close around me. I worked to keep my breathing stable. "I didn't know her because I lived very far away, in Michigan."

"Michigan!" an older boy yelled. "Do you know my Uncle Fred? He lives in Michigan!"

I laughed. It was shaky, but it was a laugh. "Maybe," was all I could say.

The tiny girl climbed into my lap. My heart was pounding, crashing against my ribs, but I stayed still. "You don't smell like Emma Rae," she declared.

I laughed again, a real laugh this time, and I heard a startled laugh from Daniel, too. "No? What did Emma Rae smell like?"

"Dirt!"

We spent a few more minutes with the kids before they became bored and ran off to the next adventure. Daniel helped me to my feet and we wandered on down the beach. "That went well," Daniel observed.

I laughed a shaky laugh up at him. "It did, didn't it?"

"You're a natural with kids." He didn't actually say it, but I could hear the silent words, *just like Emma Rae.*

"I've never really spent much time with kids. My best friend didn't have any, and neither did I. And neither of us had siblings, so no nieces or nephews."

"Did you want children?"

I swallowed, struggled to find my voice.

"I'm sorry, that's a very personal question."

"No," I said, "It's all right. Yes, I did want kids, very much. But," I hesitated, then simply said, "it didn't work out for me."

"I'm sorry," he said again.

I wanted to laugh and shrug and say, no big deal, I'm over it. But I couldn't. We walked in silence back up to the tables, and I wasted no time pouring us both another glass of tea.

It was a fun day, a good day. I met so many people that I didn't even try to remember their names, and they were all very gracious about it. When I needed a break, I simply walked away for a few minutes, and no one followed or intruded while I breathed and took strength from the rolling ocean waves. These were such nice people, easy to talk to and eager to welcome me into their small community. As the evening wore on I became more and more relaxed. Shortly before the extraordinary fireworks display, I slipped away to the Honda to retrieve a bottle of what had started out as simple wine but was now a very special Sangria, and Walter and Daniel and I toasted to the star-strewn sky.

We settled into our beach chairs, and Walter leaned towards me. "Emma, you are a power to be reckoned with," he said, his eyes gleaming.

I turned to him, startled. "Oh? And why is that?"

A smile lit up his whole face. "I thought the tea was delightful. But this wine? My dear, if you bottled this for sale, you would never have to worry about money for the rest of your life. In fact, your greatest worry might be that of being mobbed in the streets!"

I raised my glass to his again. "Here's to never worrying about money again!" I laughed, adding, "But to be honest, I've already been worried about being mobbed in the streets, from the moment I got here!"

He joined in my laughter. "Well, yes, there is that. But once people are used to you, I think you'll find they bother you no more nor less than they bother anyone else."

"I certainly hope so."

"In any case, you've got a way with herbs that, though I hesitate to say it, Emma Rae herself might envy. And I certainly hope I'll have many more opportunities to experience your, shall we say, concoctions."

I put my hand over his, not even thinking until much later how unusual that was for me. "Thank you, Walter. What a kind thing to say."

"Nonsense," he said briskly, "It's nothing but the truth."

At that, a streamer of fire whizzed up into the sky, and any reply I might have made was drowned out by the start of the fireworks display.

Chapter 10

I woke late the next morning. For the first time since arriving in California, I wanted to stay in bed. I was exhausted, drained. Too much sun, too many people, too much food and wine and noise. . . . I rolled over and dragged the quilt up over my head, shutting out the brilliant sunshine. No. Not today.

I drifted in and out of sleep, in and out of dreams. I woke sweating, stifling under the light-blocking quilt, but I just burrowed down deeper, and willed myself back to sleep. I didn't want to think about . . . I didn't want to think. Too much change. Decades of hiding . . . this was too much, too fast.

What was I thinking? That I was new? That all the problems I'd had for so long had simply disappeared because I was suddenly . . . what was I now? Rich? Change of scenery, change of self: was that what had happened? What about "wherever you go, there you are?" I was still the same person I'd been two weeks ago, the morning of my fiftieth birthday when all I'd wanted was to stay in bed, keep the lights out, be alone.

I curled more tightly into myself. The old, familiar gray had descended, swathing me in the smothering cloud of depression that I knew so well. Who was I kidding? Nothing ever really changed.

Did it?

Who did I think I was? Why was I so special that I would believe, even for a minute, that I could change my life, that I could change myself? I didn't know anyone else who ever did. And what about all those lottery winners you read about? They win millions of dollars, and three years later they're back to being broke and miserable, worse off than they ever were before. Did I really think I was better than they were, different, that somehow I would be the one to come out bright and smiling, after all the years I'd spent living in a foul gray fog?

I lay, curled and sweating, exhausted and miserable, under that colorful quilt, and tried to forget the dream of these past lovely days. Because that's all it really was, right? Just a dream. That's what life had taught me. Being with people, trusting people, loving people . . . sooner or later, that all just bites you in the butt. I wrapped that thought around me, tighter than the quilt, and forced myself back into a drowning sleep.

A touch woke me, gentle, tentative. I jumped as if I'd been shot with electricity, and slammed my mind shut against the trespass. My heart pounded, my breath came in dragging, panicked gasps. I threw off the covers: air, I need air!

No idea what time it was, but outside it was midday bright and the air tugging at my curtains was hot. I heard the doorbell, but ignored it. Again, I realized. How long had Ben been there, before he risked that invading touch?

I started to slump back into the bed, started to curl back into my miserable nest. Go away, go away, I silently told him, hunching my back toward the door.

I waited for the bell to ring again, but it didn't. Then I waited to be relieved that he'd given up and gone away, but I wasn't. Then I got annoyed that I even cared. But I did.

I sat up again, swung my legs out of the bed, felt the cool wood planks beneath my bare feet. It felt like I'd been asleep for days, weeks, years. Then I realized, I had been. I'd finally, *finally* awakened, to a beautiful world and incredible possibilities, and what did I do? I crawled back into bed, and pulled up the covers.

Why? I stood up and went into the bathroom, washed my face and then stared at it in the mirror. Hadn't I had fun yesterday? Hadn't I laughed and played and talked and walked and met people and eaten great food? So I was exhausted today, worn out and confused, so what? I'd had more fun in the past week than I'd had in years, maybe ever. If I chose it, that *could* be my life.

I'd never even thought about it before, about choices. I hadn't realized that I had chosen to be miserable. Did I like it, being miserable? No-o-o, not really. It was a habit now, really, an insidious, killing habit. But just because I was used to it, that didn't mean I was stuck with it, did it?

I went back to my bedroom and picked out my prettiest shirt to wear. I put on my alexandrite jewelry, feeling ridiculous, and grinned a wobbly grin at myself in the mirror. I pulled a brilliant, multi-colored scarf out of the closet and wrapped it around my head, and found another to tie around my hips, and I danced around the room, a crazed gypsy princess. I laughed at my own silliness, but I felt a zillion times better, and I got the message. Sure, I was used to being miserable. But I didn't have to be.

I went downstairs and made a sandwich and drank some iced tea. I sent a mental nudge to Ben, just to let him know I was okay. Then I crossed the road to my little bit of beach and sat with myself and with the ocean for a long, long time.

I rolled over and snuggled deeper under the bright quilt, but then I remembered yesterday, and sat up quickly. Not gonna do that again, no way. And I had a lot to do today, starting with going through the attic. I dressed quickly and went down to the kitchen to make breakfast, then headed upstairs.

Sunlight slanted across the old floorboards as I surveyed the attic, munching my last bite of toast, preparing my plan of attack. Emma Rae had sure been tidy! Her many, many boxes were neatly piled at the ends of the huge room, labeled and arranged so they were easy to get to in spite of the quantity. I opened the windows at either end, inviting a weak, warm breeze to move the air around in the stillness, and started work at the shadowed end. "Winter Clothes," claimed the labels on several boxes. Might as well start here, I decided.

It was strange going through someone else's things like this, someone I hadn't even known. Emma Rae's taste in clothing had been very different from mine; I could barely imagine myself wearing most of these things. And almost everything she had stored up here was both well worn and very casual. Pants with lots of pockets, jeans with the knees blown out, old sweaters losing their shape . . . I was happy not to find velour running suits. Heavy socks, gloves, scarves, hats: I found exactly what I'd expect to find in boxes marked "winter clothes." I wondered why she would even save most of this stuff. One of the hanging racks had nicer clothes, and some of these were actually beautiful, well made with good quality fabrics. They could have been fifty years old or ten, the styles were so classic. But in the boxes, there was almost nothing remarkable, nothing that wouldn't have been perfect for her treks out to the garden, the greenhouses, the Mystic Wood. And in almost every garment that had a pocket, of course, she had squirreled away dollars in all denominations. I had quite a pile of the stuff, and it was growing bigger by the minute. I set aside whatever clothes I thought I might want, but there weren't many. Especially since I got to California, I'd been wanting bright colors, sundresses, light and cheery. Of course I saw the value of cargo pants, and I did plan to keep some, but it was clear that Emma Rae and I had very different tastes.

I worked my way through what seemed like fifty years worth of saved clothes, sometimes laughing at what she'd saved and at her peculiar banking system, sometimes simply baffled at what she thought was worth holding onto. Box after box after box, and almost all of it would be quite unremarkable at any thrift shop or Goodwill.

Finally I reached the wall, where the only things left were a large leather steamer trunk, a freestanding wooden wardrobe, and a large bundle wrapped in a packing blanket. I would be glad to be done with this part of the attic excavation. But not so fast; the wardrobe was locked. Hmmm. My interest kicked up a notch. Where would I find the key? I closed my eyes and, in my mind, made a quick scan of the house. The junk drawer in the kitchen where she kept the spare keys to the cars and plane? No. The hooks by the back door where Emma Rae had hung keys to the house, the barn and the greenhouses? No. I knew all the keys that hung on her key ring; it wasn't there. Hmmm, I'd look for it later, I thought, and turned to the trunk.

No joy there; it, too, was locked. Now I was really intrigued. I stood up and brushed dust off my hands. It was way past time for a cup of tea anyway. And after the tea, I'd be ready for a little scavenger hunt!

While the tea was certainly reviving after a morning spent in the dusty attic, it didn't shed light on the whereabouts of the keys. I looked through drawers all over the house: in the kitchen, the bathrooms, the dressers and bedside stands. I took a cursory peek through all the closets, hoping something would jump out at me, a half-hidden yet obvious-to-the-mind-of-Emma Rae's-great-granddaughter hiding place. Nothing. I got a whole lot dustier and a good bit richer and much, much more curious. What did Emma Rae have that was worth locking up? For heaven's sake, she kept the keys to her cars, her plane, even her home hanging right beside the kitchen door.

From what I'd seen up until this morning, Emma Rae's life was pretty much out in the open.

Oh, well, except for the parts about hidden money, secret lovers, and other worlds, of course.

I wandered across to the gardens, looking for some magical "secret finding" herb. Nothing. But then I heard Ben, whistling softly under his breath as he worked in the back of the first greenhouse, and my heart lifted. I didn't need to be discouraged. The keys would show up sooner or later, right? Even if they didn't, I could easily get a locksmith to open the locks. I squirmed inside a little at the thought of some stranger opening the door to Emma Rae's secrets. Okay, forget the locksmith. I did an about face and headed back into the house to get a glass of iced tea for Ben, and another for myself. Maybe he'd have an idea or two. And anyway, any excuse to see Ben was a good excuse, as far as I was concerned.

"Hello there!"

Ben looked up, and a cautious smile lit his face. "Well, hello! I wondered if you'd be out today."

"Yes, well, here I am," I said, stating the obvious and handing him his tea.

"Thanks. How are you doing? Are you okay?"

I nodded. "Rough day yesterday, but yes, I'm okay."

He looked at me closely. "I'm sorry. I should have expected that."

"Why would you?"

"I saw you at the festival. Emma Rae loved festivals. They were always fun for her, but the next day was always hard on her, even though she was used to it. It's all pretty new to you."

I sighed. "The part about it being fun is new. The part about it being hard? That's old news."

He touched my cheek gently. "And yet, here you are. You pulled yourself out of it, didn't you? All by yourself."

I thought about it. "Your touch helped," I said, yet he was right. I had pretty much pulled myself out of that old, way-too-familiar abyss. That was something, something to be proud of. I grinned, and changed the subject. "Anyway, I've had a busy morning today, excavating Emma Rae's past life."

"How's that?"

"Well, to be honest it wasn't all that exciting. I've been sorting through the attic, boxes and boxes and boxes of old clothes. I can't believe she kept it all. Ben, the woman had no style!"

He laughed. "Oh she had style all right, it was just very distinctly all her own! With Emma Rae, it was definitely more about the woman than the clothes. Did you find anything you'd wear?"

I shook my head. "Not much. Well, yeah, I guess I could use it for gardening, for work or cleaning or whatever, and all those cargo pants could come in handy when I *cross over*, I guess. The pockets, you know. But for anything else?" I shook my head again. "There were a few nice skirts and blouses, and one or two dresses. But even those, nice as they are, aren't really my style."

He quirked an eyebrow at me. "What is your style, Emma?"

I laughed up at him. "Good question! I'm not sure I really have one. But after this morning in the attic, I know what it isn't!"

I hiked myself onto a stool, and took a deep drink of tea. "There's a locked wardrobe and trunk. I couldn't find the key, so of course I'm burning with curiosity. D'you know anything about that?"

He wiped his hands on a dirty towel and picked up his own tea. "Nope, her attic is a mystery to me. I didn't even know about the tea chest, remember? Did you find any more money?"

I laughed again. "Ohhhh, yeah. Living here is so much better than playing the stock market!"

"Well, so far, all of the mysteries Emma Rae has left for you have been pretty good ones, yes? So no doubt whatever's behind those locks will be worth waiting for."

Funny, I hadn't imagined anything else at all.

I'd found a recipe for scones in one of Emma Rae's recipe books and had just finished mixing up a batch and sliding the tray into the oven when I heard the doorbell. Brushing ineffectively at the flour dusting my tank top, I went and opened the door, expecting Ben. A girl stood there, a teenager. The smile froze on my face as anguish slammed over me. I rocked back and grabbed the door jam.

She looked at me. "You're Emma," she said.

"Yes." My voice came out in a whisper.

"I heard about you. I'm Katie." She reached out to shake my hand, and I loosened my grip on the door jam to take it. I felt something else as our hands met, something wild and sweet and new.

"What can I do for you, Katie?" I asked, but I already had a pretty good idea. My voice was stronger, and I concentrated on controlling my breathing.

"I used to help Emma Rae sometimes," she told me, "You know, in the gardens. Or gathering."

It seemed I ought to invite her into the house, but I couldn't do it. I stepped onto the porch, closing the door behind me, and gestured at the chairs. We sat.

"I wondered if maybe I could help you." She added after a moment.

"How old are you?"

She looked at her white-knuckled hands, tight in her lap. "Seventeen."

"Do your parents know?" I asked her.

She hunched a shoulder and slanted a look at me. "They don't mind," she said.

I sighed and took another breath, preparing. "I mean, do they know you're pregnant?"

Her head shot up and her mouth flew open. I gripped the arms of my chair as her shock, fear, confusion battered at me. Why, oh why is everyone around here so damn emotional? I breathed, trying not to be swept away.

"How did you know that?" she whispered. "I didn't tell anyone. Not even Emma Rae."

I shrugged, speechless under the onslaught of her emotions.

She didn't say anything. After a few minutes I said, "Katie, I don't really even know what I'm doing around here yet. I wouldn't know what to have you do."

"I'm real good with the riding mower," she volunteered, "And you've got plenty of grass. It's past due."

I looked around, seeing for the first time how shaggy my lawn was looking. I hadn't even noticed it. "I imagine Ben does that," I said, but if he did, I wondered, why hadn't he?

She picked at her nails, and we sat without speaking for a while. The force of her emotions was receding. I heard the timer buzzing inside and excused myself to pull the scones out of the oven. I put them on a plate and took them out to the porch, setting them on a little table. "Help yourself," I said, and went back inside to get some iced tea. I didn't want to deal with this, no, not at all. I poured two glasses full of tea and took them out. She was crumbling up a scone. I said, as gently as I could, "That's a fresh, delicious, homemade scone. If you want to eat it, please do. If you want to destroy something, please find something else."

Again her head shot up, her eyes big and startled. I kept mine calm and took a healthy bite of my own scone. Oh, yeah, it was delicious. But, "they'll be even better with honey or jam. Which would you prefer?"

She took a nibble. "Honey. Please."

Back into the kitchen. Each time I went into the house, I was afraid she would follow me. I didn't want her in my house. Let's face it, I didn't even want her on my porch. But I wasn't going to kick her off, tempting though it was.

We ate in silence. It made me nervous, because I kept expecting her to start talking, to tell me what she thought I could do for her. But she didn't, and after a while I started to ask myself what *I* thought I could do for her. I wondered if she had her own tea. But even if she did, would it be useful now, for this?

"Emma Rae warned me about this," she said suddenly, breaking the silence. "She warned me that Tom wouldn't take precautions and so that meant I had to, but I told her I wouldn't be so stupid to even have sex in the first place. So then she told my mom to get me on the pill, and my mom came and yelled at me and I told her I wasn't gonna have sex with him. And then I did. And now my mom is gonna kill me."

There didn't seem to be anything I could say to that, so I didn't. Katie ate another scone. I drank some tea.

"Ben doesn't mow," she said at last. "Emma Rae liked to do it. Maybe you like to do it, too. But if you don't, I'd like to. I'd let you pay me a little bit. I have to start making money now. The baby's gonna need things, you know."

I thought about that. I'd never ridden a riding mower. My apartment back in Michigan didn't even have a yard. I looked around again. I had plenty of yard here, lots and lots of grass. "Okay. I'll ask Ben what a fair wage would be, and that's what I'll give you. No negotiating."

"Okay. Is tomorrow okay? I have to go home now and tell my folks about the baby."

"How about Friday?" I countered, and she nodded. "Before you go," I added, "will you walk in the garden with me?"

She got up, and we went out to walk among the vegetables and herbs and flowers. Bees and butterflies were everywhere, and hummingbirds zipped around us. Katie was calm now. I could still feel her fear, but under that was determination. I pinched off a bit of leaves and gave them to her. "Eat this," I suggested.

She popped them into her mouth without question, chewing and swallowing with only a slight grimace. Then she gave me a little grin. "You aren't that much like Emma Rae, you know."

"No," I shook my head, "I don't know. I never knew her."

"She never ever gave people fresh herbs. And she talked. A lot. Sometimes it was helpful, and sometimes it was annoying. I loved her like crazy. But she sure did talk a lot. You don't talk at all. Well, hardly at all. But you bake. You feed me. Emma Rae never did that."

I gave her back her little grin. "Those are my gifts, you know?"

"You are a lot like her, too, though. It's weird. You look like her, but you don't act like her. I always felt so good with her, she made everything better." She shook her head, and I knew she was trying to shake away her sorrow. "But you've made things better, too."

I didn't know what to say. As usual. So I turned away and pinched off a little more of the herb, giving it to her. "Eat this right before you talk to your mom, okay? Oh, and give her some tea before you start."

She took the herb and looked at me, her head tilted a little, like a puppy. "I'm guessing you're not a hugger like Emma Rae was." She swallowed, and I felt her fear and sadness well up again. "But do you think you could make an exception this once?"

I thought about it for a minute. Yes, I thought. I could.

After Katie left, I refilled my iced tea and returned to the porch. That had not been fun. Once again, I was drained from dealing with someone else's emotions. No, it was not fun at all, experiencing those raw feelings battering at me, whipped again and again as the feelings ebbed and flowed. Yet I could see that maybe I'd been helpful to Katie, even though I hadn't really done anything except feed her tea and scones, and listen. And even though I was exhausted again, and shaken, underneath was something else, like a new plant pushing it's curled head up out of the ground, a feeling of satisfaction, a feeling that I had done something good, just by being present for Katie, just by listening. And besides that, I had been more grounded. I had been able to engage, to breathe, to sit with her in spite of the chaos of her anxieties.

I closed my eyes and leaned back in my chair, rocking gently. In my mind's eye I saw a plant that I'd seen in the other world. I didn't think there was any in Emma Rae's garden. That plant would help me. It would help to stabilize me, and it would help me recover. It grew near the stream. I thought about drinking that amazing, sparkling water. Maybe it was time for another visit. Maybe I'd take some empty water bottles.

Having settled on that, I allowed myself to drop even deeper into my bruised psyche. Katie would be back Friday. And, I imagined, other days after that, days that would turn into months. Unless I put a stop to her visits, I would be a witness to her entire pregnancy, to another woman, a child still, having what I could never have. She wanted to bond with me, wanted me to be her friend as Emma Rae had been. Could I do it? Did I even want to? Of all the people to come to me, to come right up to my doorstep, why this one? I had pushed this pain down so deep inside for so long, I didn't want it surfacing now, or ever. But Emma Rae's journal, her life story, had brought it up already, and now this. I felt tears running down my cheeks and I wiped them away angrily.

I jumped up and paced the porch, stalked down to the gardens, stomped along the flagstone paths. Tears were flowing freely now, and I let them. I let myself be angry. It was better than feeling the grief of never having children, that old, old grief, still so raw after all these years, cutting like a knife with a blade that never dulled. Why was it being pushed on me now, why had Katie come to me? There had to be some other crazy old lady around here that people could go to, why did she come to *me*? It was hard enough feeling my own pain, why did I have to feel the pain of strangers, too? Not to mention, how had I even known, so instantly, about the baby? I didn't even want to think about that.

I flounced back up to the porch and threw myself down in the chair, letting the tears dry. Again, I saw the bubbling, shining waters of the stream. They seemed to hold some kind of promise, but for what, I didn't know. Right then, though, I'd take about any promise I could get. Yes. It was time to go back.

July 1961

I am beside myself with joy! How can I ever thank Walter for what he has done? My hands are shaking so that I can hardly write. Walter knew of my long search for Henry; I told Mary and him about it years ago, when I first knew that we would become dear friends. Without ever telling me, he has been looking for my Henry, and he has found him! But there is more, so much more! Henry has a son, a second Henry. And, oh, this is so wonderful, the second Henry has a wife, and she has just given birth to a daughter, and they have named her Emma Rae! This is beyond anything! And she was born on my birthday, on the summer solstice! My great-granddaughter, my namesake, Emma Rae Wright, born on June 21, 1961. What a gift! I knew on my birthday that this world had shifted somehow . . . that was the day I suddenly decided to buy my property! But never did I imagine that it was something like this. I am in Walter's debt forever! And now I must go. I am going to send a card to my grandson, to congratulate him on this blessed event!

I set down the journal and stared out across the road, through the darkening sky to the ocean. That was me she had written about, me she was so excited about. All those long years ago, and so long after she had lost her Henry, she rejoiced over *me*, over *my* birth! The knowledge stunned me, as for the first time I actually thought about the fact that Emma Rae, my great-grandmother and my namesake, had really, truly loved me.

A little later, after a glass of wine and a bedtime scone, I began to wonder about that card. Had she ever sent it? I wondered. And if so, what had happened to it?

The next morning, with only a little coercion, Ben took me back to the Mystic Wood. I could have gone alone, but after the last time, and his strange confession, I wanted to be respectful of his request. I certainly didn't intend to take him with me every time I went, leave him sitting alone beside the giant while I played on the other side, but I had an idea I wanted to try out. I thought that I could form a connection between him and "Rhein's world," as Emma Rae called it, so that maybe he could keep his awareness of me even when I was over there.

"Haven't you ever gone over?" I yelled over the noise of his jeep.

"Nope."

"Why not?"

"I never wanted to," he yelled back.

"Never?"

He shrugged, keeping his eyes on the road. "I'm content with the world I've got. I'm just not that curious."

I stared at him. I couldn't imagine that. But maybe Emma Rae knew that about him; maybe that's why she'd felt safe telling him about it in the first place. Still . . . "That's it? Just not interested?"

He glanced at me, then returned his attention forward. "I admit that the thought of shoving through a tree into a whole different world is rather intimidating," he said slowly, "especially since it was really hard on her. It always took her awhile to recover; sometimes she even blacked out, like she had the day I found her. You seem to have a much easier time with it than she ever did." That was a relief! "But beyond that, ever since I found Emma Rae at the doorway, I've felt like I was an anchor for her, like I was the sensible one in the relationship, and she was more like, well, like a butterfly, I guess. Always racing here or there. I'm not like that."

"You really never even wanted to?"

He shook his head. "I don't need that kind of adventure. Working with Emma Rae every day was enough of an adventure for me, I guess. If I needed more than that, I could always hop in my plane and take off, go wherever the winds blew me. That's more my style."

It was my turn to shake my head. "I want it all," I laughed, "The sky, the sea, and other worlds, too."

He slanted another look my way. "Well, I guess it's a good thing I don't require boring, or easy. Between you and Emma Rae, that hasn't been one of my options for, oh, about twenty years, I guess."

I laughed again. Poor Ben.

The hike up was as enchanted as always. We finally entered the quiet sweetness of the Mystic Wood, and approached the giant. Ben was nervous, of course. I understood why, now, much better. But I was fairly confident that my idea would work. I didn't know how I know, but like so many things these days, I just did. Backpack slung over my shoulder, I braced myself for the passage.

"Emma?"

I turned around, smiling up into Ben's handsome face. "Come back to me," he said.

I stepped away from the tree, and stretched up to leave a kiss on his lips. "I promise." Then, my heart singing, I stepped through to the other world.

I wouldn't stay long this time. I knew how stressful it was for Ben. The first thing I did was to take out a small, lidded bowl. I knelt on the flowered ground, and gathered as much of the purple pollen as I could into the bowl. This was for Ben. Once he had breathed this, he would begin to be connected to this world, even if he never actually came over. I had bottles, too, that I was going to fill with water from that incredible stream to share with him. And while I was there, I was going to give myself a good dunking. It had felt so amazing the last time; I wanted another shot of that elixir. I was confident that sharing the pollen and the water with Ben would create enough of a connection with this world that he would be able to maintain his connection to me while I was here. I had no interest in coming here regularly without some sort of safety net. Unlike Emma Rae, I wasn't going to be falling in love over here; my feet, and my heart, were firmly planted on my side of the giant. I put the sealed bowl in my pack, patted the compass in my pocket, and set off to explore.

First, the stream. I went right down on my knees to scoop that frigid water up over my face, to drink from my shivering hands. Like lightning striking, the blast of joy staggered me. I shot to my feet and, barely even thinking, stripped out of my clothes, my socks, my shoes, and threw myself back into the stream, lying across the water smoothed pebbles and letting that glorious water wash over me. I'd never felt anything so cold, but still I lay there, soaking in the bubbling, sparkling, shining wet bliss. My teeth chattered, my skin prickled and sizzled with the cold, yet I was laughing and felt like I was being turned inside out with joy, like my insides, my heart and my soul, were expanding and bursting out through my skin.

It was probably only moments before I had to jump back up out of that frigid water and go dance in the sun, my bare feet playing over the long soft grasses that grew on the bank. Looking back, I always have to laugh at the thought of myself, naked and laughing like a lunatic, dancing in that empty meadow in that unknown world. But in the interest of full disclosure, I admit that I have done the same thing many times since, and I intend to keep doing it, every chance I get, for the rest of my —*what is sure to be a very long indeed*—life.

Once I had danced myself dry, I dressed again, filled my bottles with water, and headed back to the giant.

Ben jumped to his feet as I staggered back into our world. A book lay forgotten on the ground. I felt relief sweep through him, recognized that he was calming himself even as a huge smile lit his face. I regained my balance and we stood looking at each other for a long minute. Then a puzzled look compromised his smile. "What happened to you over there?" he asked. "You look . . . amazing! You look, I don't know, fifteen years younger or something, and all, what, glowing or something!"

I tilted my head at him and slanted him a flirty look. "Oh, really? Well, how'd you like some of that fo' yo' ownself?" I drawled.

His hands were on my arms, like he couldn't keep himself from touching me. "What did you have in mind?" he asked.

I shrugged out of my backpack, and handed him a bottle of water. "Here," I suggested, opening it, "Drink this."

I'm not sure he was even aware of what he was doing, he was still so focused on me. But he took the bottle and tipped it back, drinking deeply.

I watched intently. And the best I can do to describe it is to say that it was as though he was drinking light. I could almost trace its path down his throat and into his body. As he drank, it was like he was lighting up from the inside. When he had emptied the bottle, he looked at me and he was very, very intent.

"Ho-o-oly shi-i-it," he said softly.

This is what I know for sure. Twelve ounces of that water, and something was discernibly different about him. Maybe I wouldn't have noticed if I hadn't been watching, but I had been watching.

He touched my face, gentle as a butterfly wing. "That explains a lot," he said, almost in a whisper. His eyes were brilliant. His hand dropped to his side again. We stood, staring into each others' eyes, and though we weren't even touching, I felt closer to him, more intimate with him, than I had ever before felt with anyone. Even with my own self, I think. It was incredible, delicious, indescribable.

"How do you feel?" I breathed.

"Good," he breathed back, and then laughed in amazement, shaking his head at the understatement.

"Can you take more?"

"More water?"

I shook my head. The little bowl was in my hand. "Not water." I opened the bowl and held it up to him. The purple pollen seemed to glow. "If you think you can stand it, breathe this."

He never even broke our gaze, he simply leaned in toward the bowl and breathed in, deeply, deeply. His eyelids fluttered briefly and his eyes glazed a little, then he took a long breath, exhaled slowly, and once again dipped his head toward the bowl and breathed that pollen in. Then slowly, carefully, as though he was in a trance, he took the lid from me and sealed the bowl, making sure it was tightly closed. He dropped it. His eyes never left mine. Then he gathered me into his arms and kissed me. He kissed me like I was oxygen, or water, as though he was breathing me in, drinking me in, taking me completely into himself. And yet at the same time he was giving himself over to me just as completely, pouring himself into me. The air around us crackled and sizzled. Minutes—or days—later, he moved his lips to my ear and breathed, "Take me to your world, Emma."

And so I did.

And he let me. Ben came with me to Rhein's world. He breathed in the pollen direct from the flowers, he splashed with me in the stream, he danced with me in the meadow. All that afternoon our laughter mixed with bird song and the shushing of the winds. We never heard or saw any sign of anyone else. We played the day away in the quiet and the breezes of that young world. And as the shadows lengthened across the meadow and the birds quieted into the dusk, Ben and I lay down in the long grass and created another world, all our own.

Chapter 11

Ben had reluctantly left me after I'd cobbled together a quick supper for us. What a day, what an amazing, wonderful day! I needed space, time to breathe, time to think. I mixed up a batch of bread, stirring with a big wooden spoon of Emma Rae's and breathing in the scent of the awakening yeast, when I remembered the one last thing in that corner of the attic: the big lumpy bundle wrapped in a shipping blanket. How could I forget such an enticing package, especially when Emma Rae had been so organized about things, so tidy. It was an intriguing anomaly.

I poured out the dough and started kneading, push turn pull, push turn pull, relaxing into the rhythm I'd learned as a child in Petie's kitchen. Much as I wanted to run right up the stairs two at a time, I knew from experience that the yeast and the dough wanted at least ten minutes of steady work in order to rise to their best potential. I wouldn't cheat myself out of a perfect loaf of bread because I was too impatient to work the dough properly. Push turn pull, push turn pull . . . How might my life have been different if I had continued to make bread all through the years? The swaying of my body, the push and stretch of my arms, chest and back, the rhythm and the heady aroma almost put me in a trance. My breathing was strong and steady, and even as I relaxed into the moment, I looked forward to the scent of the bread baking, and to the first crunchy cut of the knife through the crust and into the moist, warm finished loaf. Little in my life had ever grounded me, filled me with peace and pleasant anticipation, the way making bread did, the way working in Petie's mother's garden did, the way walking in the rain did. Why, oh why, had I given it all up?

But I knew the "why" wasn't really important. What was important was that I was here, now, doing this thing that I loved, filling myself with exactly what I needed right now. This was my business, and though I'd neglected it for far too long, I was learning daily now how to take care of myself, how to meet my own simple needs.

Finally I shaped the dough into a heavy ball and set it into a buttered bowl, covering it with a well worn linen towel, and setting it at the back of the counter. In an hour or two, I'd shape the loaves and put them in the refrigerator overnight. In the morning they'd be ready to bake, and I'd have fresh, hot bread for breakfast. I scrubbed the counter top, rinsed the cloth, and at last released myself from the hypnotic routine so I could race back up to the attic.

I went directly to the farthest corner, under a dusty wedge of evening light filtering in through a window. The shipping blanket was tightly wrapped, and fastened with a thick rope that was tied in a knot so determined that I finally had to go back downstairs, back to the kitchen for a knife. I could never untie that knot.

When the cord fell away at last, I sat back on my haunches for a moment, suddenly oddly reluctant to unwrap this package. I gazed up, out the window at the deepening blue of the evening sky. I stood and opened the window, which gave a brief cry of distress, as though it hadn't been forced open just yesterday. Then I knelt again and carefully folded the blanket off and away, exposing leather so old it had cracked in long, ragged lines. My breath caught as I wrestled the leather free of the entangling blanket. It was a case, it looked like an ancient leather carpet bag. This had to be the valise that Emma Rae had carried with her when she left Alexis and her life in New York in 1931. I released the clasp carefully, afraid the whole thing would simply fall to dust under my hands. Pieces shredded away as I opened the wide mouth. I reached inside and gently pulled out the pile of cotton, dresses of fabric so fragile it was like damp tissue paper. They had already been old eighty years ago when she had worn them as a disguise. There were thick woolen stockings, and heavy, well worn boots, the kind of boots a poor woman would wear as she crossed a continent looking for a better life. A shapeless fabric hat, scraps of undergarments, a coat of a no-longer-recognizable color were all in the valise. A shabby fabric purse with a broken clasp held a few coins and a bent safety pin. I carefully, gently set all the things in a pile on the floor beside me. When the bag was empty, I ran my fingers around the inside, across the bottom. I knew this was the false bottom; I knew there was more underneath. I was surprised to notice my hands were shaking and my breath trembled. There, there was the discreet latch. The wedge of leather shifted, caught, raised up along one side. I shifted the bag so the sunlight caught inside, lighting it up to the very bottom. Empty. The secret compartment was empty.

I sat back on my heels. Such a delicious irony! Emma Rae hid money in cracker boxes, buried it in tin cans in her garden, left it in the pockets of all her clothes. Yet here, in the place specially designed for secrets, there was nothing but old, stale air. Idly, I reached back down into the bag, slid my fingers along every crease, every fold, every corner above and below the false bottom. It was just too anticlimactic. I picked up the valise and shook it, hard.

Ah, yes! Something broke loose, I heard it skittering inside. Once again I felt in the deepest corner, and this time my fingers found it. Of course. Wrapped tightly together with shredding cotton string were two small brass keys.

Too many mysteries; too much change! I needed to pace myself. I stood up, tucked the still-wrapped keys into my pocket, and dusted myself off. I had no doubt they would open the steamer trunk and the wardrobe. But I just wasn't ready for that now. My mind was far, far away, in both place and time. She had worn these things all those long years ago, to escape from a man she loved deeply, to escape to a life she could live freely. She had left everything she knew, again. This woman was my great-grandmother. Her blood ran in my veins. She had courage of a kind I could only imagine.

I picked her old clothes up off the floor and carried them over to the table by the tea chest. I put them on. I had to be so very careful not to tear the dress, the first one on top of the pile. What did it feel like, I wondered, to make the choices she had made? In loving Alexis, she had lost everything over and over again, first her parents' love, then her son, Henry. Then the half life she and Alexis shared. Bit by bit, she lost it all. But they were her own choices, and look at this life she had ended up with, this rich and apparently satisfying life she'd built for herself here, surrounded by friends and people who loved and needed her.

I looked at myself in the long oval mirror, and once again felt that strange disorientation, that moment when I wasn't sure if I was seeing myself or Emma Rae looking back at me. I looked like someone out of a movie, a time piece from the depression, *Grapes of Wrath* maybe. The clothes were faded and shapeless. Alexis had chosen well for Emma Rae; wearing these things she would have been invisible, just another hungry soul desperately looking for food and hope. I eased my hand into the pockets of the dress, and felt something in the left side.

A gold ring. Dull, worn, plain: was it part of the disguise? Had she decided she would be safer if she wore a wedding ring, that she'd be left alone if people thought she had someone to protect her, someone who cared? I slid it onto my left ring finger, rubbed it with my thumb. I stared at my reflection. Then I noticed that something was dragging down the hem of the dress, and I pulled it up to investigate. The hem had been folded over double, and something had been sewn inside. I ran downstairs for scissors, my heart beating harder than the exercise accounted for. Carefully, carefully, I teased out the stitches and unrolled the hem, my fingers stammering over the tiny bundle.

It was another ring, a very different ring. It was a man's pinky ring, by my guess, heavy gold strands woven to cradle a square-cut alexandrite. The extraordinary workmanship reminded me of the alexandrite necklace and earrings, though this design was much simpler. I tried the ring on my fingers; it slid onto my right index finger as though it had been made for it, and as it settled on my hand I felt a jolt like electricity zing through my body.

I held both hands in front of me and stared at the two rings: a cheap, gold wedding band and what had to be a one-of-a-kind man's ring, possibly a family heirloom. What was the story? My heart stuttered in my chest, and I had trouble breathing. Had Emma Rae written *everything* into her journals?

Bird song, sunshine, and a teasing breeze woke me. I'd gone to bed last night right after I'd finished forming the loaves, too overwhelmed to do any more explorations. And though I lay sleepless for hours as the events of the day twisted through my restless thoughts, I awoke now full of excitement. As soon as I had the bread in the oven and a cup of tea in my hand, I would open the locked wardrobe and chest. And after that, Ben would be coming for breakfast. Could it get any better than this? I jumped out of bed, pausing only long enough to touch the two rings I'd stashed carefully in my bedside stand, threw on shorts and a T-shirt, and raced downstairs to light the oven. I danced impatiently around the kitchen waiting for the water to boil and the oven to heat. Then, tea sloshing in an oversized mug, I headed back to the attic.

First the wardrobe. The lock was rusty and reluctant, but finally clicked open at my gentle persistence. The hinges cried out at the stiff movement of the doors. I carefully peeled back layers of plastic that shrouded the hanging garments, and my breath caught in my throat. Whoa! Now *these* were worth saving! Sheer fabrics, opalescent colors, intricate designs . . . there could be no doubt: these were the clothes she had worn in New York, ninety some years ago, when she was the paramour of Alexis Alexander Mikhailskovich, kin to the tzar of Russia. She'd never mentioned him sending them to her, but clearly she hadn't brought these with her from New York. One dress, a glorious pale ivory that shimmered like captured moonlight, was crusted in glimmering seed pearls that swirled across the bodice and in twisting vines down the skirt to pool at the tea length hem. Another, deep blood red, was accented with rivers of what surely must be garnets. And there was a velvet gown of a blue so rich it was like midnight, with a neckline that plunged down between the breasts, where the fabric was gathered in a crystal brooch carved in the shape of a hand, from which it dropped in graceful drapes to the floor. I pictured Emma Rae, myself, in such a dress, and had to retreat to a chair to catch my breath. As if the dresses alone weren't enough, on the floor beneath them were neatly stacked all the matching shoes, carefully bundled in velvet bags made for the purpose. I could not begin to imagine what such things were worth.

I recovered quickly enough, though my breath stayed shallow with excitement. I opened the trunk, and my breath caught again. Her lingerie! Silk stockings, bras and panties and corsets so fine they caught on my skin. Peignoirs, silk nightgowns, jeweled slippers, also wrapped in velvet. Unbelievable. How had the young woman who wore such things evolved into a living mystery who ran around the countryside in ratty cargo pants?

My heart pounding with excitement, I stripped out of my shorts, T-shirt and undies and carefully selected a set of almost invisible silk bra and panties. Then I slid the blue velvet gown off its thickly padded hanger and over my head. The fabric was heavy, but it settled onto my body like a living second skin. I'd never worn anything so incredibly sensual. The matching shoes had slim, crystal-studded straps and heels. I put them on, caught my hair up into a loose knot at the back of my head, and twirled in front of the mirror.

Wo-o-ow. Who *was* that woman? I grinned, I fluttered my eyelashes, I tried on a sexy smile and a runway walk. Then I just laughed in sheer joy. Never in a million years had I ever imagined I could look like that! Or feel like that. It was incredible. I gathered that amazing fabric up in my hands and headed carefully down the stairs to check on the bread. I probably should have taken that gown off and hung it back up in its safe cocoon. But really? Are you kidding me? No-o-o way!

We'd reached a more casual place, Ben and I. He only knocked as a courtesy before letting himself into my fragrant kitchen. "Emma?"

I stepped out of the pantry. Oh, for a camera! His jaw dropped and his eyes popped. Then he just stayed that way for a long moment, giving me time to sashay across the kitchen and take his face in my hands before leaning in for a long, thirsty kiss. His hands came up to my waist, settled gently on the velvet, pulled me closer.

"Good Lord, Emma," he breathed when we came up for air, "Are you trying to kill me?"

"Oh, no," I murmured back. "I like to think of this as *living!*"

He shook his head against my neck, chuckling softly. "Is it always going to be like this?"

"Oh, no," I said again. "I will definitely not wear a velvet gown to breakfast every morning." I kissed him again, touching his lips with my tongue, and he gripped me more tightly, responding in a most satisfying manner. I pulled back just enough to add, "I've got silk and satin as well!"

After breakfast, Ben went out to the greenhouses, and I changed into something more suitable for gardening. In the workshop I scrounged around for pots, finding a cache of round bellied terra-cotta pots in a variety of sizes. I bundled them out to the garden, looking for plants that might thrive inside. In Emma Rae's house, my house, there were no plants. There were no personal pictures, photographs, keepsakes. The house had been well lived in, that was evident from the wear on the couches and chairs, the worn blankets folded neatly across the backs. It was evident by the fact that every window on the first two floors opened smoothly, cleanly, without complaint. The broom in the closet was shaggy from use, the dishcloths were faded and thin.

But Emma Rae had done little to set her stamp inside, to personalize her home in any significant way. The crazy quilt on her bed was the strongest statement in the house, next to her shabby clothes and her mud covered boots. Emma Rae had not been an indoor kind of woman.

My apartment back in Michigan didn't reflect my personality, either. I'd used some of the money from my divorce to buy decent, comfortable furniture. I'd bought beautiful dishes to keep me company during my solitary meals. But I'd never painted, brought in plants or flowers, set out photos or knick-knacks. Things like that from my marriage had gone straight into storage. Even if I'd loved them once, I hadn't wanted to be reminded of all I'd lost.

Here, in the sunshine and the bright, fresh ocean air, I was ready to make my mark. My old apartment was dark, with small, high windows that had been painted shut long before I'd moved in. This tall house by the sea had lots and lots of big windows. I could walk through the house and enjoy the changing outside light at every hour of the day and night. The generous counters in the kitchen had resurrected in me an almost forgotten love of preparing food. The deep window over the sink, with its wide sill, had plenty of room for pots of herbs, violets, ivies. I could pot up cherry tomatoes for the balcony and start every day with a sunbright bite before I even washed my face. I could hang ruby-toned feeders from the eaves and share my private space with hummingbirds and butterflies. I might train trumpet vine and wisteria, honeysuckle and wild roses, up the sides of the house, luring winged creatures from up and down the coast to visit while I drank my morning tea, my evening glass of wine.

Once upon a time, after my husband had so clearly shown that he preferred the touch of others to mine, I had shut myself away from touch of any kind. Not only did I shy away from the hands and arms of my family and friends, but I'd stopped taking pleasure from the soft body of bread dough, from the cling of rich soil, from the voices of birds and the song of bees and the whisper of the wind. I had pulled closed the drapes, over my windows and across my heart, and retreated into a cold, silent vacuum where the only sound was the cut-off cry of my own starving soul.

As I patted the near-black earth around the pale roots of herbs, seedlings and flowers, I couldn't imagine how, let alone why, I had made those choices. With the sun warming my shoulders and a salty breeze lipping across the back of my neck, such withdrawal seemed inconceivable. Thank God.

I stretched back and looked with affection at my assortment of small clay pots, each cradling a new little life. We would grow together. We'd fill my house with life, and scent, and a new kind of belief in what was possible every day. Katie was coming to mow today. I'd ask her to care for these plants while I was gone. It would help us both, I thought, for her to do that for me.

I walked through the garden, looking for other plants I might enjoy inside, kneeling to dig when I found one. I leaned into the freshly turned dirt and breathed deeply. Memories flooded my mind. Petie chasing a dragonfly and laughing, her mom looking up from her weeding, laughing. Petie and me chasing each other around the garden with huge, brilliant orange carrots covered in thick, moist dirt, screaming and laughing. So much laughter in those days, sun-risen sweat dappling our faces, cheeks flushed bright red with heat and exertion, our hearts singing just because we were alive and together and everything was so good in our world.

Later, we'd hauled—complaining all the way—bushels and bushels of red, ripe tomatoes, or sweet, sunhot strawberries, or whatever was on the schedule that day, into the kitchen and started up the "cauldrons," as we called Petie's mom's big canning pots. Our hands and faces covered with juices, we'd throw ourselves into the magic of transforming dirt-crusted stuff from the yard and garden into delicious food that would sustain us all for months to come, foods that would bring the flush of hot summer sun back to our cheeks and our memories even on the coldest, darkest, snowiest days of a long, cold winter.

All those sweet memories flooded my mind as I worked in the dirt around an unknown plant. I imprinted its image on my mind: miniature flowers that seemed to wind and twine all around each other in twiggy clumps. I broke off a leaf and smelled its spicy perfume. I tasted it. Yuck! The topmost flavor was comparable to a good, thick mud. But underneath was a sweetness I recognized from my own tea, though this fresh taste was brighter. This was the herb that brought on happy memories, I realized, the herb that had soothed my heart when I first learned of Emma Rae, and that I hoped would smooth my dad's heart when I told him about her and her unbroken love for his father, and him, and even me.

Only after all that did I let myself see the name that Emma Rae and Ben had assigned this powerful little plant: tangle flower. Ah, another gem from Rhein's world.

I leaned back on my haunches, stretching my back. There was so much to learn! I was eager to learn it all, while at the same time I struggled with feeling overwhelmed. Was I kidding myself? Could I really just step into the larger-than-life footsteps of Emma Rae, take up where she left off? Maybe if all I had to deal with was learning the attributes of a bunch of otherworldly plants, not to mention all the already known herbs and plants of my own world. But there were also all the people, people like Katie, who would come to me for advice and expect me to have solutions. Could I do the one without taking on the other? Could I retire behind the Two World Teas banner and not become involved in all the messiness of dealing with real people? Yet here I was, already thinking about Katie as if I had some responsibility for her. And, oddly enough, I kind of liked it.

I thought back on my years of isolation and depression. What if someone had been there for me? Yes, Petie was always there, but she had no more understanding of how to deal with my problems than I did. And she had plenty of her own to deal with. But what if I'd had someone like Emma Rae, someone who could make a cup of magical tea for me that would soothe the edges of my anguish, and then let me tell my story, in my own time and in my own way? And then, what? Did she wrap up the stories, tie them in a bow, and hand them back, all tidy and neat? Somehow I doubted it. And even if she could, what then? After she sent people home, did she go up into her lovely room, fall across the bed and weep out all the agony that had been dumped on her? Did people understand the pain and exhaustion that came to Emma Rae when she absorbed their emotions?

I brushed my hand over the leaves of the little herb, breathed in another deep breath. I remembered sitting in the dark with Petie. There was an empty wine bottle on the scarred table between us. She was talking, telling me details about her most recent crazy date, laughing a little wildly. I hadn't heard the wildness at the time. "Good old Petie," I'd thought, thinking she was only there to try and cheer me up. But now I remembered how my heart had been breaking for her. In spite of the cheerful, funny way she told her stories, I was never convinced that she was happy living the way she did, dancing from one relationship to another, always looking good and sounding good. Now I recognized that it all had a hollow undertone. Did she suspect I heard it? Did she hope I did? Did Petie need saving as much as I did?

I shook out the tension in my shoulders. Talk about the blind leading the blind! I stood up and began to walk slowly through the beds, holding a vivid picture of my dearest friend in my mind and in my heart. It was time for me to start making tea.

May 31, 1969
Alexis is dead!

June 1, 1969
Alexis is dead. I cannot believe it. My head keeps whirling and my heart races; my mouth is dry and I feel as though I may vomit. I have felt this way since yesterday, since I learned . . .
I did not sleep at all. I sit here in my lovely home, and in my

attic is a brass-bound steamer trunk, and the very wardrobe that I used in New York almost forty years ago. They scream into the silence that Alexis is dead. Furthermore, that for many years he has known exactly where I am, and has never tried to contact me.

But why would he? I left him, and I never even let him know I survived the long journey, never even let him know I was safe.

I have to try to put my thoughts in order. I cannot remember ever feeling so . . . so shredded!

Yesterday I spent with Rhein, my beloved Rhein, who lights my heart with sunshine and fills me with laughter and joy. We played in his world, and gathered herbs. . . . The herbs from his world have wonderful healing attributes in ours, and I have been using them in my teas with excellent effect. In any case, we had spent a normal day together; that is, another "best day of my life."

I was home in time for dinner, and was just putting together a salad when I heard a truck in the drive. Two men were here, quite upset at the late hour. It seems they had underestimated the drive from the city, a common enough mistake. They were delivery men, and they brought—I can still scarcely believe it!—they brought my clothes from New York, from my time with Alexis! Not everything, of course, but my entire wardrobe, still full of the gowns and dresses I wore for him, as well as a trunk full of my lingerie. I look at these things and I can scarcely remember wearing such feminine, impractical garments, yet they were once a part of my everyday life!

The men brought me a letter, also. And the newspaper clipping: Alexis' obituary.

I am stunned. I made this new life, and it is a good life. I so seldom even think of Alexis these days, but now I feel that a knife has been plunged through my heart. He is gone. He is *dead! I look at his picture in the newspaper clipping. It is the picture of an old man! But I am still young! Oh, Alexis, how I loved you!*

It had been a long time since I'd seen the mark of tears on Emma Rae's journal pages, but this entry was hard to read in places, so smeared were her words. I gently opened the papers that were tucked into the book. There it was, the obituary: Alexis Alexander Mikhailskovich, aged 73, died in his bed. . . . Yes, he was an old man. I could barely see traces of the laughing young man Emma Rae had so often sketched into those early journals.

And there was a letter. "*To my long lost friend, Emma Rae,*" it began.

> *As you see, Dear One, Alexis has left us. Do you even care? But you must! I remember your tender, loving heart. I remember how you wept, so many times, for my brother, and how you clung to us both when you hardened your heart and left us so many years ago.*
>
> *I never blamed you! But I missed you. Oh, how I have missed you! Even though we were not permitted to be friends, knowing that you were there, that you were bringing joy to my brother's life, brought sweetness to mine as well.*
>
> *I am not the only one who missed you. When you left, you took Alexis' joy with you, and it never came back to him. No longer did his eyes smile even when his lips were still. No longer did he play with words and tease, no longer did he catch me up in a dance whenever he felt too happy or excited to be still. All of that exuberance went West with you, and never returned.*
>
> *I did not know he knew where you were, or I would have written to you many times over the years, not as an ambassador for Alexis, but as your friend, who loves you still.*

In the last days of his illness, Alexis called for me and told me he had found you years ago. He told me that you live in California and that you appear to be happy. He told me that you never married another. He told me that, though he tried, he never found your Henry. He thought that if he could have found him for you, you might have returned to him. He asked me to send your things to you. He told me, over and over again, to tell you that he was sorry, that he was a coward. . . . I don't know what he meant, but he kept repeating it, he made me promise. And so I promised, and I tell you now, also, Alexis never stopped loving you, not even for one minute. All these years, he has kept your little house. It is where he always went when life was too much for him. In these last days, he simply moved there. Sadly, no one cared. His wife died some years ago, and he has long been estranged from his children. And I . . . I was glad to visit him there. After all these years, a trace of you seems to linger in those rooms still. And there Alexis died, in your bed. I pray he has found some peace at last.

I chose only the best of your things to send. If this was wrong, I will send everything to you. All the furniture, the pictures, everything is yours if you desire it. This is what Alexis wanted.

Dearest Emma Rae, I hope you will write to me. My life is too quiet, and with Alexis gone now, it will be quieter still.

I love you, dear friend.

Your

Sophia

Saturday morning Daniel had planned to come up and help me in the attic, but I called and cancelled. The discoveries of the last days had left me wrung out. He was driving me down coast tomorrow, back to San Francisco, and first thing

Monday morning I was boarding a flight back to Michigan. We could catch up on the drive. Today I didn't want any company. I thought about getting back to work in the attic by myself, but I couldn't seem to face that, either. Today was a good day to spend quietly. I would wander through the rooms of my house and think about my possessions, my furniture, all the things in my apartment and in storage back home, and start to decide what to bring back with me and what to leave. I felt ready now, at long last, to deal with the things I'd left in storage since the divorce. I couldn't think of anything I wanted to keep, any more than I wanted to keep the sad memories any longer. It was time to let all of that go. As for the furnishings in my apartment, I did have some things I wanted to bring here. My living room furniture, though not the very highest quality, was in better shape than the disparate pieces Emma Rae had collected. I would continue to use her bedroom furniture, but mine could go into one of the spare rooms. My pots and pans, my kitchen gadgets: all of that would come with me. It was clear that none of those things had much importance to Emma Rae, and hers could go to the thrift store or, more likely, a dumpster.

Ben had said he'd water my new little potted plants, set out on window sills around the house, but instead I'd asked Katie. She had come to mow yesterday, as agreed. Her eyes were swollen and red, which I did my best to ignore as I took her a mid-mowing snack of tea and muffins. I imagined she'd be happy of a place to escape to legitimately.

As I walked around my house, wandered in the gardens, walked barefooted through the fresh-cut grass of my property, I thought about this new life of mine. I'd only been here two weeks. I was going "back home" now, back to the town I'd lived in my whole life, back to my parents. Thank God, I thought, it was only for a week! I felt a whole new understanding of the concept of purgatory.

Chapter 12

Petie drove slowly, peering in the gloom of the airport arrivals area at the travelers waiting for rides. She thought she saw Emma and started to pull over, but no, it wasn't. The woman could be Emma's twin, though, she looked enough like her. But her hair was deeper red, and she carried herself straighter, with more confidence than Emma had ever had. Petie pulled back into the traffic just as the woman looked up, caught her eye and waved. It *was* Emma!

Oh, well, too late, she was caught in the moving traffic and would have to circle around one more time. This would have been a great time for a choice word or two, but Petie was too startled to swear. What had happened to Emma?

Petie had heard the change in Emma's voice when they'd talked on the phone, but figured it was just due to all the excitement and changes. Anyone would sound revved up, going through what Emma was going through. But something deeper than that had to have happened to have fooled Petie into not recognizing her best friend of over 40 years.

Petie felt a strange wrench in the pit of her stomach as she steered back around the loop, back into the tight quarters near the curb. *What* had happened to Emma?

She threaded in between an oversized black SUV and a little red and white mini to snatch a place by the curb. She popped the trunk and jumped out just as Emma wrestled her bags over to the car. Emma's face was lit up in a laugh. "I can't believe you drove right by me!" She let go of the suitcase handle and launched herself at Petie for a hug, staggering her.

"Whoa girl, holy shit, you trying to kill me here?" Petie laughed, returning the hug. "I didn't even recognize you! I thought you were your own twin or something, but not you for real."

"Yeah, there's a lot of that going around these days," Emma grinned, tossing her carry-on into the car. They each grabbed an end of the large bag and hefted it into the trunk, then dashed to their respective doors and hopped into the car. Emma barely had her seat belt on before Petie was inching back into traffic.

"Girl, what have you done to yourself?" Petie asked, "Did you dye your hair? Get a face lift? Have sex?"

"Oh yeah, what*ever*!"

"Well no, for real Emma, you look amazing. What's been going on?"

Emma stretched as well as she could in the cramped quarters of the car. "Oh, so much! It has been crazy! Did I tell you I'm learning to fly?"

"To fly? You mean, like, a plane?" Petie sent an astonished look at Emma.

"Yeah, a plane. I actually own one, a little bitty two-seat plane, all my very own."

"No effing way!"

Emma was laughing, still laughing, like she hadn't stopped once since Petie had pulled over. When was the last time Petie had seen her like this? Tenth grade?

"I know, it's insane," Emma said. "I've got a truck and a Honda CRV, too. And greenhouses and a barn and a house, not to mention the whole tea business! And the ocean, and the woods, and, and, and oh, Petie, you are gonna absolutely love it out there!"

"Who are you? Where's the real Emma, the one who never leaves her apartment?"

"Oh my gosh, I know, can you believe it? And I have to admit, sometimes I still really don't want to leave the house. But I've learned so much about myself, stuff that explains so much."

"You've only been gone two weeks, right? Or did I pull a Rip Van Winkle here and didn't know it?"

Emma giggled. "Has it only been two weeks? It feels like about two lifetimes. But I can tell you this much, it hasn't been nearly long enough. I can't wait to get back, either. Coming back here was about the hardest thing I've ever done. And I probably wouldn't have, if I'd thought you'd come without me fetching you."

Petie's eyebrows lifted. "Really!?"

"You truly have no idea."

That much was obvious. Emma kept talking, but Petie had a hard time concentrating on the words. For years she had been trying to snap Emma out of that damn self-imposed coma she was in. Now, suddenly, Emma had awakened, and in a big way. Petie felt like she was sharing her car with a total stranger. She was happy for Emma, for sure. But at the same time, and for the first time, Petie felt just a little bit lonely, even with Emma right here beside her.

$$* \quad * \quad *$$

Wow, this was a change! Usually Petie did all the talking, about her latest date or what book she was reading or a new club she'd been to or some crazy thing that had happened at the bar she worked at. Now I was the one with so much to say, and it just kept rolling out. But after a bit I slowed down to say, "Petie? You okay?"

She glanced at me. "Yeah, I just can't get a word in edgewise," she chuckled.

I looked at her sharply. Oh, boy. Was it always going to be this way for me, from now on? "What's going on?" I asked

"What do you mean?"

"I mean something's wrong. Is something bothering you?"

She sent me a longer glance, checked the road ahead and swung her gaze over me again. Silence stretched. Then she sighed, and let a small smile play at the edges of her mouth. Her eyes met mine. "Well, hel*loooo,*" she said softly. "I remember you."

"What do you mean?" it was my turn to ask.

"You reminded me of someone just then," she said, now keeping her eyes on the road. "It took me a minute to remember who."

She left me dangling until I couldn't resist the bait. "And?" I prompted, "Who?"

Again she cut her eyes my way. "This smarty-pants red-headed kid I used to know in grade school."

That confirmed my own thoughts on the matter. I sighed. "Has it really been that long?"

"Pretty much. Oh, she showed up now and then when I was married, but after that? Gone. Haven't seen her since." One more sidelong glance. "And yet, she lives! Fresh from California, living and breathing, ladies and gentlemen, please join me in welcoming back *Emma Rae Wright!* She sees all, she knows all. . . ."

"Oh come on!" I interrupted, "I wasn't that bad!"

Her smile lit up her whole face. "No, you weren't bad, not at all. Oh, well, annoying sometimes, when I wanted to hide something from you. But I've missed that girl, for so long, in fact, that I even forgot I missed her." She let go of the steering wheel to reach over and grab my hand. "I am so glad to see this. Welcome home, Emma."

"Mom! Dad! I'm home!" I yelled, just like I used to back in high school.

I heard a shriek from the kitchen, and the squeaking of Dad's chair in his office, and they both came hurrying out.

"Oh, honey, I've missed you!" Mom said around a giant hug. "Why didn't you call?"

I held her tight for a long minute before letting go, then turned to hug my dad. He wasn't a hugger, never had been, but I hugged him anyway, and after a moment he relaxed a fraction and almost hugged me back.

"Oh, gee whiz," I answered Mom's question, "there was just way too much to say in a phone call! It is a whole different world out there!" (Ain't that the truth?)

I had a bombshell to drop on them, and I honestly didn't know how they'd take it, me moving to California. They had no clue what had been going on. My folks had never been the best communicators, and in that respect, at least where they were concerned, I was no different. The stuff I had to tell them, it was better to tell them up close and personal. Not that I intended to tell them everything. Oh, no.

It was late afternoon. Petie had picked me up from the airport and taken me to my apartment, where I'd stayed only long enough to drop off my luggage and pick up my car. I'd invited her to go to my folk's house with me, but she declined; she had lots to do, since she was helping me pack up my apartment in the coming week, and then she was driving cross country with me, all the way back to Northern California.

"We're so glad to see you, honey," Mom said, hustling me into the kitchen for a lovely cup of instant coffee, always ready. Dad followed along behind. "You'll stay for dinner, of course."

"Of course, I'd love to," I grinned.

She put the kettle on to boil, and I said, "How 'bout we have tea instead of coffee? I've got some really great stuff you can try."

I looked at my dad. He gave me a little smile. "I've missed you, Emma," he said. Then, apparently embarrassed by such uncharacteristic effusiveness, he turned away to get the cups out of the cupboard.

What a dinner that was! Mom, even without any advance warning, had managed to heat up some chicken, whip up some instant mashed potatoes, open a can of gravy, and chop up a head of iceberg lettuce for salad. I thought of all the different kinds of lettuce I had growing on the shady side of my house, the thick pepper bacon I got at my little market, the herbed breads I baked from scratch, and chuckled at myself. It sure hadn't taken me long to become a food snob.

We kept it light as we ate. Mom talked about her garden club, making strong mention of the new grandbabies that were arriving for her friends. One of Mom's greatest tragedies was that I had never managed to reproduce, though I got high marks for many years of trying. I told them Petie's news, filled them in on my first cross country flights, and talked about the 4th of July festival I'd gone to at Boast Point. Dad, as usual, restrained himself to the occasional grunt or chuckle.

Finally (breaking from the after dinner instant coffee tradition), I brewed up another pot of tea for us all, and a plate of cookies was passed around. We relaxed back away from the table. Mom and Dad looked at me expectantly. They had stretched the limits of their patience, and it was time for their reward. But oh, Lord, where to start?

"Well, folks, it was all true. I've inherited a fortune."

Exclamations and excited questions flew at me, just as I'd expected. I laughed and made shushing motions with my hands. "Okay, okay! This is the story," I began as they quieted. And then I told them about the big old house overlooking the ocean, and my Honda and my truck and my fabulous little airplane. I told them about the gardens and Two World Teas.

Though Mom had lots of questions and opinions, Dad didn't say much. But when I talked about Emma Rae, about all she'd done for people and how much they loved her, he slammed his hands down on the table, shocking Mom and me into silence. "That is not possible!" he roared. "First of all, there is no way Emma Rae could still be alive. But beyond that, she was a horrible, selfish woman! She left my father, with never a backward glance! She left him to be raised by those two dried up, miserable parents of hers!"

I let the silence settle, and then I said softly, "Dad, I don't like to contradict you, but that simply isn't true."

He started to yell again, but I put my hand up and talked louder, "No, Dad, trust me, it isn't true, that isn't what happened! She kept journals, and I've read them, every one from 1917 until 1969. I'm still reading. And it wasn't what you were told, what Grandpa was told."

I got up from the table then, and fetched the early journals from my room. I put them directly into my dad's hands, and after I sat back down, I told the story of Emma Rae and Alexis and Henry. "It's all in there," I summed up at last. "Even the marks of her tears."

Dad was stunned. "How can you believe it?" he said at last. "What makes you so sure it's true?"

"For one thing, I've read her words. I've felt her anguish, and learned the things she did to survive. And also," I pulled the flat wooden box out of my lap, and went to kneel beside my dad. I opened the box and set it on the table in front of him. "There's this. She kept it, all these years. It's from Alexis, your grandfather." Dad's stunned eyes didn't move away from the astonishing alexandrite and diamond set until I said softly, "How do you like that, Dad? You're descended from Russian royalty." I showed them the ring, too, that I was wearing on my right forefinger. After I'd first put it on, I'd barely taken it off except to work in the garden.

He looked at me then for a long moment. I saw shifting behind his eyes, I felt the struggle taking place. Then, still not speaking, he pushed away from the table and went into his office. I looked at Mom and she looked back at me, her eyes wide, but neither of us spoke. What could we say? I started to stand, but then he was back, a small yellowed card in his hands.

"I haven't looked at this in fifty years," he said, "but I guess it's time now." He opened the card and eased out an old, old photograph. He put the photograph in my hand. "I found that picture in my father's things when he died." It was old and faded, but I could still make out the face. It was so like my own, even though this was the face of a very young woman.

"Emma Rae?" I asked, and he nodded, turning the picture in my hand so that I could see the back. Scratched across in pencil it said only, "Mother."

"You were twenty-three when your grandpa died," Dad said, "and this picture looks just like you did then. I knew it had to be Emma Rae. I was amazed to find it. As far as I ever knew, my father hated that woman for leaving him."

I nodded, staring at the picture. We could have been alone, Dad and I. Then he handed me the card. On the front was a beautifully rendered pencil drawing of a baby. I knew that deft touch. And inside was bold, slanted, familiar handwriting. "Congratulations on the birth of your daughter," it said, "May she fill your life with joy!" It was signed, "Emma Rae Wright." And at the very bottom, in a tiny, timid script, like a nervous afterthought, was written, "your grandmother."

I rocked back on my heels. "Holy cow, Dad." I stood up. "You knew she was alive."

"Fifty years ago," he said.

"You never said anything," Mom chimed in.

He shook his head. He looked so bewildered. "I didn't know what to say, or what to think. I showed this to my father, and I honestly thought he was going to have a heart attack. If I hadn't snatched it out of his hand, he would have torn it to shreds right there. In fact, he tried to get it back; he ripped the envelope out of my hands, and in moments it was in pieces. It was horrible! But I saved this. I couldn't ever seem to get rid of it, but I never wanted to see it again, either. I put it away and did my best to never think of it. Until my father died, and I found the picture." He sighed deeply. "There'd been an address on the envelope. If my father hadn't destroyed it, I could have contacted her."

So much pain! Emma Rae's parents had caused generations of pain with their hard hearts.

Dad patted my hand gently, and got up. "I have to think about this. Please excuse me," he said. "Do you mind if I take all this?" he asked, gathering up the picture and the card, the journals and the jewels.

I shook my head. "Take all the time you need, Dad."

He started to walk away, but he stopped and, without looking at me, he said softly, "Thank you, Emma." Then he went into his office, closing the door behind him.

My mind was full of the conversation with my mom and dad when I got back to my apartment. I unlocked the first door, grabbed my suitcases from where I'd left them at the bottom of the steps, and headed upstairs. As I climbed, every step seemed harder than the one before it. It felt as though the actual air was getting heavier and heavier, pushing against me, shoving me down. When I finally reached the landing, the oppression weighed me down so that I could barely catch my breath. I fumbled with my keys again, finally getting the door open.

The dark apartment seemed full of ghosts. I couldn't think. I stood at the threshold, dropped my luggage, grabbed the door jam. What was happening? Breathe, Emma, breathe, I told myself.

Wow. It was crazy! I had felt so great in California, even as I'd struggled with all the new experiences and people, even as I'd learned about Emma Rae and about myself. Re-entering "My Life as it Used to Be" felt awful! With a shaking hand, I turned on the lights.

Everything looked the same, but it all looked different. How had I lived here all these years? The carpet was stained and brown, old and nappy even before I'd moved in. The walls were yellowed from the cigarette smoke of long ago tenants. My Walmart lamps weren't very bright, my decorating was minimal at best. The air seemed much too stale, as though I'd been gone years instead of weeks. I went to the kitchen, the brightest room in the house, and struggled to open the window over the sink. All the other windows were long since painted shut. I had a tiny balcony, and I opened the door to that, desperately trying to create some kind of movement in the air. I turned on the exhaust fan over the stove, and listened for a minute to its asthmatic wheezing. Then I collapsed onto my couch and just sat there, staring into the gloom, feeling it penetrate my skin and sink inside me, filling me, numbing me.

I knew I should get up, fix some tea. But I didn't have the energy. Tomorrow, I told myself as I sagged down onto the couch. Tomorrow.

Emma.

Emma!

EMMA!

The gentle nudge turned into a bump, and then a shout in my head. I struggled against it, but it was insistent. *EMMA!!!*

I'd fallen asleep on the couch. The heavy humidity of July in Michigan weighed down the air. It must be close to noon. I searched for my purse, dug inside. My cell phone was dead. Of course. I'd forgotten to charge it last night.

EMMA!

I squeezed out onto my miniscule balcony, gasping for breath. Two weeks in California, and my lungs had forgotten how to breathe in the thick Michigan air. Ugh.

I eased myself open to Ben's insistent query, just enough for him to know he had my attention. I could feel his relief. But I didn't have the energy to deal with him right then. Gently, gently, I closed my mind to him.

This was dangerous. My own self was calling out to me now, shaking me from a depth I'd never known I had. Get up! Make tea! Get up!!!

Once upon a time, two weeks ago, I hadn't even been able to hear the cry of my own soul. Now I couldn't ignore it. I hadn't been prepared for this, I hadn't realized what it would be like, coming back to the place where I'd been so miserable for the last ten years. But my new strong self was not giving up without a fight. And plug in your damn phone! she ordered. Bossy bitch.

I got up. I put the kettle on. I dug out my packet of tea and my phone charger. And when the phone was plugged in, I called my mom. "Hi, honey!" she answered, bright and perky. "How are you? How did you sleep?"

For a tiny minute there, I almost lied to her, just like I had been lying to her and Petie and myself for the last uncountable years. But I stopped myself.

"Not so good, Mom," I said. "I need your help. Can you come over?"

There was a moment of silence. I had never once, as an adult, asked my mother for help.

"I'm on my way," she said, and the phone went dead.

That was a very tough week. I sometimes think that I never would have pulled through if my mom and Petie, and even my dad, hadn't rallied around, bringing flowers and music and candles and Chinese food. I sometimes think that the oppression in that apartment would have defeated me, and I would have just slid back down that greasy slope into the abyss of depression and not come out again. But every time I started to slide, someone would show up and help out. And when it wasn't Petie or Mom or Dad, in the quiet of night or the earliest morning, Ben would nudge at my heart. After the first few days I called him, just to hear his voice, and to apologize for shutting him out. He hated it when I did that, yet he let me set the pace, he respected my boundaries. Knowing he was there, feeling his support from all the way across the country, was a huge help to me.

At other times I feel confident that, since I'd experienced something so different, since I had become reacquainted with light and laughter and hope, I wouldn't have been able to give myself up to it so completely again. Sooner or later, I tell myself, I would have found my own way out.

Most likely, the truth is a combination of the two. I'm glad I'll never know. They rallied, I rallied, and together we got me sorted and packed and out of that apartment once and for all. I had painted the walls there with my despair, throughout the years my tears had watered the air in every room. Maybe if I'd been able to pry open the windows, replace the carpet, repaint the walls, put in new light fixtures . . . But thankfully, I didn't have to try any of that. I could just leave. And with their help, I did.

We went through everything in my apartment and storage space, had a garage sale on Saturday, and sold, threw out or donated everything that I didn't want to cart across country. The rest we loaded into a rented moving truck. It was surprising how much stuff I really didn't care about, and even so, how much was left to transport. Mom and Dad came by every day to help me, and I think we talked more in that week than we had in the last thirty years combined. In the evenings, after work, Petie would join us, and after sharing dinner with us, Mom & Dad would head home.

They weren't thrilled that I was moving all the way to California, but they had already come to the conclusion that it was just plain senseless for me to do anything else, once all the factors were taken into account. And I hadn't even talked about Ben. Much.

Something about my dad had changed in the days I'd been back. He seemed to be softening somehow. He normally had his head buried in a book, newspaper or crossword puzzle. But now I'd often notice him sitting with the newspaper on his lap forgotten, his eyes unfocused and gazing off into a distance I couldn't see. At first I wondered if age was catching up with him, but Mom disabused me of that notion. "Honey," she whispered to me, "you don't know what this means to your dad, this news about Emma Rae. All his life he's waited to be left, just like his dad was. It's been a constant, nagging issue even in our marriage, to be honest. Knowing that she didn't just walk away, that her love remained constant after all, and for all these years, has really changed him. You just don't know!"

And when the time came for me to say goodbye, Dad himself opened up to me, something he had never done before. "Emma, thank you for standing up to me, and for telling me about Emma Rae. I'd like to keep the journals for a while, if that's okay?"

I nodded yes.

"I've made copies for you of her picture and the card she sent when you were born. And I think you should take these back with you." He handed me the jewels.

"Are you sure, Dad? Mom would look mighty fine wearing those."

He grinned a sly little grin I'd never seen before. "Yes, she does."

"Oh!" I said, shocked, and changed the subject. "Do you want me to send the rest of the journals?"

"Yes, when you've finished them. There's no hurry. I have the ones that are most important to me."

His voice was so relaxed, and his expression so calm, I realized for the first time how tense he had always been. My voice caught a little as I put my arms around him. "I love you, Dad. I'll miss you."

One more surprise: he wrapped both arms around me and gave me a long, tight hug. He had never hugged me like that before. "I love you too, Emma. And maybe Mom and I will surprise you with a visit one of these days."

"Oh, Dad, that would be so great. But don't surprise me. Let me fly you out first class! I'm sure there's plenty of money left in the attic!"

Petie and I were both excited about the trip; neither of us had ever really seen much of the country at all. I hadn't done any travelling, and Petie hadn't done much. We'd be driving right through the heart of America on Route 80, stopping whenever we felt like it, detouring if we wanted. Petie, who hadn't taken a vacation in years, had asked for three weeks off, and much to her surprise, it had been granted with a minimum of fuss. We figured it could take us up to a week to get to California (depending on how many detours we took), and then we'd have two weeks to hang out in San Francisco (which I hadn't even done yet), go shopping, and then play in my new neighborhood. All in all, we were downright stoked.

That road trip was one of the greatest experiences of my life. It was fun, it was different, it was me and Petie, together again like we hadn't been since high school, since before we'd met and married the jerks. And this time we had the wisdom to appreciate our blessings, and each other. We blasted music, we sang and joked and stopped at crazy little out of the way tourist traps and generally acted like lunatics. And beyond that, we talked. And talked. And talked. Petie told me how worried she'd been about me since just a few years into my marriage. She'd seen me changing, becoming more withdrawn and tense. And after the divorce, instead of recovering I just continued to get worse.

"Emma, when you called me from California, I heard a note in your voice that I never thought to hear again. It was all I could do not to scream 'Hallelujah!' right in your ear! Your Emma Rae sounds like a bit of a crackpot, but she's got my undying devotion for bringing you back to life, you hear me?"

I was ashamed of how I'd hurt her, and I knew my parents must have experienced the same concern. But all I said was, "Emma Rae was not a crackpot!"

Petie laughed, a rippling trill of a giggle, "Oh, no! Not at all! The woman is a million years old, mixes herbal potions like some old-time witch, and buries money in the yard!"

"Well, when you put it like that . . ." And Petie didn't even know the really weird stuff!

We spent a slow and easy week getting to California, and then spent two days in and around San Francisco, doing the tourist thing. Lombard Street, Fisherman's Wharf, the trolley and Alcatraz all got a piece of us. At the advice of a woman we met in a hat shop, we spent a day at a spa in Berkeley, getting wrapped, manicured, and pedicured. We both got our hair cut, and Petie bleached her tips. After that, we were so jazzed with our gorgeous selves that we just had to do some shopping in the funky downtown, making sure we had plenty of sundresses, hats and bathing suits. Another day took us back up the coast with the occasional stop for farmers' markets, pottery studios and second-hand shops. I'd never had any surplus money before, and it was obvious to me that, if I kept on like this, I'd be back in that situation before the year was out. But for these few weeks, I allowed myself to indulge and play like I never had before. After all, up North in the hood, population about a thousand, there wasn't a whole lot to spend my money on anyway.

We drove through Boast Point late at night, and I thought of Walter and Daniel, each in their lonely homes, grieving over Emma Rae. I was looking forward to having them over for dinner while Petie was here. Of course, I'd invite Ben too. Just thinking about it was exciting. How long had it been since I'd hosted a party? Well, it was about damn time now. Before we'd left the metropolis behind, I'd left a message at Connor, Black and Connor for the Misters Connor, setting a date, and Petie and I were planning the menu. I was thinking what herbs I could use, and how.

"Yeehaw! I hit the jackpot!!!" Petie's voice sliced through the soft morning air. She was in the workshop looking at Emma Rae's gardening books while I worked at picking the tomatoes, zucchinis, beans and peppers that had ripened while I was back East. What on Earth was I going to do with all this stuff? And the season was just beginning! It looked like an emergency lesson on preserving was in order, and I was happy that Petie was here to give it to me. If my not-so-secret plan was successful, we'd be putting up fruits and vegetables together all through the harvest.

I stood up, stretching my back, and headed over to see what all the shouting was about, but I hadn't gone far before Petie came dancing out of the workshop, waving a book and, big surprise, a fist full of bills. "One THOUSAND dollars!" she yelled. "Who knew reading could be so enriching?" She doubled over with exaggerated hilarity over her dumb joke. "Can I keep it, can I? Can I? Huh? Can I?" she sang, skipping in circles around me.

I couldn't help laughing. "Sure, go ahead. I'm sure there's more where that came from."

She stopped laughing. "Emma, you can't just take this stuff for granted, you know. There's got to be an end to it somewhere!"

I shrugged. "Well, then I can sell the family jewels."

"Emma!" she shrieked, appalled. "You wouldn't!"

I laughed again. "Of course not, silly," I reassured her. "What were you reading?"

"Benjamin Franklin!" she said, cracking herself up all over again. I hadn't remembered she could be so silly. I liked it.

"No, really," I grinned at her.

"I don't know, it's something about plants. It's got pictures, and recipes and stuff. I'm guessing it's Emma Rae's writing?"

I took it from her. Sure enough, it was Emma Rae's familiar script. Was it more tea recipes?

Not exactly. I flipped through it, getting increasingly interested. She'd sketched detailed pictures of plants, of their leaves, stalks, root systems. I recognized some of them. They were not, so to speak, of this world. And beside the pictures, she'd written about their growing habits, different ways to use them, and what other plants went well with them. There were some recipes, and some general guidelines. "Greygreen Fuzzleaf," read one, "Bitter as gall." Ew, I knew that one! "Brings clarity, reveals heart's desire. But be careful, both the leaf and the knowledge can be hard to swallow. Honey smooths the bitter taste, Little Stickleaf can soften the knowledge. Not good in baked goods, okay in tea if used in small quantities." Hmmm, forget about the thousand dollars, this could be a very valuable little book. Ben would be pleased to see this.

As though conjured by my thoughts, the jeep rolled into the yard. Petie glanced at me, taking in the look on my face, and grinned mischievously. "Ah, this must be Ben."

"Behave yourself," I cautioned her, as we went to meet him. But maybe I should have been talking to myself. Just looking at him climbing out of the jeep had my heart racing and heat rising in my cheeks. And elsewhere.

After Ben joined us, we finished up in the garden and went inside for lunch. I was right; Ben was very interested in Emma Rae's book of "unusual" herbs and their uses. Then after lunch, Petie insisted she wanted a nap and some time by herself. She was used to living alone, and for the past week we'd been to-gether 24/7. She needed a break, she said, and I was happy to take her word for it so I could steal away with Ben. We took the opportunity to go up in my little plane. I could tell he had something on his mind, and I realized that, though I wouldn't have called it clairvoyance, I'd had this connection to him right along. Was this so different from what he felt, from the things he "knew"?

We flew along the coast, high above the waves. Oh, how I loved this, the wind in my hair, the lightness of the air, sharing this with Ben. It was wonderful. It would have been perfect, in fact, if I hadn't been so aware that something was bother-ing him. But I knew him now, well enough to know that he'd talk when he was ready. So I did my best not to think about it, and just to enjoy the ride. Soon he'd swing east and find a clear stretch of beach to land on. We were headed back to the Mystic Wood. There was an herb there, I'd seen it on the riverbank, and though I hadn't paid attention to it at the time, lately I'd been dreaming about it. There wasn't any of it in the gardens, and I really, really wanted to try it. And anyway, after a week away, I was ready to go back. As we soared above the waves, I thought about our last visit, when Ben had gone across with me, and my heart raced. Would he come with me again today? Would we splash naked in the stream, dance in the meadow? Would we come back to our world younger than when we left it?

We were flying parallel to a long, narrow beach. It was a popular place; even on a weekday afternoon there were lots of people, lying on oversized towels, playing in the surf, throwing frisbees. Ben's voice came over my headset. "This is where it happened. Right here is where Emma Rae's plane went down."

Whoa! I hadn't expected that! It suddenly occurred to me that I'd never asked, never even wondered about the details beyond what Daniel had told me. A shiver raced through my body. Had there been people on the beach that day? What must it have been like for them, seeing her plane go down? And what had it been like for Ben, flying along beside her? I reached out and grabbed his hand, giving it a hard squeeze. I realized that I would never know her, other than what I read in her journals. I was sorry about that. From everything I had heard or read, she was an amazing woman. And she had done so much for me. I would have liked to have known her. I sighed into the wind. At least I did have her journals. I wondered again where the last one was. Surely I'd find it someday? But even if I never found it, I'd learned so much about her in all the books she had left.

We banked to the right, and I recognized the beach we'd landed at before. Once again, it was empty of people. Ben brought us down in a smooth landing, barely jolting as we hit the hard-packed sand.

We got our packs, and headed across the beach into the woods. "I'm sorry about Emma Rae," I said. "I know she really meant a lot to you."

"Thank you. It's been tough. Watching her plane go down . . ."

I reached over and took his hand again, holding it as we walked. "You don't have to talk about it if you'd rather not."

He shook his head. "No, I do have to talk about it." He sounded very firm. I looked sideways at him. He seemed more determined than grief stricken.

"Okay," I said, "That's fine."

"I would swear you to secrecy about this," he said, "but no one would ever believe you, so I think I'm safe here."

"What are you talking about?"

"Emma Rae didn't go down with her plane."

"What!? Then where is she? Why . . ." I remembered all the things I read in her journals. "Oh. My. God. She's . . ."

"She's with Rhein."

"How is that possible? Who was in her plane?"

"Well, she was. I don't know how they did it. She was in it one minute, then she flew into this weird, really low cloud and there was a flash, almost blinded me, and then her plane was falling, right down into the water."

"What makes you think she wasn't in it? What makes you think it wasn't just an accident? Ben, what you're saying is crazy!"

"I know it is! And I wouldn't believe it myself, not for a minute. Except she wrote me a letter. When I got home that day, it was waiting for me with the rest of my mail. She told me all about it, what she was going to do and why. I don't understand how she did it, but she wrote that she was going to take her plane up, and she was going to take a 'left turn at Cloud 9.' Those were her exact words. She said not to believe my eyes, she was just taking an unusual detour."

"I don't believe it."

"I don't blame you. I can show you the letter if you want."

I stared at him. "What a horrible thing to do to people who love you!"

He nodded slowly. "Yes, it is. But there were extenuating circumstances."

"Now you sound like Daniel! What's that supposed to mean?"

He negotiated over a fallen log, then held out a hand to help me. "It was actually more like a preemptive strike."

"A preemptive strike? What do you mean?" I demanded.

"Emma Rae is sick. She thinks she might have cancer."

"She *thinks*? She *might*? What's that supposed to mean?"

"She wouldn't go to a doctor. She never goes, ever. She thinks they're charlatans at best, killers at worst. But in any case, she's very sick."

I stopped. So many thoughts raced through my mind. Ben turned, took three steps back to me. I couldn't speak. He took my hands in his, and continued, looking directly into my eyes. "She couldn't stay here and do nothing. But if she had stayed here and got medical help, chances are she had chemo, radiation, slow and agonizing death to look forward to. She thought that maybe, if she went over there, if she stayed over there, under Rhein's care, she might get better. And even if she didn't, she wanted to spend every last minute with Rhein. Living in both worlds had gotten too hard for her."

"But why fake her death? Wasn't there a better way? What if she gets better? She could come back!"

He shook his head. "She didn't want that. No one gets closure that way. This way, no one would wonder. People could grieve. And she could get on with healing. Or dying. With Rhein."

"But that's just crazy!" I protested. "I don't understand why she had to fake her death! Wasn't there any other way? Couldn't she just tell people she was moving or something?"

"She could have," he said. "Except for you."

"Me? What does any of this have to do with me?"

"You don't get it?" he asked. "She wanted you to have everything. Free and clear. No mess. No taxes. She set everything up for you a long, long time ago. She'd planned all along for you to have it. She had tried for years to get the courage to contact you. But though she was the most courageous woman I ever knew, she just couldn't seem to do that one thing. And she also thought, well, she thought she would have died years ago. She never expected to keep on living, and living, and living."

I just stared at him. I couldn't take in what he was saying. Only one thing was penetrating my fog. "Emma Rae is alive?"

He smiled a little. "Probably."

"Is there any way to know?"

He shook his head. "Not that I know of. I suppose you could try to find her over there."

I thought about that. "Did she tell you to tell me?"

"No. She said for me to tell you about Rhein's world only if you had her gifts, if you'd use the knowledge wisely. She trusted me for that."

"Wow. Doesn't she want to meet me?"

"Oh, honey," Ben gathered me into his arms, "I don't think it's that simple. I think the one thing she was afraid of in life was that you wouldn't want to meet her, or that you wouldn't like her."

"How could I not like her?!" But then I remembered. Her own parents had betrayed her in the most appalling ways. Alexis, who claimed to have loved her so much, had let her walk away. And though she had sent that card to my dad when I was born, he had never responded. Maybe I could understand her fear.

"Well," I said stubbornly, "I would like her. I *do* like her."

Ben took my hand, and we started walking again. "There is a way you might be able to tell her that."

"Like what? Leave her a letter at the tree? She may never even go there again."

"That's true. But I was thinking of something a little closer to home."

"Yes?"

"You could tell your mirrors."

"What!?"

He laughed. "Your mirrors. Don't they ever seem a little . . . odd?"

I stopped again, whirling to face him. "The one by the front door?!" I said, "The one in the attic?"

"Smart lady," he smiled. "Years and years ago, Rhein gave her those. They're from his world. I think they're supposed to be something like windows, or, I don't know, skype. So they could be together somewhat even when she was home over here."

"No-o-o," I said. "I don't believe it." After a minute I turned and started walking again. But I did believe it. I knew it was true. That sly Emma Rae.

Tuesday morning I had recovered enough from our trip to wake just before sunrise as I had gotten used to before my trip back East. I snuck down the stairs on tiptoe so as not to wake Petie, but before I even got to the kitchen, I smelled fresh coffee. Petie was waiting, a giant grin on her face. "Maybe you can greet the morning without an artificial stimulant, but me? No way!" she laughed.

"Bring it along if you must," I advised, "but if we don't get a move on, we'll miss it." As I crossed the kitchen, I passed by the coffee pot and instead grabbed a bunch of the herb I'd brought back with me yesterday from Rhein's world. I was glad I'd picked so much. I couldn't seem to get enough of it. Fortunately, neither Ben nor Petie would touch it; they wouldn't even taste it. I believe they both used the exact same word when I offered them some: Yuck! Oh, well, their loss. I was more than happy to eat it all myself.

Petie raised her cup to show me that she'd used a travel mug, and we headed out the door into the silvery light. We'd only been back two days, and she'd already been to the ocean three times: once as soon as we got home, in spite of the fact that it had been almost midnight, and she'd gone yesterday while Ben and I were gone. Then after a late dinner, she'd dragged me down again, to watch the sunset. I didn't really need much dragging, to be sure, but it seemed that Petie was even more enamored of the wind and the waves than I was.

At first I felt awkward with her beside me. Whenever I came down to greet the dawn, I played along the edge of the waves and sang, wordless tunes that formed in my head as I splashed and danced. Would Petie think I'd lost my mind? But after the first few minutes, while we both stood still and silent on the beach while the waves lapped at our feet, I decided I didn't care. The ocean was singing to me, and I had to sing back. I shrugged and grinned at Petie, slid out of my flip flops, and headed into the waves.

When I finished my ritual and full light played across the water, I finally turned back toward the beach. There was Petie, sitting like a statue, a blanket wrapped around her and her hands wrapped around her coffee cup. "Ready for breakfast?" I asked, breathless, as I danced back toward her.

She stood up, gathering the blanket around herself. "Ready, my strange friend," she laughed.

I shot her an offended look, but she waved a hand to calm me. "No, no, don't get worked up. You know as well as I do that you're a freak. But you're my freak, and I love you. You can play and sing out there all day for all I care."

"You didn't have to come, you know."

"True, true," she said, "but I wouldn't have missed it for the world. And now I'm ready to start the day. If I hadn't gone with you, you'd have to drag me out of bed and put an IV coffee drip in me before I could function. Now that's all taken care of."

She had a point there. Today was going to be a very busy day. We'd planned our dinner for Daniel, Walter and Ben for tonight. Last night Daniel had called to invite himself and Walter to come up for the day. He knew we had a truck full of my stuff, and they offered to help us unpack, and rearrange the house. The offer was too good to pass up. They were coming at nine. We had time for leisurely showers and breakfast, and I could get some muffins baked for them. After that it was full steam ahead for the rest of the day.

And it was a good day. I'd already planned how to arrange things to accommodate my furniture, so that was mostly just muscle work. Ben joined the party, too, and Petie and I got to spend the morning telling the men what to move where. The afternoon was spent unpacking the smaller stuff. Petie and I worked in the kitchen, replacing Emma Rae's things with my own, reorganizing, talking and dreaming of all the cooking, baking, and canning I (and hopefully *we*) would be doing in this space, while the others unpacked and carefully piled stuff up in the other rooms, to be sorted out as time allowed.

Daniel took Petie to the grocery store in the late afternoon, and then she and I made homemade pizza, just like we used to back in high school. Walter surprised us by joining us in the kitchen and making a fabulous salad (though when I tried to sneak in just a bit of my new favorite herb, there was a loud and unanimous outcry against it!). And after the long, hot, busy day had wound down and the dinner dishes were done, after we had switched from iced tea to wine I had infused with mint and some other, more secret ingredients, Walter pulled out some photograph albums, and we settled down to listen to reminiscences of Emma Rae. Walter was quite the amateur photographer, and he knew how to tell a good story. At times Daniel, or even Ben, quibbled laughingly with him about details. We spent a marvelous couple of hours, and I felt like I knew Emma Rae so much better than before, even after all I'd read in her journals.

Then a new face showed up in the pictures, an old woman with a sweet, sad face. There was something evocative about the face, though I had no idea who it was. "Who's that?" I asked, touching the photo.

Daniel leaned closer to see. "Oh, isn't that Miss Sophia?"

"Sophia!?" I asked sharply, as Walter nodded.

"She was a friend of Emma Rae's from New York," Walter confirmed. "She came to live with Emma Rae in, oh, the early seventies, I think it was."

"She was a grand old Russian lady," Daniel said, faking an atrocious Russian accent.

I was stunned. Sophia had come to California? Of course I knew she'd written to Emma Rae, but I hadn't had a chance to read further in the journals. This had never occurred to me.

"Emma?" Ben said, touching my hand. "Are you all right?"

I shook my head to clear it, then looked closely at Walter. "Do you know who Sophia was?"

"Not exactly," he said slowly. "I just knew they'd been friends years earlier. Sophia was very quiet, she mostly kept to herself. She died in 1977, I think it was. I never really understood their connection. It was one of Emma Rae's little mysteries. But they were very devoted to one another. Even though Sophia was sick for quite some time, Emma Rae was devastated when she died."

"Do you know who Alexis was?" I asked.

Ben and Daniel shook their heads, but Walter said, "He was Sophia's brother, yes?"

"Yes," I said slowly, then made my decision. "He was Sophia's brother. He was also, well, Alexis was my great-grandfather."

The room was silent. Finally Walter whispered, "How do you know this?"

"She kept journals," I answered softly. "From the time she was seventeen, she kept journals. They were all here, and I've been reading them."

"But Miss Sophia was an old lady!" Daniel protested. "She was almost eighty when she died!"

I nodded. "Yes. So was Emma Rae at that time. They were the same age."

"This is," Walter started, stumbled, tried again, "this is very difficult to believe."

I stood up. "Just a minute, I'll tell you all about it, but let me get something." I hurried up to my bedroom to retrieve the alexandrite jewelry. When he saw the box, Walter's eyebrows shot to his forehead.

"These jewels were a gift from Alexis," I told them. "He said they were family heirlooms, and he wanted her to have them in case their son was ever found. Their son was Henry, my father's father." The men looked baffled, and I hurried to open the box before I even sat down again. But the latch caught, and as I struggled with it, the whole thing slipped out of my hands, bounced off the edge of the coffee table, and crashed to the ground. The silk cushion flew out of the box and the jewels skidded across the wood floor.

But I wasn't looking at the jewels. Wedged tightly into the bottom of the box was some sort of paper, like a folded document. It had been hidden beneath the thick silk padding that had protected the jewels. With trembling hands I pried it loose, and unfolded the heavy parchment paper.

"My Emma Rae, my beloved, my heart," the handwritten letter began. I looked up quickly, tears suddenly blurring my vision. "I'm sorry," I said, "I need . . . I need a few minutes alone, please." I got to my feet, trembling. "Petie, will you please, um, make tea or something? I'll, uh, I'll just, um, please excuse me," I said, and ran out of the room, back upstairs, all the way up to the attic. I sat in the soft chair. I could see my reflection in the mirror . . . or was it Emma Rae? "Did you know about this, Emma Rae?" I whispered. And then I read the letter out loud, my voice husky.

My Emma Rae, my beloved, my heart,

If you are reading this, you are gone, and I have never found the courage to tell you the truth, the truth that would have kept you with me forever. Know at once, then, that I have lived my life as a coward, and as my punishment I have lived it without you, the only one I have ever loved. But is that true? For if you are reading this, my darling, then I have loved my position in the bosom of my family, and my place in society more than I have loved you.

This is the truth that I have kept from you all these years. We are married. You are my wife, not just in my heart as I always told you, but by law. The first night we loved, the night before your father first took you away from me, do you remember? I remember everything! I wanted you so passionately, and you were afraid, as you should have been. To smooth away your fears, I brought in my friend and he performed a ceremony, do you remember? I told you that it was as if we were married, to reassure you of my love. You thought it was merely a play for your benefit, but you let it be enough.

Emma Rae, my friend was in fact a priest. The ceremony was legitimate. And the ring that I gave you that night, the ring I forbade you to wear in public, was my seal and vow, the ring of my father and his father and his father before him. If you had ever been seen wearing that ring, anyone who knew my family would have known instantly that you were my wife. But I was a coward! Having survived the desolation of my country, I could not risk being shunned by my family and my society, as I surely would have been had I not submitted to their wishes in the matter of my marriage. So I told them that I had lost the ring when I escaped, and I did as they required; I married the Countess. But that was a false marriage. Only my friend Karl knew the truth, and he pled with me not to continue the charade. But my fear was greater than my love.

You are my true wife. Our son Henry is my heir. I have never stopped loving you. But alas, neither have I ever stopped being a coward. I write you this letter, and I conceal it, in hope and in dread that one day you may find it, and know the truth, and come back to me, that you will take the decision from me, and force me to be the man for you and for our son that I am too weak to be.

My heart, I will go to my grave loving you. Please Emma Rae, I pray that you can forgive me.

Your husband,

Alexis Alexander Mikhailskovich

I looked at the ring on my forefinger, the ring I'd worn ever since I found it sewn into the hem of Emma Rae's paper thin traveling dress. This ring would have told the world that Emma Rae was married to a prince of Russia, that her son Henry was legitimate, that he was the heir of the family Mikhailskovich. The alexandrite jewelry that I had just spilled across my living room floor would confirm it, I was sure. If I chose, I could, even now, have my father proven as the heir. I wondered if the family had prospered in the new world, or had lost everything as had so many others. I glanced back at the mirror. I almost hoped Emma Rae hadn't heard my impetuous reading. What difference could it make to her now? But then I remembered her grief when Alexis had died and I knew, it would indeed make a difference.

I folded the pages again and went slowly back downstairs. So many explanations to be made! Maybe Petie had already started; I'd told her as much of Emma Rae's story as I knew on our long road trip. But in any case, after this incredible revelation, I imagined this was going to be a long night.

Even so, I couldn't help but grin a little. So, Emma Rae. Even your secrets have secrets.

I am too old for slumber parties! I thought as I crawled out of bed the next morning. I had predicted correctly; it was a very long night. By the time I had told Emma Rae's story, and Walter had added his corroborations, it was after 2 a.m. Walter was exhausted to the point of staggering. With my own furniture added to Emma Rae's, I had plenty of beds and couches, and Daniel and Ben both agreed with me that it would be better for him to just stay here. After that it was but a minute to convince Daniel to stay as well.

Ben had made his escape, but from the muffled noises I heard coming from the kitchen, I guessed he was back already, and making himself useful. Ah, yes, my nose informed me, coffee, at least, yes and bacon! I slid silently into the room, crossing and sliding my arms around Ben before he knew I was there. "You are a prince among men," I said into his shoulder, adjusting so the apron knot at his back stopped poking me in the belly.

He turned in my arms, putting down a spatula to hug me. "And don't you forget it!" he grinned before kissing me soundly. After returning the kiss with great enthusiasm, I extricated myself from his embrace to help myself to a pinch of the mystery herb.

"I don't know how you can eat that stuff," Ben said severely. "I know I've never seen it before. Emma Rae didn't use it. How do you know it's safe?"

I shrugged. "I don't know what you're talking about; it's fabulous. You tried everything else, why not this?" I ate another bunch.

"No, no, no. I'm drawing the line on this one. Uh uh, no way."

"Well, that's fortunate, anyway, 'cause there's none left."

"You ate it all? Already? Emma, you're liable to make yourself sick at that rate. We picked a ton of the stuff!"

"Well, we're gonna have to get some more," I said simply, going to the cupboard to pull out ingredients for waffles. Yes! I thought, my own waffle iron!

"You're going to have to get it yourself. One of us has to run the business, you know?"

"Hmmm, someone not get enough sleep? A little crabby are we?" I teased, putting myself back in his arms.

"Hey, hey, none of that!" Petie said from the doorway, "You'll make me lose my appetite!" I looked up and laughed. Her short hair was sticking up in spikes, and she was wearing Tasmanian devil pajamas.

"Great look!" I grinned. "Did you forget we have a house full of men?"

She shrugged and reached for the coffee. "I'm sure they've all seen Tas before."

I looked at her long legs. Those pajamas were short! "I was more concerned with them seeing the other devil!"

She grinned up over a steaming cup, started to say something, then stopped herself. I raised an eyebrow at her, but only got a saucy smile in reply.

"Oh, re-e-eally?"

Petie laughed. "Mind your own business, Miss Know-it-all!"

"What is going on here?" Ben asked, totally baffled.

"Nothing!" Petie and I answered in one loud voice, and then dissolved into grade school giggles. Oh, yeah, it was great having Petie here. And if that look was anything to go by, the chances of her coming back again, even if only for regular visits, had definitely improved. Nice!

I looked at myself in the mirror. Daniel had invited Petie to go back into town with him and Walter after breakfast, and he'd give her the grand tour. She had readily agreed. Ben had gone out to work. I also had work to do, tea to package and ship, upkeep on the garden. But I was feeling a pull to Rhein's world so strong that I couldn't settle down at all. I'd get some more of that herb while I was there, I justified to myself.

I'd run upstairs to get my backpack and different shoes, and had caught a glimpse of myself in the mirror. Now I was stuck there, looking. Who are you? I asked my reflection yet again. That face looked ten years younger than the face I was used to seeing. The hair was deep glossy red and curly; no gray showing at all, though a short month ago I'd had more than my share. My skin seemed almost unlined, tight and youthful. I tried to convince myself that I was imagining the changes, but I knew they were real. Something very powerful was happening in my body. I had a sudden awful thought: I hope my menopause doesn't stop! After my long and disappointing years of childlessness, I had greeted the onset of menopause with great relief. Those constant monthly reminders had remained painful. But now that I thought about it, I realized I hadn't had a hot flash in, well, I couldn't remember the last one. Hmmm. And my mood was certainly much improved. Best not to think about that at all, I decided as I turned away from my reflection. Once again, I thought about the plant I'd been eating so much of. Ah, I thought, maybe that's it, a natural hormone balancer.

I took my time in Rhein's world, exploring a little further than I had before. If I focused, opening myself, I experienced a clear awareness of Ben, and I knew my idea had worked. Either that, or just finally getting him over here had done it. Either way, he'd always be able to keep his connection with me, which I knew was a great relief to him. I played in the stream, drinking deeply and once again plunging myself straight in to lie in the frigid rushing waters, and then filling several bottles. I danced in the meadow and sang to the unnamed birds I saw. I gorged on the strange little herb, and filled several large plastic bags to take back with me. I kept my awareness open while gathering other plants as well, some to dry, some to root. Once again, I saw or heard no sign of people. Was Emma Rae still alive? Did she know I was here? Would she want to see me if she did?

For the first time in this other world, I felt a little lonely, and decided it was time to go home. As I headed back to the giant, I thought again about this wonderful new life I was living. My relationship with Ben was amazing, so unexpected and satisfying. I felt that Daniel, Walter and I were going to be good friends. I even enjoyed Katie, and looked forward to getting to know her better. She and her parents were having a tough time, trying to redefine their relationship and adjust to the idea of the coming baby. And Petie: I was so happy she was here! There was no knowing if she would choose to move here or not; she was unpredictable. But I would do my best to convince her to make the move. I laughed and did another little song and dance as I neared the giant. Yes, this was a good life.

Then I saw it. At the foot of the giant, almost buried in the white and purple flowers, lay a book. I knew it instantly: Emma Rae's last journal. I sat down abruptly, almost afraid to pick it up. But of course I had to. Quickly, fearfully, I fanned the pages. The first half of the book was mostly Emma Rae's spiky writing, interspersed with her lovely drawings. That was expected. But near the end of the book, she had written less and drawn more, until by the last few pages there were almost no words at all, just sketch after sketch after sketch. I was enthralled. Here was the giant, drawn from both worlds. The stream, and lightly shadowed over the water, almost like a ghost, was a figure. Was that me? No way to know. Then the pictures moved away from places that were familiar to me, showing trees, plants, landscapes I might recognize if I ever saw them. Then—a surprise!—a path, a bridge, rustic houses! Could I find these places? Had Emma Rae left me a map?

Also there were faces. One I knew was Rhein. Women's faces: Rhein's sisters? I was too impatient to spend time studying the images. I was overwhelmed with excitement, and possibility. Then I turned to the last page.

A simple sketch, like so many I'd seen: a plant, leaves and stem and roots and flower. I recognized it at once; I had three big bags of it in my pack, and no doubt flecks of it even now were stuck between my teeth. I squinted at the tiny writing at the lower left corner of the page.

"Very thirsty plant, thrives by streams and other bodies of water. Grows profusely, needing little care. Does not normally appeal. Only known use: superb nutritional support during pregnancy and breastfeeding, when it becomes irresistible."

The book dropped from my hands. I stared across the meadow. I sat motionless for endless minutes. And then I threw my head back and laughed, and laughed, and laughed.

✳   ✳   ✳

Ben straightened up and stretched his back. He was almost done for the day, almost ready to brush off his knees, scrub the dirt out from under his nails, and head into Emma's house to pilfer a glass of her amazing herbed wine. He opened his mind to her more fully, enjoying the gentle knowledge of her even though she was in Rhein's world. He felt her happiness; she was always so happy over there.

He walked toward the house, feeling the sun warm his shoulders and loosen his stiff back. He felt a sudden ripple in Emma's energy, like an electric shock, and then he was caught in a mad crash of joy, so powerful that it staggered him. He felt her laughter course through his entire body, and with it a sudden, astonishing knowledge.

He stood motionless, his mind blank with surprise. Then a smile twitched at the corner of his mouth. Ahhh, so that's it! he thought, that's what that was! And then he, too, threw back his head and joined Emma, so close by in another world, in joyous laughter.

Acknowledgments

There are countless people involved in the successful completion of a novel. I imagine that each person I've ever encountered has contributed, in some way, to this one. My thanks go to every one. Then there are those whose participation is more easily recognized. I would like to acknowledge of few of them by name.

First, last and middle is my sister Beth. Without her, it is highly possible that I would be a gypsy living out of my van (not that that would be a *bad* thing . . .). She provides me with endless games of Skip-bo, fried zucchini, episode after episode of Bones, Castle, and NCIS, and more love, encouragement and support than can ever be measured. She listens to me long after I've begun to bore even myself, and is very convincing when she insists she's still interested. She sat and knitted while I read the entire manuscript out loud to her. She is priceless to me.

My friends Angelica, Jack, Jamie and John (listed here alphabetically because each of them is *THE* most important) have loved and supported me for years, whatever I've been up to. They have each provided countless hugs, made space for my tears, joined me in laughter, and in all ways been extraordinary friends. I am so lucky!

Jamie also was with me when I first encountered the amazing place referred to in the story as the Mystic Wood, where I took the cover photo. Without that highly entertaining camping trip, there might have been no story.

When Vic saw the previously mentioned photograph, he told me, "This can't be used for cover art." Then he took it away and used it to design a cover to be proud of. After that, he proceeded to help me wrap up the whole project in fine style. His help was invaluable, and his friendship is a gift.

Thank you to Walter, a superb estate attorney, who made sure that the details of the inheritance are accurate. I named Emma Rae's longtime friend and lawyer after him. Both Walters are excellent attorneys, and are handsome, wise, kind and generous. As far as I know, the resemblance between them ends there.

My thanks also to people who provided any kind of proofreading or editing help, including Beth, Judy, Mom, Malena, and Walter. And to Renee, who gave me a piece of writing advice that radically changed the story.

Unending gratitude to the people without whom, really and truly, none of this would have happened: Mom and Dad, thank you for giving me life, for raising me well, and for loving me always. I love you back.

21900461R00150

Made in the USA
San Bernardino, CA
10 June 2015